*   *   *

CONFLUENCE

* * *

CONFLUENCE

Murder in the Mountains

JIM OGLETHORPE

Edited by Alice Oglethorpe

* * *

DEDICATION

*Dedicated to the brave men and women that first settled the Youghiogheny
River Valley*

*   *   *

ACKNOWLEDGMENTS

The Turkeyfoot Valley Historical Society
Floyd Pullin for telling his story of life in the mountains
The University of Pittsburgh for the help of their archive and librarians
My wife Jean and daughters Alice and Laura for their encouragement
and support

PREFACE

"Confluence" is my second Joe Zajac story and a bit different from my first, "Leisenring No. 1". That story took place for the most part in the Connellsville area, and focused on the immigrant miners and cokers that lived in the company towns. I wrote it as a labor of love to my hard-working ancestors and to the glory days of my hometown.

I'd decided to set my second story in the Youghiogheny River Valley and originally was going to title the work "Murder on the Yough". But I didn't want to have another title that was hard to pronounce for folks not from western Pennsylvania. So "Confluence" it became. The title refers not only to the city, but other "Comings Together" that occur in my story.

Fair warning to all of you readers from Confluence. While much of the story is set in the middle Youghiogheny area, and some in Confluence itself, it is not heavy of the history of the town. I do think it generally reflects the area at the turn of the 20th Century, and I've worked hard to make it historically accurate.

Joe still lives in Connellsville but his adventure takes him from Confluence and Ohiopyle to Altoona, with stops in between at Dawson, Brownsville, Uniontown and Scottdale. And as he's a college student at the Western University of Pennsylvania, he spends his Tuesdays and Thursdays in the City of Allegheny and Pittsburgh.

For this book I tried to imagine what it would have been like to be a man of 30 living in 1901. To that end you'll find Joe dealing with some of the issues of the day, and his own intellectual awakening as he attends school. It's nothing too heavy, but an important part of the book to me.

In the end, "Confluence" is the story I had to tell this time. I've one more Joe Zajac story in mind, "Three Rivers - Murder in the Mill". Then we shall see what becomes of my friend. It's been fun to know him.

PROLOGUE

MAY 28, 1754
DAWN

John Harkins was cold, wet, and anxious. *Least the rain has stopped,* he thought to himself. A thin fog clung to the ground as he and a small band of men marched along a wooded trail. Travelling over wet, rocky ridges and ravines, the slog was slow and hard. Next to him was his mate, Peter Bell. The path was treacherous in the dim dawn light.

"John, I wish we'd not signed on with George. Better we'd stayed in Alexandria."

"Too late now and we'll be earnin' that sixpence today I wager."

Ahead of them stretched their group: a ragged line of Virginia Militiamen, led by 22-year-old Lieutenant Colonel George Washington, perhaps 40 men in all. In front of Washington and leading the way were a dozen Mingo Indians, their leader Tanaghrisson, known as the Half-King, at the fore.

As they marched, John thought of Alexandria. *Work was hard to find and rare was a roof over my head. Was a vagabond life we led.* The sixpence sounded like easy money to the 18-year-old, decent pay for a walk in the woods. Instead here he was, about to shoot, and get shot at.

Their destination had been the western frontier of the American Colonies of England, deep in the mountain range that defined much of their border.

Their mission: defend the territory against the attempts of the French to establish control of the region. The forks of the Ohio were the key to the ambitions of both. This morning they were scouting for a French detachment led by Joseph de Jumonville. Although there was no formal war between the two countries, the frontier was a hostile place, the Indian allies of each side a threat to the other.

Washington raised his arm and the line stopped. The Half-King and he conferred, then orders passed back the line. Their Captain, Adam Stephen, huddled with his men. "Jumonville camps a hundred yards hence in a glen, his back to a rock wall. We approach from the front. The Indians are moving to the rocks. No noise now and don't fire until you receive your order."

John ducked behind a tree, relieved himself, and checked his musket load. The line moved out. As they approached the glen, the men separated to the flanks and crept forward, soon within range. A few of Jumonville's men were stirring, most still asleep. Peter took another step, his foot landing on a fallen branch. The cracking sound echoed through the still forest.

One of the French moved for his musket. "Réveiller! Réveiller!" Soon all were up and going for their arms. Peter raised his gun. "What are we waiting for?" Washington quietly observed the scene. No order to fire was issued.

One shot rang out. The man with the musket fell. For a moment no one moved, no sound was heard. Then a second shot, and the woods exploded. A few French returned fire, many more were cut down. Jumonville ran to the front and took a shot to the chest. "Hold fire!" Washington finally called out, his first command of the engagement, and the action ended.

Washington approached Jumonville and was joined by the Half-King, carrying a tomahawk. One of the French spoke English. "We are not at war! We are a diplomatic mission to deliver a message. You English are intruding on French lands."

The Half-King approached a sagging Jumonville, his shirt stained red. Standing tall, he spoke: "You are not dead yet my father." With a quick swing, his tomahawk cleaved the skull of the Frenchman, who fell at his feet. Reaching down, he pulled the brain from Jumonville's head, laughing as it disintegrated in his hands.

A great roar sprung from the Mingos. In a rush they fell on the wounded French, slaughtering many, mutilating the dead. Finally, Washington fired his pistol in the air. "Enough, the battle is won."

*   *   *

JULY 3, 1754
7:00 PM

John Harkins was again cold, wet, and anxious. He and Peter huddled near the stockade of Fort Necessity, a hastily built wall of logs in the middle of a meadow. Woodlands pressed close, filled with French and Indian musketeers. The 400 men inside the compound had been under steady fire all day. A heavy rain fell.

A shivering Peter spoke lowly. "George will be getting us all killed I wager. They say it's the brother of the Frenchman killed at the glen, bent on revenge."

John shrugged. "I'm near to starved anyhow and if the rains don't soon stop we're all drowned. We sit here in the lowest part of the meadow."

Washington's men had been marching around for weeks, dragging wagons and equipment over rough and untracked mountains. Deciding that an advance to the forks of the Ohio was impossible, he retreated to the fort. A French and Indian force of over a thousand, led by Joseph de Jumonville's brother Louis, was on their tail.

John threw his musket into the mud. "We are without hope. There's no dry powder to be had." Nearby some of the men had broken into the rum supply, many already drunk.

Peter threw his musket down and stood up. "If we are to die in this mud hole, might as well be happy." He ran toward the supply hut. A shot rang out and he fell. John leaned back against the stockade, afraid to move a muscle except to weep for his friend.

A bit later the shooting finally stopped. From the woods a message was called. "Voulez-vous parler?" The French wanted to talk. Washington and his men huddled, weary heads nodding. An officer was dispatched to parley with the enemy. He returned after several hours with two documents. Then

Washington and his officers huddled again. The documents were modified, signed and dispatched to the French.

Washington stood on a box and addressed his mostly drunken command. "The fighting is over. We leave on the morrow."

It was a ragtag band that straggled out of Fort Necessity the next morning. The French troops stood between them and the Indians, unhappy with such a benign ending. They had taken casualties and thirsted for revenge. What was left of the Virginia Militia made their way south along the Nemacolin Trail towards Wills Creek. Many more of them would die along the way.

The rain had stopped, the day sunny and warm. As he trudged along, John gazed at the green forests that covered the Allegheny ridges. *Truth be told, I'm fond of these mountains.*

Chapter 1

＊　　＊　　＊

The Allegheny Mountains of western Pennsylvania once defined the end of civilization, the lands beyond a wilderness where the Iroquois ruled. But the white man came eventually. They found life hard there, especially in winter. To survive, those mountain people formed a rugged community: self-reliant, insular, and hard working.

This winter of 1900 was a particularly harsh one, testing the mettle of even the toughest mountain folks. The snow started falling early in November, followed soon after by the arrival of frigid Arctic air. By mid-December, the Youghiogheny[1] River was mostly ice covered, the streams that fed it frozen solid. The snow lay three feet deep, drifts making even rail travel a challenge. Most of the lumber mills, tanneries, and other businesses that lined the Youghiogheny valley from Confluence to Ohiopyle had shut down, but not all.

Paxson Boyd was, by any measure, a man of these mountains. Big and burly, his weather-beaten face mostly hidden behind a full beard, he rode out of Ohiopyle. Astride a workhorse, his destination was a small sawmill, one of the few still operating. The Boyd family had been lumbering (and making moonshine) in these hills for almost 100 years, his great-great grandfather an early settler. Paxson learned the trades from his father at an early age and had

---

1　Pronounced *Yock a gain e*

passed both on to his son. Now, at age 50, he was wearing out. Of necessity, he'd work to the end.

* * *

A few miles away at that sawmill, five men gathered. One held a gun, another a length of rope, a third jumped around excitedly. The three circled a sad looking fellow, his hands bound. The fifth man stood, head bowed, at the side.

"You just need to be honest with us, Homer. We're not looking to hurt you, nor Clyde here."

The bound man shook his head. "I already told you. No one knows nothing."

The excited one grabbed the rope. "He's a liar. I bet he'll talk with some encouragement." He tied a noose around Homer's head and dragged a chair over. "Stand up here."

* * *

Boyd was now riding up a rough track. The snow here was packed down from heavy sled traffic but still the horse struggled. His ride huffing and puffing, Boyd stopped for a bit. *One more hill to climb*, he thought, *damn snow won't let up*. It had started up again around noon this last day of December, the dark grey clouds promising even more to come. He brushed the snow and ice from his beard, took a deep breath, and moved on. *The best thing Pappy left me was this Union suit.* A guttural growl sounded. At once the horse reared. "Easy. Easy." Snorting and pawing, he stilled. Ahead on the path was a big black cat. *Panther. Wonder what's got him up?* The panther stood, eyeing the horse and rider. "Get! Get!" The cat took a step toward them. *Might be he's hungry.* Paxson pulled a pistol. "Easy boy, easy." He stroked the horse's head and fired a shot into the air. The cat leaped from the trail and crashed through the woods. *That's about a big of one I've seen in a while.*

* * *

The men in the mill heard the shot. As the three turned, Clyde made a break for it. Homer, the rope now tied to a beam, stood on tiptoes. The excited one turned and tackled Clyde, both rolling into the chair. The line pulled taut with a jerk and a crack. Clyde was getting the better of it until soundly struck from behind. He now lay motionless.

"You boys happy now?" The one with the gun pointed to Clyde. "Hide him in back. Untie Homer's hands and let him hang. We got to get out of here."

* * *

The sawmill, and hundreds of acres of adjacent woodlands, was owned and operated by Henry Brooks. *If'n I didn't owe Henry I'm damned if I'd be to work on New Year's Eve* Paxson thought. The Brooks operation had a contract with the H.C. Frick Coke Company to supply the lumber used in their coal mines, and the mining continued despite the weather. There were two sled loads of ceiling posts ready to be delivered, Paxson's job to transport them to the B&O Railroad siding near Ohiopyle. Although an experienced teamster, his skills would be tested dragging the heavy loads down the steep mountain trail. *Even a horse knows it's too damn cold to be out.*

Paxson crested the hill and stopped again to let the horse catch his breath. The sawmill, consisting of a steam engine and several roughhewn wooden buildings, sat about a half mile away, in one of the many little hollows that ran down from Laurel Ridge. He could still barely see it through the falling snow, but should have been able to hear it by now. A steam powered sawmill was a noisy place but today the woods were silent. Only a thin strand of smoke came from the steam engine. *I hope Half-moon ain't drunk and passed out. If them sleds ain't loaded there'll be hell to pay.*

He was referring to Homer "Half-moon" Harkins, who along with one of his mates was supposed to be running the mill today. Although experienced with the saw and a hard worker, Half-moon was known to be fond of the bottle and, on occasion, other people's property. He'd been sober for the last few weeks, thanks to an extended stay in the Fayette County jail. But he'd fallen off the wagon before.

As Paxson approached the mill, a sense of unease came over him. He saw one loaded sled but the other was only half full. Stopping in his tracks, he crouched down and surveyed the surroundings. *Where's the other horse?* The little stable was empty but he could see some tracks leading away from it, and down a path behind the mill. Pulling out his pistol, he continued on. *No time to be getting the woolies.* Just outside the main building stood the steam engine, its firebox cold enough to touch. He entered the saw room, which likewise showed no signs of recent activity. *Not much mill work done here today I'd say. Where in tarnation is Half-moon?*

The wind had picked up and the snow was finally slowing down. With no small amount of foreboding Paxson moved on. A workroom lay behind. Lacking windows, it was dark inside. But there was enough light to see Half-moon, swinging slowly from the rafters, a noose around his neck. A chair lay on its side underneath. Paxson lowered his gun and slowly backed out of the room. *Don't need no doctor, he's dead as a door nail!*

Chapter 2

* * *

J oe Zajac set down his pen and rubbed his eyes. Grim faced and tight lipped, he stared at the ledger sheet in front of him. He'd been working on it for an hour but still could not get it to add up. *Who knew bookkeeping was so hard,* he thought. Locking his fingers behind his head, Joe closed his eyes and slid down in the chair. His head ached.

"No sleeping on the job Joe."

He opened his eyes and smiled. In the office doorway stood a tall, slim woman with auburn hair. Peggy Patterson, his lady friend, was the former bookkeeper for The Star, one of the most popular taverns in Connellsville, Pennsylvania. Owned by her father Andy, it had been Joe's favorite watering hole since he moved to town. "You made this job look easy Peggy but I swear I'd rather mine coal."

Peggy smiled back. "Practice makes perfect. Daddy taught me bookkeeping when I was only 15 years old." She walked behind the desk and glanced at the sheet. "What seems to be the problem?"

"I'm off by 81 cents."

Peggy took off her coat and hat. "Let me take a look."

Joe rose from the chair and let her sit down. "Be my guest."

Peggy straightened up the stack of bills and started comparing them to the sheet. In a few moments she stood up and handed him one of them.

"Here's your error. You entered the bill from Yough Brewery as $2.90. It's really for $2.09."

Joe's face reddened a bit. "I should have caught that. Thanks Peggy."

"You're welcome Joe, and thank you for your help. Maybe you were just up too late last night ringing in the New Year."

She was right about that. While Peggy had stayed home with her ailing father, Joe, along with his friends Lloyd McCormack and Johnny Davidson, had celebrated at The Star, staying until it closed. "That's the first time I've been up past midnight for a long time."

It was shortly after 2:00pm Tuesday, January 1, 1901. Although open, The Star was almost empty, only a few men standing at the long bar. "I haven't had lunch yet. Care to join me?"

"I've eaten already. Would you like me to make you a roast beef sandwich?"

The Star was famous for their roast beef sandwiches and Joe had eaten many. "I likely could find room for one," Joe said with a smile.

Joe and Peggy left the office, he taking a seat at his favorite table in the rear, she heading to the kitchen. The Star was one big room, with the bar on one side and a collection of assorted tables and chairs on the other. The space featured a tall ceiling covered with embossed tin tiles and a well-worn wooden floor. A low cabinet stood behind the bar, its top covered with an assortment of whiskey bottles, all reflected in the mirror behind. A brass foot rail ran the length of the bar, with matching spittoons placed every few feet.

Joe, a former policeman from Philadelphia, moved to Connellsville seven years earlier to work for the H.C. Frick Coke Company. As a plainclothes member of the Frick Police, he was mostly involved in security and theft prevention But last August he became caught up in a murder investigation and a related conspiracy to blow up several Frick mines[2]. The experience had changed Joe, who left Frick's employ with an injured foot and a $5,000 reward for saving the day.

Connellsville was a boomtown as the 20th century dawned, sitting on top of a vein of coal that bore its name, "The Connellsville Seam." Soft, easily mined, and low in sulphur, the coal was well suited for the manufacture of

---

2 See Joe Zajac's first adventure *Leisenring No. 1*

coke, the fuel of choice in the iron and steel mills of Pittsburgh. A hundred coal mines fed 20,000 coke ovens along the seam, their release obscuring the skies of Connellsville and all of Fayette County with a hazy cloud. But the smoke seemed a small price to pay for the prosperity that accompanied it.

Peggy came out of the kitchen with his sandwich, thin slices of roast beef piled high between thick slices of rye bread. Joe's mouth watered as he eyed it. "Would you like a beer to wash it down?"

Joe shook his head. "I had enough last night for two days." He waved to the bartender. "Hiram, pull me a root beer."

Peggy sat down and watched Joe take a big bite, letting out a low "umm" as he chewed. "I've never seen a man who enjoyed food more."

"That bookkeeping works up an appetite."

Peggy retrieved Joe's root beer then sat in silence as he polished off the sandwich, washing it down with half of the glass. Leaning forward, arms on the table, he let a contented sigh. "How's your Pop?"

Peggy frowned, her face dropping. "No better I'm afraid. He did eat a good breakfast though. Thank God he's a tough old bird." Andy had been ailing since June, and since then it had fallen upon Peggy to manage the tavern. For the last few months Joe had, for the most part, taken on that job. "When do your classes start up again?"

Joe had decided that, at age 30, he'd use some of the reward money to attend the University of Western Pennsylvania. He was a "Special Student," not working toward a degree, but permitted to take as many classes a semester as he wanted. His first semester, which ended just before Christmas, he studied Rhetoric and Ancient History. "My first day is next Tuesday. I've scheduled two more classes, Philosophy and American History."

Peggy leaned forward, taking Joe's hands in hers. "I'm so proud of you Joe. It takes a lot of resolve to start college at age 30."

Joe looked her in the eye and gave a little squeeze. "I've your encouragement to thank for that as much as anything. That, and Frick's reward money."

The door to The Star blew open with a bang, followed by a gust of cold wind and a big man in a long coat. He pushed the door closed, brushed himself off and removed his furry hat and coat. Joe recognized him as Henry

Brooks, a lumberman from the mountains. He was an old friend of Peggy's. Looking around, Henry spotted them and headed their way.

Peggy and Joe both stood up, Peggy speaking first. "Why Henry Brooks, what brings you to town on New Year's Day? We haven't seen you here since the snow started."

Henry smiled at Peggy, then turned to Joe. "I'm looking for this fellow. I hear he's the best detective in Fayette County."

Joe laughed. "I don't know about that Henry. All I did was damn near get killed a couple of times before I got lucky. Besides, what would a lumberman need with a detective?"

They all sat down at the table, Henry silent for a bit as he composed his thoughts. "One of my men turned up dead yesterday. It looks like he might have done himself in but I'm a might suspicious. There's been other goings on too."

"What can I do to help?"

"Can you come up to Ohiopyle with me tomorrow? I'd like to show you where the man was found. You can look at the body too. He's on ice."

Joe turned to Peggy. "Can you cover for me here?"

"Sure Joe, please do what you can to help Henry."

"Okay Henry, what's your plan?"

"Meet me at the B&O station. The local leaves at nine. I'll fill you in on the way up the mountain."

Chapter 3

＊　　　＊　　　＊

Joe awoke just before 7:00am Wednesday morning and half an hour later he left his two-room apartment on Pittsburgh Street, two blocks from The Star. A frigid dawn was just breaking. Bent against a stiff wind, his breath leaving a white trail, he hurried down Main Street. *At least it stopped snowing.* His destination was City Lunch, where he ate breakfast most every day. He walked through the front door a few minutes later, a little bell announcing his arrival. The place was nearly empty. Joe could smell bacon being fried and bread baking. A few moments later the owner, cook, and dishwasher, Tony Molinari, poked his head out of the kitchen. A small man with a big mustache, Tony and Joe had become good friends over the years.

"Joey, you early today. Give me a minute, I be right with you."

"OK Tony, no hurry."

City Lunch was a popular spot. Not fancy but always clean, the food was simple and well made. Breakfasts and spaghetti were the specialties of the house. A counter ran down the left side. Faded red and white checked tablecloths covered a dozen wooden tables on the right, a row of grimy windows behind them. Joe walked to the rear and took his favorite seat at the end of the counter.

Tony reappeared, a cup of coffee in his hand. "Why you up so early? Ever since you quit Frick you eat at 8:30."

"I got something to do today Tony, taking a train ride to Ohiopyle."

"Why you go up there? I bet the falls are frozen already."

"Doing a favor for a friend Tony. How about you fry me up a couple of eggs, over easy, and some of that bacon I smell. What's in the oven?"

"I got some fresh biscuits ready to come out. You want?"

Joe smiled and nodded. *He knows I love his fresh biscuits.* At times he thought Tony could read his mind.

Joe drank his coffee and thought about the day ahead. *I don't know what Henry thinks I can do. I'm no Sherlock Holmes.* But he'd promised Peggy he'd help. *I've never been to Ohiopyle. At least I get a train ride out of it.* He pulled a small notebook and pencil from his pocket and made a few notes. He headed up a page "Henry Brooks." Under that he wrote "Other problems."

Tony reappeared again, a plate in each hand. "Here you go Joey, mangia." On one plate were the eggs and four slices of thick, crispy bacon. The other held two fat biscuits, sliced open and buttered.

"Thanks Tony. This should keep me through the morning."

"You welcome Joe. Nobody appreciate my cooking like you."

Joe dug in with his usual enthusiasm. In a few minutes both plates were clean. Hearing the bell, Joe looked up to see one of his best friends, Johnny Davidson, walk through the front door. A member of the Connellsville Police Department, he'd also been involved in the troubles at the Leisenring No. 1 mine in August. He saw Joe and joined him at the end of the counter.

"You recover from New Year's Eve?"

"A night with you and Lloyd is always a good time Johnny, whatever the price. And since I gave up the whiskey, mornings aren't the problem they once were. I was back at The Star by noon, working on the books."

"Joe the saloon manager. You sure you don't want to get back into the policing business? I could put a word in with the chief."

Joe smiled and shook his head. "No thanks buddy. I'll not be in the tavern business forever but I'm done with policing. What's new in town?"

"The cells were filled with drunks yesterday but not much else is going on. It's even too damn cold for the crooks."

Tony showed up with another cup of coffee and a plate with two dough-nuts. "Here you go Johnny, the usual."

Johnny ate one of the doughnuts and drank half of the coffee. "What are you up to so early?"

"I promised to do a favor for a friend of Peggy's. You know Henry Brooks?"

"Brooks Lumber, up Ohiopyle way?"

"That's his operation. He showed up at The Star yesterday. One of his workers turned up dead New Year's Eve. He thinks it's suspicious, been hav-ing some other problems too. We're leaving for Ohiopyle on the nine o'clock train."

"That's a pretty spot in summer. Ever been?"

"No, it's my first visit."

"Take a stroll down to the Ferncliff Hotel if you can. It's quite the summer vacation spot and close to the station."

"Don't know that I'll be doing much strolling in this weather."

"I spent two summers in the mountains when I was a kid, loved it there. Mom had an old aunt lived up one of the hollows. The mountain folks are a different breed, don't care much for strangers and quick to take offense from city people. Keep to the beaten paths is my free advice."

"I'll take it Johnny. Time for me to get going." Joe dropped a quarter on the counter, put on his hat and coat, and headed for the door, waving to Tony as he left. "See you tomorrow buddy."

The B&O station was only three blocks away, but by the time Joe got there he was about frozen. The sun was up, the sky cloud free, except for the ever-present haze. Joe entered the station and bought a ticket for the nine o'clock train to Ohiopyle and points south. He took a seat on one of the tall-backed wooden benches and waited for Henry. At ten of nine he walked through the door, bought his ticket and joined Joe on the bench.

"Morning Joe. Thanks again for agreeing to help."

"You've been a good friend of Peggy's. I'm glad to oblige."

"There's more than meets the eye here I'm sure."

The stationmaster called out. "Arriving on the southbound tracks, local train 117 with service to Ohiopyle, Confluence, Frostburg, and Cumberland."

"That's us Joe." They both arose and exited the station, standing on the platform as the train approached. Bell clanging, the train pulled into the station with a screech and a hiss. A short train, it consisted of the engine, tender, a mail car, and three passenger cars. The conductor stepped down and the arriving passengers left the train. Joe strolled up the platform, where the engineer was inspecting the steam engine, oil can in hand.

"Morning buddy. What's new on the B&O?"

Turning from his work, the engineer frowned at Joe. "Nothing but trouble, up and down the line. Tough weather for running a railroad." He turned back to his work. Joe took a minute to inspect the engine, an old 2-4 model with a wooden cowcatcher. As the conductor called "all aboard" he hurried to the end car, where Henry stood by the steps.

"Thought you were going to ride up front with the engineer."

"I'd do it. I've always loved trains." They climbed the steps and entered the car from the rear, taking two empty seats in the middle of it. With more clangs and hisses, the train left the station.

The trip to Ohiopyle was only about 20 miles south but it was all uphill, the tracks following the Youghiogheny River on the east bank. Joe watched out the window as the train left town, passing some familiar sites, including his favorite fishing hole. In a few minutes they were out of town and climbing into the Allegheny Mountains. The river was mostly ice covered, only a narrow band of open water visible in the middle. Snow had been pushed into high banks along the sides of the tracks as the railroad struggled to keep the line clear.

"Where did you grow up Joe?

"I was born in Poland and came to America with my father in 1885. I lived in Scranton for a few years, then Philadelphia. How about you?"

"Born and raised in these hills, couldn't think of anywhere else I'd want to be."

"I've come to call Connellsville my home, hope to stay here." Joe looked out the window for a bit more then pulled out his notebook and turned to Henry. "You said you've been having some problems?"

Henry drew a deep breath and shook his head. "More than problems. I think someone is out to put Brooks Lumber out of business. It all started in September with some little things, equipment going missing, saws sabotaged, thinks like that."

Joe made a few notes, nodding. "It's gotten more serious?"

"In early October someone started spiking my big trees. Joe, I've got one of the largest stands of old-growth hardwoods around here, some of them almost a thousand years old I'd say, valuable timber. My father bought up most of the land 50 years ago or more, before the demand for lumber went sky high. You know what happens when someone pounds a few spikes into one?"

Joe shook his head. "Don't know much about lumbering."

"If you don't see it, which is hard to do, it plays hell with the saw blade. The first time it happened, the blade exploded, shutting my mill down for a week. The next time some of the saw pieces struck the operator in the leg. He liked to bleed to death before we got him tied off and into town. He lost the leg though."

"What else?"

"Men not showing up for work, men who been with me for years. Steam engines damaged, wagons stolen, all sorts of mischief. Then, in mid-December, after the heavy snows and cold weather set in, my timber started disappearing."

"Disappearing?"

"Started with some smaller trees, from out of the way corners of our holdings. They'd come in, cut the trees down and haul them out, doing maybe a wagon load at a time, never hitting the same spot twice. Then they started on the big ones. What happened to them I have no idea. They'd be too big to move very far without cutting them up some. There was never any evidence of that."

Joe made a few more notes then put his notebook away. "Know anyone has a grudge against you? Made any new enemies lately?"

"None that I'm aware of. The Brooks have lived in these hills for 75 years, been friends to most all of the old families. But mountain life is changing, plenty of strangers showing up, working the mills and mines. I've had to run a few squatters off of my land."

"Tell me about the dead man."

Henry smiled. "Half-moon Harkins was quite a character, but to tell his tale I might as well tell you the story of the Harkins family, as much as I know of it."

Chapter 4

＊　　　＊　　　＊

"Tickets, tickets please." The B&O conductor worked his way down the car collecting tickets, pausing at their seats. "Morning Henry."

"Morning Isaac. Seems like we're slowing down some."

"There's been a bit of drifting. We need to take it easy until we clear it, should be in Ohiopyle before eleven o'clock."

The conductor moved on. "The conductor a friend of yours Henry?"

"I ride this local at least once a week, have for years. Isaac has always been the conductor."

Joe took out his notebook again. "The Harkins, they've lived in the mountains for a long time?"

"You could say that. Legend has it that the first John Harkins fought at Fort Necessity with George Washington in the French & Indian War."

"Don't know much about that. When was it?"

"Started in 1754 as best I recall, ended in the early 1760s. We learned some about it in school, but not much."

"Don't know hardly anything about those days."

"Didn't I hear Peggy mention you were studying down at the University of Western Pennsylvania?"

"I am, going to take a course in United States history this semester."

"I was lucky, got to finish high school. Most of my friends had to go to work early, some didn't get any schooling. But then I had to go to work helping the old man."

"So John Harkins stayed here after the war?"

"No, the colonial governors of Virginia and Pennsylvania agreed this would stay Indian land. But that didn't hold long. By the mid 1760's the white man was moving in at a steady pace, John Harkins the first one to settle in the Yough[3] valley. The land was mostly deserted. Even the Indians didn't want to live here."

Joe contemplated that for a moment, looking out the window at the frozen river. "Can't imagine what that might have been like. How'd they survive winters like this?"

"God only know Joe. A man had to acquire many skills: farming, lumbering, carpentry, hunting, fishing, and the like. If you couldn't make it, kill it, or grow it, you'd likely freeze or starve to death. And many did. The closest place to get supplies was Cumberland and that was a hard trip, nigh unto impossible in winter. It took a tough man to survive and John Harkins was one, by all accounts. Legend has it he killed a panther with only a knife and his bare hands."

"He was a big man?"

"Don't think so, just wiry and mean, a trait he passed on down the line."

"He raised a big family then?"

Henry smiled. "There's where the story gets interesting. He raised two families with two different women. His first wife he brought up from Virginia, just after settling in here. I think her name was Mary. They had two children, John and a daughter. Mary died giving birth to the girl. Ever since that day there's been at least one or more John Harkins hereabout, the name passed down to the first son."

"The current John Harkins, he still lives near Ohiopyle?"

"About halfway between there and Confluence, a place the locals call Harkins Hollow."

---

3 Pronounced *Yock*, rhymes with *lock*.

Joe noticed that the train had picked up speed. He could see the engine as they rounded a curve, black smoke pouring from the stack as it climbed the grade. "What about wife number two?"

"He married a Delaware Indian woman, don't know where they met up with each other. Her Indian nickname was Touches Leaf. She was a big woman, taller than John I suspect, and she bore him many children. The first was a boy they named George, after George Washington most likely. And ever since that day there's been one or more George Harkins hereabout."

"How'd you come to know so much about the families?"

"I know both of the current elders fairly well. My father bought land from them. I went to school with children from both "The Johns" and "The Georges," as the two branches of the family are known. I've even seen The Book."

"The Book?"

"The first John Harkins started a book at some point, used it to record the family history, and the history of the settlers that came after. He kept an eye out for new settlers, ran off ones he didn't like. He was all the law there was for many years."

"Where does Half-moon fit into the family tree?"

"He was a George."

"Why'd they call him Half-moon?"

"Because he was half-crazy I guess, at least he acted that way. He knew how to run a saw mill though."

"What else can you tell me about the families?"

"It's easy to tell them apart. The Johns are generally smaller, especially the men, and have blue eyes. The Georges' men are bigger, some of them over six feet tall, and have brown, almost black. eyes."

The conductor made his way down the car again. "Next stop Ohiopyle, five minutes."

"That's us Joe. Better button up tight. It's always a bit colder up here."

The train soon pulled into the Ohiopyle station, Henry and Joe stepping off into a stiff wind. Joe pulled the ear lugs down on his hat, buttoned the top button of his coat, and wrapped his scarf tightly around his neck. "How are we going to get to the mill?"

"My sleigh is across the river at the livery."

Joe and Henry strode off at a brisk pace, following a snow-packed path across the Yough bridge and into the village of Ohiopyle. They entered the stable, where a few men huddled around a pot-bellied stove. Joe joined them while Henry got the horses hitched to his sleigh. In a few minutes they were ready to go.

The sled was a small two-seater, open to the elements. They climbed aboard and left town back across the bridge and tracks. Joe huddled against the cold, shivering.

"There's a blanket behind the seat Joe. We need to pick you up some long-johns."

Joe dug for the blanket and wrapped up, the thick wool cutting the wind. "Where are we going?"

"We'll stop and see the body first, then on to the mill."

"Why haven't his kin claimed it?"

"Half-moon was the blackest sheep in a fairly rotten branch of the Georges family tree. His folks are dead, one brother shows up around town on occasion, he has a few no-account cousins. It'll be up to me to bury him I suspect. I haven't had time to get the news to the current George Harkins Senior."

A few minutes later they stopped at a stone building, half sunk into the side of a hill. "This is our ice house Joe. My cousin runs it. Half-moon is inside."

They entered through a low door, dim light filtering through two small windows. Henry lit a lantern and led the way. "He's right back here."

Joe followed him to the rear, where he saw the body, stretched out on a bench and covered with a canvas tarp. He unwrapped his scarf and took off his gloves. "It's warmer in here than it is outside."

Henry nodded, and removed the tarp. "Have a close look Joe, tell me what you see."

Half-moon appeared to be in his fifties, tall and skinny with a full, unkempt beard and long hair. His clothing had been removed, except for his long underwear, which was stiff looking and filthy. Joe stepped forward and, for the next few minutes examined the body. "Let's get those long-johns off."

The body was dirty and bore many scars. Joe examined the front carefully. "Help me flip him over."

With Henry's help they flipped the body over and Joe continued his examination. "What do you make of this Henry?" On the back of his neck was a small tattoo of a spider.

"Not much, just a black spider."

"Mean anything to you?"

Henry shook his head. "See those bruises across his shoulders? Looks like he's been clubbed."

Joe nodded. "And that mark around his neck, it's not very noticeable. You'd think even a suicide would struggle at the rope. And look here." Joe held up first one arm then the other. Both wrists were badly abraded. "What do you make of these?"

"Don't know what to make of them."

"They look like more rope burns."

Joe dug out his notebook, made a little drawing of the tattoo and a few other notes and put it away. "I've seen enough. Let's go to the mill."

After throwing the tarp back over Half-moon's body, the two men left the icehouse. Joe smiled as they left. "Don't suppose he'll be needing those long-johns anymore. How far away is the mill?"

"The turnoff is about a mile or so up the road, the mill about two miles further up a rough lane. I hope this little sleigh can handle it."

Joe bundled back up and away they went. "Where's this road end up?"

"Connellsville, but it's a long, hard trip in the winter."

It didn't take long to get to the turnoff, the road well-packed from the traffic into Ohiopyle, but once they started up the lane the going got slow. The strong winds had knocked down some branches and caused some drifting, which got worse as they entered an area that had already been cleared of trees. In places, the track passed very close to steep drop-offs. Despite the cold, Joe could feel himself starting to sweat. They came to a spot where there were drop-offs on both sides. Henry stopped the sleigh. "Why don't you get out."

Joe climbed down and followed on foot as Henry slowly maneuvered the sleigh past, then stopped. "That's the worst of it Joe. The mill is on the other side of this hill."

Joe climbed back aboard and they were soon at the mill. "Anyone here since you found the body?"

"I was here most of yesterday morning with a few of my men. They stayed the rest of the day. Other than that no one that I know of. It took a while for the fellow that found the body to ride back out. I guess someone could have come by New Year's Eve."

"He work for you long?"

"Yes, he's a teamster. Rode a horse in to drive a sled load of posts out. First thing he noticed was the other horse stabled here was gone."

"Where do you think it went?"

Henry pointed to a faint trail leading away from the mill. "My best guess is into the woods. There's a rough path leads on to Confluence."

"Let's see where the body was found."

They entered the mill, Joe's first time in one. "Half-moon was working alone?"

"No, he had a helper, don't know who it was though. Most likely a cousin. There's been no sign, or word from him. Half-moon's body was found in the back." The sky had darkened again. Henry took a moment to light a lantern and they entered the storeroom. "The body was hanging from the middle rafter. The chair on the floor was lying on its side under, just where you see it."

Joe sat the chair upright under the rafter. "How tall do you think Half-moon was?"

"Almost six feet I'd say."

Joe noticed that the rope was still attached to the rafter. "You cut him loose right at the neck?"

Henry nodded and pointed to the rear. "Used that ladder to get to him."

Joe got the ladder and placed it next to the chair. "Got any more rope?"

Henry retrieved a length from the other room. Joe climbed the ladder, took one end of the rope, held it to the still-attached length, and let the rest fall. "Mark where the rope hits the chair."

Henry did and Joe climbed down. "Let's measure the rope."

They laid the rope on the floor and Joe stepped it off and turned to Henry. "Seeing as how that length of rope is about seven feet long, and Half-moon was only six feet tall, it's not likely it was a suicide. I'd say he was clubbed, bound and then somehow hoisted up, probably using this ladder."

"There's another one should be around here somewhere, most likely took two men to do the job."

"Let's take a walk down that path a bit."

The two men headed down the path and entered the woods. Here, the snow hadn't blown as much and faint hoof prints could be made out. There were no signs of human tracks. "Looks like you were right Henry. Whoever took the horse must have rode them out this way."

The two walked on for another hundred yards until they exited the patch of woods. The blowing snow had obliterated the tracks here. Henry stopped and turned around. "Let's go back before we get frostbit."

They retraced their steps and exited the woods, just in time to see their sleigh go over the top of the hill. Henry ran down the road a bit before stopping, throwing his hat to the ground. "Son of a bitch." At that moment it started to snow again. Henry picked up his hat and trotted back. "Sorry for dragging you into this. I'd advise against us following them. Looks like we're in for more snow, and it's soon dark. We best hole up here for the night."

Joe sat down on a stump, watching the snow falling faster. *Peggy is going to wonder what happened to me.*

Chapter 5

By now the sun was low in the sky, the snowfall just a shower. It would soon be dark. Henry was busy at the steam engine, building a fire in the box. *Looks like a locomotive without wheels,* Joe thought. "Not much wood in the pile Henry. Will it last the night?"

Henry pointed to a loaded sled, waiting to be hauled out. "When these scraps are gone we'll start burning those posts. There's more than enough."

Joe inspected the engine. A large wheel was affixed to the top of the boiler, a belt around it leading into the mill. He went inside to inspect further, where the belt turned a smaller wheel, linked to the saw in the same way. Various leavers controlled the saw blade. A feed line with rollers extended out the other direction, a small stack of logs piled at the end of it. That wall of the mill was open. His inspection complete, he rejoined Henry, busy feeding wood into the firebox. "Nice work Henry. Guess we won't freeze to death."

"Likely not. Once the boiler heats up it'll stay fairly warm all around it. We'll have to sleep in shifts though to keep the fire going."

The sun had set, darkness descending on the mill. Without a cloud in the sky the night promised to be a cold one. Joe edged closer to the boiler, already warming up. *Wish we had that blanket from the sleigh.* "I'm going to inspect the storeroom again." He went back inside, hoping to find anything that could be used as a cover.

"There should be a lantern in there, hanging on a hook by the saw. We'll need that."

Joe found the lantern, lit it and entered the room. *Let's see what we've got.* There was a container of kerosene by the door, which he moved out near the saw, and a pile of tools. Other than that the front of the room was mostly empty. Moving on, the light revealed a heap at the far end, covered by a canvas tarp. *Not a blanket but close enough.* He grabbed an end and tried to pull it free of whatever it was covering. *It's stuck under something.* He set the lantern down, knelt, and, grabbing one end, pulled hard. The tarp pulled free, exposing a pair of boots. Joe dropped the tarp and jumped to his feet. *It's another body!* "Henry, come on in here."

Henry entered and saw the tarp. "Good work Joe. That'll come in handy tonight."

Joe pulled the tarp off of the body. "And I don't think this fellow will be needing it. He's already stiff as a board. Let's pull him out of here." Henry grabbed one foot, Joe the other, and together they drug the body from the storeroom. Joe retrieved the lantern and they inspected the body. The man was small in stature, and wearing ragged work clothes. "I think we found Half-moon's helper. Recognize him?"

Henry knelt down with the lantern. "He's unfamiliar to me, don't think I've ever seen him working the mills."

Joe eyed the man's high boots. *I need a pair of those.* "Let's roll him over." The rear of his head was flattened, his hair matted with congealed blood. "Looks like whoever clubbed Half-moon gave him a dose of the same medicine." Dried blood covered the man's neck. Joe pulled out his handkerchief and rubbed. "No tattoo on this fellow."

They rolled him back over and went through his pockets. Joe pulled a round metal object from the man's coat. "It's a pocket watch." He handed it to Henry, who fiddled with the case, finally popping it open.

"Look here Joe." He handed it back. The silver case was engraved, with a panther on the outside and "JH 1880" on the inside. "Know who this belongs to?"

"From what you've told me I can guess. Now how in the hell did that fellow end up with John Harkins' watch?"

A muffled crack rang out, followed by a "ping." Henry grabbed Joe, "Stay down. That's a rifle shot." He blew out the lantern and, reaching inside his coat, pulled out a pistol. They backed slowly toward the storeroom. Another crack echoed, followed by another ping. "He's shooting at the boiler. We need to get as far away from it as we can!" They moved to where the body had lain, crouching against the wall.

"Why didn't you tell me to bring a gun?"

Henry shrugged. "Never thought to advise it. I've been carrying mine since the troubles started." Silence fell on the scene, a near-full moon lighting the clearing. "He's likely moving in."

Joe suddenly had to pee and started to get up.

Henry grabbed his arm. "Stay put. I gotta go too. Piss your pants if you need to, but keep down." Another crack and ping, the sound closer.

Henry grabbed the tarp and pulled it over them. "We need to lie flat, as close to the wall as we can get."

Lord help us. Joe and Henry huddled close to the wall.

Another crack, but no ping, just a loud hiss. Henry whispered, "He got it."

With a loud boom the steam engine exploded. The mill shook, then fell, the roof collapsing. Somehow the rear wall held. Dazed, and with ringing ears, Joe coughed in the dust.

"Shhh," Henry whispered. He started moving some of the fallen roof boards until a small peep hole was cleared. The saw mill was demolished, a fire starting to grow in the ruins. "Here the bastard comes."

Joe could see their sleigh coming down the hill. It stopped close by and a man with a rifle got out. He studied the scene and, apparently satisfied, walked around the destroyed steam engine. Shaking his head, he turned toward their hiding place. Stopping first by the body, he sat his rifle down and started going through his pockets.

Henry nudged Joe, finger across his lips.

Finding nothing, the man stood, looked around further, then entered the storeroom, his rifle at the ready.

With a loud "bang, bang, bang," Henry fired three shots. The man stood for a second, fired one wild shot with his rifle, then fell over.

"Let's get the hell out of here." Henry started pushing through the fallen roof. Joe snapped out of it and began pushing his way out too. Soon they were both free.

The fire was spreading. Soon the ruins would be engulfed. Henry ran for the sleigh. "Pull this bastard out of there. He's coming with us."

Joe grabbed the man by both feet and tugged him free. Then he returned for the rifle. Henry pulled the sleigh close and together they stuffed the body behind the seat. By the time they were done, both were blood-smeared. Climbing aboard, Henry drove the sleigh up the hill, the mill ruins roaring behind them.

"Hold on a minute." Joe climbed down and relieved himself next to the sleigh. Henry laughed, then joined him.

Chapter 6

*   *   *

It was almost seven when Henry pulled into the icehouse. "Might as well add him to our collection of stiffs. Wait here." He went to the back door of the house, knocked, then entered, exiting a minute later with another man carrying a lantern.

"Joe, meet my cousin Bob."

"How do. Your cousin leads an exciting life."

"Don't I know it. That's why I'm in the ice business." Bob opened the door to the icehouse and sat the lantern down. He and Henry hauled the body inside, then returned. "You fellas look a might chilled. Let's go warm up."

Joe's stomach rumbled. *Haven't ate since breakfast!* He followed the brothers into the kitchen of the house, where a coal stove gave off welcome heat. The men took off their coats, hats, and gloves then sat down at a wooden table, Joe grabbing the chair closest to the stove. "Bob, I hate to be a bother, but somehow we managed to skip lunch. I'd pay dearly for a bite."

"A cup of this old coffee should warm you up a bit. How about some ham and eggs?" Bob pulled two mugs down from a shelf and filled them from a metal pot sitting on the stove. "Now can you please tell me how I've ended up with two dead men in my icehouse."

As Henry told the tale, and Joe sipped his coffee, Bob retrieved a thick piece of ham from the icebox and dropped it in a cast-iron skillet. In a second one he fried four eggs. In just a few minutes Henry and Joe were shoveling it in. Bob sat and watched them eat.

"That's some story. How'd you get mixed up in this Joe?"

"Henry is a friend of a friend."

Henry smiled. "Bob knows Peggy. If I knew it would turn out like this, I'd not asked you to."

Joe cleaned his plate with a heel of bread. "Much obliged for the grub. I was about to fall over." He turned to Henry. "I thought my gunplay days were behind me, but now that I'm mixed up in this I intend to see it through. We need to find out who's behind this."

Henry nodded. "I think it's time for you to meet the Harkins clan." He pulled out the pocket watch they found. "Still running. It's after eight, no way for you to get back to Connellsville tonight. Let's pack up and get you a room at The Ohiopyle House. On the way we can stop at the telegraph office. You can let Peggy know what's going on. We can visit John Harkins in the morning." The two men rose and bundled back up. "Thanks for the help Bob."

The night had grown even colder. Joe looked up at the clear sky, his jaw dropping. "I've seen stars in the sky before but nothing like this." A wide band of light spread across the night sky, a glowing smear, each star invisible, joined in a celestial display.

"That's the Milky Way Joe, tens of thousands of stars all crowded together. You'll never see such a thing down in the valley, too much smoke and light."

Joe gazed up until he started getting dizzy, contemplating the night sky. *So beautiful. Makes a man feel small.* He took a deep breath. *The air, so crisp and clean.* He turned to Henry. "There's a lot I've not seen Henry, and a lot I don't know." He looked up again. "This makes the day worthwhile, even if I nearly got blown up."

Henry laughed again. "You're a funny fellow Joe, a good match for a serious-minded woman like Peggy. What say we take a closer look at that fellow before calling it a night." They entered the icehouse, their attacker dumped on the floor next to Half-moon.

There was nothing to distinguish him, just another mountain man with a beard, dressed like most of the others around Ohiopyle. His plaid coat was bloodstained, with three small holes in it. "Looks like you hit with all three shots."

"Growing up I learned that accuracy with a firearm can be a matter of life and death, especially if you're facing a panther or bear. Same goes for human predators I'd say."

Joe rolled him over and, sure enough, there was a spider tattoo on his neck. "Another Black Widow. Looks like there's a gang of them." He bent and examined it more closely. "This tattoo is fancier, more finely drawn than the other. Let's see Half-moon's again." Rolling him over, they inspected it again. "This one looks homemade. And the mark on the back isn't red like his."

Joe dug out his notebook and wrote "Tattoos in Fayette County."

"I've had enough Joe. Let's call it a night."

Chapter 7

*   *   *

Joe was dreaming and it wasn't a good dream. He was in an icehouse, and so cold his teeth were chattering. *Got to get out of here!* He searched for the door, only to find it guarded by a man wearing a plaid jacket with three bloody holes in it. Carrying ice tongs, he moved toward Joe, opening and closing them as he advanced.

Joe awoke with a start, freezing but in a sweat. He could see his breath. *Where the hell am I?* Slowly, the events of yesterday came back to him. *Damn crazy dream.* He was in a room at an Ohiopyle hotel. *It's cold in here.* Looking around, he saw frost on the inside of the window, a dim light visible outside. He pulled the woolen blankets up around his neck.

As the dream faded, Joe calmed down and his chills passed. *Can't stay in bed all day.* Throwing back the covers, he was dressed in a minute and left the room. He found his way to the lobby. A fireplace filled one wall, radiating a welcoming heat. Sitting close to it, Joe warmed up, and planned his day.

It was 7:30 by the clock on the mantle, Henry was due to arrive at eight. *Enough time for a big breakfast.* Leaving the warmth of the fire with some reluctance, Joe approached the front desk, a grey-haired woman behind it. "Morning ma'am, where can a fellow get a bite?"

"The Ohiopyle House dining room is famous for its breakfasts." She pointed down the hall. "Tell them Ethel sent you. Breakfast comes with the room. I recommend the buckwheat pancakes and venison sausage."

"Much obliged." *Deer meat, don't see that at City Lunch.* Joe followed the hall and down a few steps, the small dining room mostly empty. Another grey-haired woman approached. "Can I help you?"

"Ethel sent me. I stayed here last night."

"Well then, breakfast comes with the room." She handed Joe a menu. "Sit where you like. My name's Valeria. Give me a holler when you're ready to order."

A pot-bellied stove sat along the front wall. Joe sauntered toward it and took a seat at a table for two. *I reckon Henry will've ate already. No sense waiting for him.* He opened the menu. The breakfast special was "The Full House," three buckwheat pancakes, two eggs, venison sausage and biscuits. Valeria was coming his way, a cup and small pot of coffee in her hand. "You look like you could use a hot drink. Made up your mind?"

"Deal me a Full House if you please, eggs over easy."

Valeria smiled. "You won't regret it. I made the biscuits and Ethel's husband shot the deer and made the sausage."

Joe poured himself a cup of coffee and took out his notebook. *There's no tattoo parlor in Connellsville I know of.* A trip to Uniontown, the county seat of Fayette County, was in order. *I'll see if Sheriff Miller knows anything about these Black Widow boys.* Joe and the sheriff had worked together in August, together foiling a plot to blow up the Frick mines.

Valeria soon delivered his meal, a platter piled high with the buckwheat cakes and eggs, a smaller plate with sausage patties and the biscuits. "What else can I get you honey?"

Joe's eyes widened, the pancakes were as big as the platter. "Maybe some jam?"

"Be right back."

Joe didn't wait, digging right in. The pancakes had an earthy, nutty taste, new to Joe. The sausage was a bit stronger than he was used to but well-seasoned. Valeria returned with a bowl of apple jelly. "This is the best I can do for you this time of year. Everything to your liking?"

Joe nodded, his mouth full. Swallowing, he took a sip of coffee. "Breakfast is my favorite meal and it don't get much better than this."

"Well, come back and see us again then."

Joe looked up to see Henry walk down the steps to the dining room, coming his way. "Morning Joe, sleep well?"

Before he could reply Valeria spoke up. "Hello Henry. Nice to see you as usual. You eat yet?"

"I did but I've got room for another cup of coffee."

"Coming right up."

Henry sat down, eyeing Joe's mostly empty plates. "That's a big load. What do you think of our mountain cooking?'

"My friend Tony has some competition. And since you liked to starve me to death yesterday I'm taking no chances." He shoveled in the last bite of sausage and eggs.

Valeria returned with Henry's coffee. "Here you go." She looked at Joe's two empty plates. "I swear, I've never seen such an appetite. Had enough?"

Joe nodded as he finished chewing. "Should hold me until lunch." Valeria cleared the plates, smiling. "I'm ready to go see the Harkins."

Henry shook his head. "Not quite. If you're going to be running these ridges with me, we need to get you dressed for it. There's a store just up the street we'll stop at first."

Together they hustled up Front Street to the next block where a sign announced "Whipkey's General Store & Dry Goods." The front windows were filled with everything from rifles to long underwear. Henry pointed to a red, one-piece pair. "That's what you need Joe, a good old Union suit."

Joe followed Henry into the store, an old man behind the counter reading a newspaper. "Mornin Jacob."

The old man looked up and nodded, "Hello Henry. Can I help you?"

"My friend needs some cold-weather gear. We'll just poke around a bit." He turned to Joe. "Let's start in the long-johns department." They headed to a table in the corner, piled high with various garments. Henry held up one of the red one-piece suits. "What do you think Joe?"

Joe took the garment, examining it closely. It was made of flannel, had about a dozen buttons in front and a rear panel that could be unbuttoned. He frowned and shook his head. "Don't think so Henry. Might slow a man down in an emergency." He sat it down and picked up a two-piece set made of grey wool. "How about these?"

"They're nice and warm but can get a mite itchy for some folks, takes some getting used to."

Joe picked up another set, red flannel but two-piece. He held it up, gauging the size. "How about these?"

"Good choice. Warm, but not itchy. Now let's get you some boots. Jacob, got a pair of high-tops back there for these big feet?"

Jacob disappeared into the back room returned with one pair. "Might be a bit big. I'd get a pair of those wool socks to take up the slack."

Henry nodded, "We'll take them, the long-johns and the socks. Joe, since I drug you up here it's on me. Jacob, put them on my bill. I'll settle up tomorrow."

They left the store with Joe's new winter gear and went back to the hotel. Joe returned to his room and donned his long johns and new footwear. Carrying his old shoes, he joined back up with Henry. "I'm ready to meet the Harkins."

Henry's sleigh was parked next to the hotel. They boarded and with "Heya" and a snap of the reins they departed, back over the bridge and the tracks, then turned onto another road heading south. "This road runs all the way to Confluence. We'll be going about half way."

Joe viewed the scenery as they left town, travelling along the Yough and the railroad tracks. The riverbank was dotted with various commercial enterprises, the first a fairly large structure just out of town. The wind from the northwest blew a noxious smell their way. As Joe's stomach turned a bit he began breathing through his mouth. "That's as foul an odor as I've smelled since I came upon a skunk been hit by a train. What goes on there?"

"That's the tannery, a rough place to work. Ever wondered how the leather you're sitting on is made?' Joe shook his head. "It's not pretty, starting with when the hides are delivered."

"They'd have to pay dearly to get me to work there. I'm 'bout to gag."

"Work is so scarce up here they don't have any shortage of men, even at a dollar a day. You want I'll arrange a tour."

Joe frowned and shook his head. "No thanks."

Travelling past the tannery they soon left the toxic fumes behind and passed into open country. The Yough valley ran between several ridges, with evidence of active lumbering operations on both sides of the river. Here the river was frozen solid. The sky was clear, temperatures still below freezing. Joe could see a few plumes of smoke rising here and there along the way. "Many people live up in here?"

"Five hundred maybe, between here and Confluence, a good portion are Harkins, or related to them one way or another."

Joe took a deep breath, the air cold but sweet. "Beautiful country Henry." He could see the river turning west, meandering around a flat plain. Shortly thereafter they crossed a small bridge. To the east a frozen stream headed up a hollow. Henry turned the sleigh up a rough trail and stopped.

"Welcome to Harkins Hollow Joe. This little stream's called Rock Creek. The Harkins live up it about a mile or so. We're better off hiking in. Doesn't look like there's been much traffic here."

Joe climbed down from the sleigh and surveyed the narrow track. Packed down from mostly horse traffic, the snow was still loose in spots. Henry tied their horse to a tree and they departed. The snow was deeper than Joe's boots. Marching in silence, they made slow progress up the grade. After fifteen minutes of walking Joe was panting from the effort. "Let's stop for a bit, let me catch my breath."

They stopped in the middle of a small clearing. Set back away from the road stood a tiny log cabin, smoke rising from a stone chimney at one end. As they rested, the door opened and a man appeared with a rifle. Raising it to his shoulder he shouted, "State your business!"

Henry took of his hat and waved. "It's me, Abner. Henry Brooks. We're going in to see John."

Abner nodded, lowered his weapon and went back inside.

"I guess you could say Abner keeps an eagle eye out for anyone heading up Harkins Hollow. He's married to a Harkins woman, works in the family trade."

"What trade is that?"

"The Harkins have a few irons in the fire. Abner works in the whiskey operation. Remember this Joe: Strangers aren't welcome back here. It's been like that since the beginning. Abner's likely to shoot first and ask questions later."

Joe nodded. "I've caught my breath. Let's move on."

Another 15 minutes brought them to a smaller hollow branching off. At the end Joe could see a two-story wooden-frame home, stone chimneys smoking at both ends. A covered porch wrapped around the front and sides. "That's a mighty fancy place for up here in the middle of nowhere."

"Yes indeed Joe. It took all of the summer of '98 for them to cart in the materials and build it. Inside it's as fine a home as you'll find here about."

As they headed up the hollow Joe saw the front door open. A young man stepped out onto the porch, rifle in hand. *Son of a bitch! I guess that's the way the say hello up here.* They both stopped.

Henry took off his hat once again and waved. "It's Henry Brooks, Hawk."

The man waved them on, set the rifle down, and waited for them, arms folded across his chest.

Henry turned to Joe. "There's currently three John Harkins. That's the youngest of them. His family and friends call him Hawk. Do us both a favor and let me do the talking."

They were soon on the porch, young John Harkins eyeing Joe up and down. "Who's this?"

"Hawk, meet Joe Zajac. He's a friend from Connellsville. Is John Senior and your father home? We have something that belongs to your family."

Hawk nodded and picked up his rifle. Opening the door he waved them inside. The entrance led into a big room, nicely warmed by the fireplaces.

To the right several chairs and a sofa sat in front of one. To the left was the kitchen. In the middle two men sat at a dining table, silently staring at them.

Henry took of his hat, gloves, and coat. Joe followed suit and kept quiet. "Morning Buck, morning John. Sorry to interrupt your day."

At one end of the table sat an old man, small in stature, clean shaven, with long white hair. At the other sat a younger carbon copy, but long brown hair pulled into a ponytail. "What brings you to the hollow in the dead of winter?"

Henry reached into his pocket and pulled out the watch. Walking to the table he sat in in front of the old man. "Is this yours?"

The old man picked it up, nodding, wound it and put in in his pocket without a word. John Junior jumped up, his chair crashing to the floor behind him. "Where'd you get that from?"

"That's a long story. Can we sit a spell and tell the tale?"

Chapter 8

*　　　*　　　*

John Harkins nodded, eyeing Joe up and down. "Have a seat then and tell your story. Who's this fellow?"

Henry and Joe sat down, one on each side of the table. "This here's Joe Zajac. He's from Connellsville. I've asked him to look into some troubles I've been having at my mills."

"What kind of troubles?"

"Tools and equipment gone missing, mills damaged, trees spiked, lumber stolen. Been going on for a few months."

John looked at the old man and nodded, then back to Henry. "What good's a city feller gonna do for you up here?"

"He's got a good head on his shoulders and some experience with investigations."

"Go on then."

"You know Half-moon works for me on occasion."

"On occasion he's not in the coop, or otherwise up to no good."

"He's a good mill man if he's been sober for a while, and up to this point never gave me a reason to suspect he'd steal from me. I've been hard pressed to keep up with my mine orders and mill men have gone scarce."

"Half-moon had the watch?"

"No, he was found dead on New Year's Eve. It was made to look like he hung himself but we know that's not likely."

"No surprise there, and I'll be shedding no tears. He was bound to come to a no-good end. Who had it then?"

"His helper, a fellow I never met before. He's dead now too, and the body likely burned up."

While Henry told the story, Joe looked around the room. On one wall there was a gun rack, above it the head of a buck white-tail with an enormous rack. On another hung a few old pictures. In the kitchen, an assortment of pots and pans filled a third wall. Joe's eyes turned to the old man, who was eyeing him with a little grin. Hawk Harkins stood in a corner, also watching Joe, but he wasn't smiling.

Henry had finished his story. "And that's all I know John. When did Buck's watch go missing?"

"Just before Christmas. We were all out, Pap and I picking up some supplies. Hawk was making a few deliveries. My Mayme was visiting with her sister. We got back early afternoon, saw the front door was open."

The old man spoke. "They wasn't your ordinary thieves neither. Left the guns and such."

Joe fished his notebook and pencil out of his coat pocket and started writing. "Did they take anything else?"

The old man stood up, shaking his fist. "The God damn snakes stole 'The Book'!"

Henry turned to John. "How'd they get past Abner?"

"Likely came down from the back. There were some tracks."

"Any idea who might have done it?"

The old man slammed his fist on the table. "Only one man would take pleasure from it, George Harkins."

Henry turned to John. "You having troubles with the other side of the family?"

John sat grim faced. "You know we've always been rivals, but respectful generally speaking. They stay on their side of the valley, we on ours. But that state of affairs has changed of late. And Half-moon being tied up in this watch business adds to it."

"How's that?"

"I guess it started at the Harvest Fair last year, at the rassling match. Many a year it ends up with the two families going at it. This year it was young George against Hawk."

Hawk spoke up. "Just like in '99, when I whipped him fair and square."

Buck smiled. "They's always got the size on us but we're quicker."

"And I was whippin him again until he got dirty. The prick kneed me in the balls."

John spoke in a low voice. "Then slammed him down, broke my boy's arm."

Hawk nodded, rubbing his right forearm. "Still hurts, but his day will come."

"Since then it's got worse. They's running their 'shine into our territory."

Buck spoke up. "Anyone fool enough to drink their corn squeezins don't know good whiskey. That junk can't hold a candle to our rye." He walked over to the kitchen cabinet and pulled out an earthenware jug. After pulling the cork he raised it and took a swallow. "Ahhh, now that's good whiskey." He returned to the table and sat the jug in front of Joe. "Have a taste if you're so inclined."

Joe glanced at Henry, who nodded slightly. *Guess a little won't kill me.* Grabbing the jug in both hands, he raised it to his lips and tilted, a generous portion filling his mouth. He swallowed, wiped his lips with the back of his hand, and slid the jug to Henry. *That's better than Old Overholt!!* He felt the liquor travel to his stomach. "Much obliged Mr. Harkins. That's a damn smooth drink."

He gave Joe a smile and a wink. "Call me Buck son. Everyone else does. They's too damn many John's around here."

Henry took a slug, and passed the jug to John, who did the same. Hawk came to the table, took a swallow, and returned the jug to the cabinet. "I need to check my trap line. Be back by supper time." He left the room through a hall in the rear.

John stood up. "Someone's been jumping them too. I got work to do. We're much obliged to you Henry for returning the watch. I gave that to Pap for his 50th birthday. Let me know if the Harkins can ever be of help." He likewise departed down the hall, and entered a room off of it.

Buck stood next. "And I have to use the privy. A shot of rye always gets me going." He also headed down the hall and out a door at the end. Joe and Henry got up, donned their coats and walked out the front door. "What did you think of the Harkins clan Joe?"

"I liked the old man. Hawk seemed a bit stand-offish, John all business."

"That about sums them up. Old Buck is as fine a fellow as you'll find."

"Why do they call him Buck?"

"He's always been one of the best hunters hereabouts, takes his share of the big bucks every year. That 26-point head on the wall was one of his more recent kills. He's still a sure-shot."

Joe and Henry retraced their path out of Harkins Hollow and were soon back at the sleigh and heading toward town. "We'll get you on the one o'clock to Connellsville. You got any thoughts on how to proceed?"

"I'll go visit Sheriff Miller tomorrow and see if he knows anything about these Black Widow boys. I'd like to get a picture of the fellow that attacked us."

"I can do that. My wife got me a Brownie for Christmas. My cousin has a darkroom. I'll take shots of both tattoos too."

"What's a Brownie?"

"The latest camera from Eastman Kodak. It's just a cardboard box with a lens but it takes nice little pictures."

"I could use a map of the area, showing your timber holdings and the spots where you've been having your problems. See if anything jumps out at us. Can we keep the bodies on ice for a while?"

"Don't think anyone will be wondering about Half-moon. I'll get those pictures taken this afternoon and see if Bob can develop them. I have a fellow going to town later on today. If I can get them done I'll have him drop them by The Star. Anything else?"

"I'd like to meet the other branch of the Harkins family. Think we can do that on Saturday?"

Henry nodded. "I thought the same. I'll meet you at the hotel around eleven."

It was almost noon when they reached Ohiopyle train station and climbed down from the sleigh. "Joe, you've been a big help already. If I'd known this would turn violent I'd have never asked. What's your fee for dangerous detective work?"

Joe laughed. "I'm happy to help, no charge. Just pay for my train tickets and keep me fed."

Now Henry laughed. "I'd rather pay you than feed you, but if that's the deal, fine by me."

They entered the station and Henry bought Joe his ticket for the one o'clock train, and another round-trip ticket for Saturday. "We've got some time. You ready for lunch?"

"I think I'll wait until I get back to town. Let me get my shoes and you can get on with your business."

Joe retrieved the shoes and tucked them inside his jacket. "See you on Saturday."

Henry waved as he drove out of town. Joe went back inside the station, the clock showing 12:15. *I've got time to do a bit of exploring, could use a little stretch of the legs.* He left the station and noticed the arched entrance to the Hotel Ferncliff just across the street. *It's a bit warmer today, Johnny said it was worth a look.* He crossed over and passed beneath the arch, where a wooden boardwalk cleared of snow lead away from the entrance. *It's not a long walk, I can see it from here.* A few minutes later he stood in front of the hotel.

The Ferncliff was a four story wooden structure with a mansard roof. A broad porch wrapped around it. The boardwalk continued but was still snow covered just past the building. Joe walked up to the front door, intent on taking a peek inside.

"The hotel is closed son." Joe turned to see a stern-faced, big-bellied man with a white beard standing behind him. His open jacket showed he was wearing a holstered revolver. *I guess these folks can't say hello without being armed.*

"Yes sir, I can see that. I was just wanting a look through the window."

"Well I'm sorry but I can't be allowing that. The owners have a 'No Trespassing' policy when we're closed for the winter. I'm charged with enforcing it. You lost or something?"

"Just waiting for the one o'clock back to Connellsville. I'm in town on business."

"What kind?"

"Helping Henry Brooks out."

The man's firm look softened. "Well alright then, why didn't you say so? Me and Henry go way back. His Pappy and me was good friends."

I guess Henry knows everyone in town. Joe descended the steps, arm outstretched. "I'm Joe Zajac."

Removing his glove, the men shook hands. "And I'm Marshall McNutt, caretaker of this fine establishment. Pleased to meet you Joe."

"This looks like quite the place. What's it like in the summer?"

"Well son, the folks from Pittsburgh come up here by the thousands over the vacation season. A dollar train ride lets you leave the smoke behind for a few days. We've 50 modern rooms here, all filled most every weekend. Some folks stay a week or more."

"What's the attraction?"

"Other than the clean mountain air, we've got a dance hall, bowling alleys and a fine restaurant. And the peninsula has some of the most abundant plant life to be found for miles around. Now that I know your credentials I'd be happy to show you the insides."

Joe checked his watch. It was a quarter till one. "Much obliged Mr. McNutt, but my train's due in a few minutes. I'll be back in town on Saturday, maybe then."

Marshall nodded. "I'll be here. If I don't see you coming, just come around to the back door and ring the bell."

"See you then."

Joe departed with a wave, returned to the station and was soon travelling back down the mountain.

Chapter 9

* * *

As the train descended toward Connellsville, Joe's thoughts wandered. *The Milky Way, what a sight. Won't be forgetting that. Made the trip worth it even if I 'bout got blown up.* He thought of his father and uncle. *Wonder if they ever saw it.*

At 30 years of age, Joe had lived a life that was at times hard. But he also considered himself quite blessed. Born in Poland in 1870, he only remembered his early days in bits and pieces. His family lived in the country, their home a one room thatched roof hut. His father Karol was a peasant farmer, working the land for the man who owned it. For his efforts, he was housed and received enough food to keep them all from starving. Of his mother, Helga, he remembered very little. She worked hard too though, he remembered that. A frail woman, she got sick and died when Joe was only 13. Two years later, he and his father came to America with dreams of a better life.

Karol was fortunate: He had an older brother, Stanley, who had come to America many years before. He lived just outside of Philadelphia, where he operated a butcher shop. He was able to support them until Karol found work in a coal mine near Scranton. Though that life was also tough, they always had food on the table and a roof over their heads. Joe was able to stay in school, and enjoyed learning.

A year later, Joe's father was killed in a mine explosion. His uncle took him in, and Joe was able to graduate from high school near the top of his class. He worked in the butcher shop for the next year. Then, at Uncle Stanley's insistence, he moved out on his own after finding work as a Philadelphia policeman.

At 19, Joe was living what he thought was the good life. He earned a decent wage and developed a taste for hard liquor, along with a quick temper, especially when the two were combined. His spare time was spent mostly in saloons and dance halls. It was at a saloon near Police Central in early 1894 that his life quickly changed. A drunken argument with an older cop led to a fight. Joe knocked the fellow out, he fell, struck his head on the bar rail, and died on the spot.

Life on the force was unpleasant at best after that. While absolved of any wrongdoing, he still felt responsible. Shunned by his fellow officers, Joe grew unhappy. He'd learned that liquor and a quick temper was a bad combination and would always carry regrets.

An advertisement in the local paper led him to work in western Pennsylvania as a plain-clothes member of the H.C. Frick Coke Company police force. Arriving in the summer of 1894, he eventually settled in Connellsville, at the heart of the "Connellsville Coal Seam."

In August of 1900, he was called upon to investigate a murder at the Leisenring No. 1 coke works. In the process he uncovered a larger plot to blow up the mines of his employer. While solving the murder mystery and foiling the plot, his eyes were opened to the plight of the immigrant workers, and the fortunate circumstances of his own life. He soon left the employ of Frick.

The best part of the summer of 1900 was Joe's meeting, and falling in love with, Peggy Patterson. Their relationship, quick to develop, had stagnated of late. Peggy was caring for her sick father, Andy, and Joe was attending to his studies.

Joe pulled out his little notebook and started writing.

Picture and map
Friday-Sheriff Miller

CONFLUENCE

Tattoo Parlors
Black Widow Boys
Saturday-Ohiopyle, take revolver
Tuesday-start classes

Looks like I'll be staying busy. Somewhere in there I still have to keep up with the books at work. He stared out the window and watched the telegraph poles flash by, his thoughts wandering again before settling on something he'd learned in his Ancient History class, a thought attributed to Socrates. He turned to a fresh page, writing it down. *The unexamined life is not worth living. That's been stuck in my head since I first heard it. Do I believe it? I lived many a year without examining mine. Why start now?*

His thoughts turned to the events of August. He hated to admit it, but that madman Kurt Straub had affected him. *He helped open my eyes to the plight of those poor folks working for Frick. I examined my life and I'm glad I did. There's more to life than drinking and running around.*

"Connellsville, next stop Connellsville, five minutes." The conductor worked his way down the car, pulling ticket stubs from the seats of the departing passengers. Outside, the ground had levelled out, the foothills of the Alleghenies left behind. A few minutes later Joe saw the railroad trestle where he'd last seen Kurt Straub, the man behind last summer's plot, falling into the Youghiogheny. *His body never did wash up.*

Joe got off at the station where a boy was selling newspapers.

"Read all about it. Frick payroll robbed."

Joe bought the "Connellsville Courier," this week's edition just published. He read the first few sentences of the lead story. The Frick paymasters had been robbed on their way to the Standard mine near Mount Pleasant. He shook his head, tucked the newspaper under his arm and headed toward City Lunch. *Someone else's worry, not mine. A bite to eat, then get cleaned up and go to work.*

The restaurant was almost empty when Joe arrived, Tony sitting at the counter with a bowl of soup. He turned and, looking Joe up and down, gave a big laugh. "Look at you, one day in the mountains and you a mountain man. Where you get those fancy boots?"

Joe looked down at himself. He still had on the high boots and his coat was stained with dried blood. He also needed a shave. "Ended up staying the night Tony, ran into a bit of trouble. Can you get me a bowl of that soup and a cup of coffee?"

Tony got up and headed to the kitchen. "Sure boss. Trouble again? I thought you all done with that."

Joe gave him a shrug and took his usual seat at the end of the counter. While waiting for his soup he changed into his city shoes, took off his coat and hat, and opened up the paper. In a minute Tony returned with a bowl of minestrone and a plate of bread. "Here you go my friend. Enjoy." He placed the meal in front of Joe and sat down beside him. "Say, I almost forgot. Your old friend, Mr. Thomas Lynch from Frick, he stop by for breakfast this morning looking for you. He wants you to give him a call."

Joe's spoon stopped in mid-air. "He say what he wanted?"

"He wanted waffles but I no make today so he settled for pancakes, ha ha ha!"

Joe shook his head and smiled. "You're a funny fellow Tony."

Joe continued eating while he read the paper and Tony returned to his bowl of soup. From the account of the payroll heist it had been well organized and violent. The road to the mine was blocked by a broken-down wagon where a fellow was working on one of the wheels. When the Frick wagon stopped, four masked men jumped from the woods and attacked the two Frick men. Both had been pistol whipped and knocked out, one sent to the hospital with a broken arm. The article mentioned a similar robbery near Latrobe the week before, the target a smaller mine run by J.C. Whitney. *Tom Lynch is a decent fellow. I'll give him a call later on. I reckon that phone line we had put in at The Star will prove handy.*

Joe finished up his soup, wiping the bowl with his last piece of bread. He left a quarter on the counter, picked up his new boots, and left with his coat over his arm. "See you tomorrow Tony." Joe strolled up Main Street, the sidewalks all now clear of snow and crowded with shoppers. *It's warmed up considerable today. The snow's starting to melt.* The street was a slushy mess, with delivery wagons parked all askew up and down the block, shoveled snow crowding their way. The piles already sported a black sooty crust, thanks to the heavy locomotive traffic on the B&O tracks a block away. The tracks for the streetcars were clear though, one turning the corner as he crossed the street.

By 3:30 Joe was cleaned up and walking through the front door of The Star. The place was already busy, a noisy pack lined up along the bar. Although there were many other saloons along this stretch of Pittsburgh Street, there was no shortage of drinkers. In a few hours the area would be a place for women and children to avoid. He saw Peggy in the office working on the books, her auburn hair piled in a loose bun. She looked up as he entered.

"Hello Joe, glad to see you made it back in time for the night crowd. You'll be glad to know I've finished yesterday's bookkeeping for you."

"I'm much obliged for that Peggy. How's Andy doing?"

"A bit better today, but still weak. I did get your telegraph. What kept you over?"

Joe sat at the chair in front of the desk. "It's a long story. Your friend Henry has got some troubles. We're sure the fellow was murdered, and he wasn't the only one. We found the body of his helper stashed at the mill." *No sense telling her all the details. She has plenty on her mind already.* "Ever see the stars up there?"

Peggy smiled. "You mean the Milky Way? Yes I have, on several occasions. It's quite the sight isn't it."

"Surely is. It got me to thinking, about how big the universe is and such. Made me feel small, but…. a part of something special."

Peggy smiled and reached across the desk, taking his hands in hers. "You're turning into quite the philosopher Joe. When do you start class?"

Joe's heart warmed at her touch. He gave her hands a little squeeze. "On Tuesday, then back on Thursday. And I told Henry I'd come back up there on Saturday."

"Life has gotten busy for us both, but this will pass." She returned the squeeze, then rose from her seat. "Time to go check on Daddy. I'll see you tomorrow." She retrieved her coat, hat, and muff, all in a matching shade of blue. "I almost forgot. Do you have plans for Sunday?"

"Just church in the morning."

"Plan on an early dinner at the Patterson's house. Just come by after church. My mother's sister, Margaret Foley, is coming for a visit. I want you both to meet. I'm her namesake and she's quite the woman."

"Your mother was a Foley. Aunt Margaret never married?"

"No Joe. She's the Headmistress at Miss Ellet's School for Girls in Pittsburgh. I've always admired her independence. She's been a big influence on me too."

Joe stood up and helped Peggy with her coat. Turning, they shared a brief kiss. "Then I'll wear my best suit and be on my best behavior. Give my regards to Andy." He accompanied her to the door and watched as she walked up Pittsburgh Street.

Chapter 10

✳   ✳   ✳

Joe returned to the office and cleared off the desk. Looking at the telephone, he thought of Mr. Lynch. *He's a decent enough fellow, treated me right. Might as well see what he wants.* Raising the earpiece to his ear, he gave its cradle a few taps.

"Operator."

"Hello Liz. Can you put me through to Scottdale?"

"One moment."

Our world is changing fast, with telephones, phonographs, moving pictures, automobiles and the rest. The Scottdale operator came on the line. "Number please."

"Can you put me through to Mr. Lynch over at Frick headquarters?"

"One moment."

"H.C. Frick Coke Company, Mr. Lynch's office."

"Joe Zajac calling for Mr. Lynch."

"He's here and expecting your call. One moment please."

After a few seconds, Thomas Lynch, President of the H.C. Frick Coke Company, came on the line. "Mr. Zajac. Thank you for the call. I was wanting to catch up with you this morning."

"I was out of town last night, just got back. What can I do for you?"

"I was hoping we could meet. There are some matters I'd like to discuss."

"Like your payroll robbery?"

"I see that bad news travels quickly. Yes Mr. Zajac, that and a few other matters."

"Read all about it in the Courier early edition. What makes you think I can help?"

"Your prior efforts were a success. I regret that the company lost your services."

"Why would I want to help? I'm not interested in coming back to work for Frick."

"That I'd rather wait to discuss face to face. I don't trust these telephones for sensitive discussions. I can return to Connellsville tomorrow if you're available."

"I have plans for the morning, but how about I come over your way in the afternoon?"

"I'll be here all day. Come at your convenience Mr. Zajac."

"You can still call me Joe. See you tomorrow."

"Thank you Joe."

He hung up the telephone and mused. *Should have my head examined for even going over there but I guess I owe him that much. It'll be good to see some of my old friends in the office.*

Nell, the waitress at The Star, stuck her head in the door. "We just pulled a beef roast out of the oven. Can I fix you a sandwich while it's still warm?"

"Much obliged Nell. I'll be out in a minute. Put it at my table with a beer if you please."

"Will do."

Joe started to get up, then sat back down, picking up the phone again. *Might as well take advantage of this modern convenience.*

"Operator."

"Put me through to Uniontown please Liz."

"One moment."

"Uniontown Central, number please."

"Can you put me through to the courthouse, Sheriff Miller please?"

"One moment."

The phone rang four times before being answered. "Who is it!" Joe recognized the gruff voice.

"Hello Tom, it's Joe Zajac."

"Zajac, you got a damn telephone now too? What the hell have you been up to?"

"Been taking it easy since August. Congratulations on your reelection."

"Thanks to us busting up 'The Reapers' gang, it wasn't even close. What can I do for you?"

"I'd like to come up tomorrow morning. You going to be in?"

"Until midday. What's going on?"

"I'm working on a problem for a friend, a murder up in the mountains."

"Come on then, I'll do what I can."

"Thanks Sheriff."

Joe hung up and got out his notebook. After adding the new appointments, he adjourned to his table, where a roast beef sandwich and beer awaited him. Halfway through he saw his friend Lloyd McCormick come in. While about Joe's height, he was at least 20 pounds heavier, with copper colored hair and a bushy beard. His hat of choice, a brown derby, sat at an angle, almost resting on his ear. He spied Joe and joined him.

"What say Zajac, where you been?"

"I was up in the mountains for a couple of days, spent last night in Ohiopyle."

Nell came over when she saw Lloyd. "What's your pleasure?"

"A shot and a beer. And a couple of your pickled eggs. Joe, you need a shot?"

"No thanks Lloyd, I already had a taste today, some genuine Harkins Mountain Rye."

"Never heard of it. Better than Old Overholt?"

Joe nodded. "Damn smooth. I was just being sociable, still off the hard stuff."

"Mind if I join you?" It was Johnny Davidson, out of uniform and off duty.

Lloyd gave a deep laugh. "The gang's all here."

Nell returned with Lloyds eggs, and a shot and a beer for him and Johnny.

Lloyd raised his glass. "May the hinges of our friendship never grow rusty." The three friends raised their mugs and drank deep. Then Lloyd and Johnny fired their shots, and polished off the rest of their beers.

Johnny waved Nell over. "Three more beers if you please." The three men had been good friends and drinking buddies since shortly after Joe moved to town almost three years ago. The Star became their favored drinking spot. Lloyd was the superintendent at a brick factory, a booming industry thanks to their use in construction of the coke ovens. They were even being used to pave the streets.

Joe enjoyed Lloyd's love of life and old Irish sayings. "What's new Big Red"?

Lloyd gave them a big grin. "Well, you gents are looking at a fellow 'bout to get hitched."

Joe and Johnny both stared at the big man silently for a moment, mouths dropped open. Then as one they rose and started pounding him on the back and shaking hands. "Never thought I'd see the day," said Joe. "Hats off to you," Johnny added, as he flipped Lloyds derby to the floor.

Nell approached with their beers. "What's going on here? You three looped up already?"

Joe shook his head. "Big news Nell, our boy here is getting married."

Nell rolled her eyes, "Oh Lordy. Give the girl my sympathies."

Lloyd had met Edna Johnson a few months back. She was a few years younger, and as tiny as he was big. They made an interesting couple, she on the quiet side, he outgoing to say the least.

The three raised their glasses again, Johnny toasting. "To Edna and Lloyd." With a clink and a swallow, the coming union was endorsed.

Joe still couldn't believe it. Lloyd had always been the most carefree among them, content to live a life of pleasure. He'd seen a few women off and on but none for very long. "What's gotten into you buddy?"

Lloyd shrugged. "We've been seeing each other longer than I'd stuck with any woman before. On New Year's Day she asked me what my intentions were. Hell, before I even thought about it I asked her to marry me. After all these years of drinking and running around I'm just ready. We want to start a family." He paused for a moment to take another swallow. "And as my Pappy used to say, 'There's no cure for love except to marry.'" He finished the rest of his beer. "That's it for me tonight. I'm going over to Edna's for dinner." The three stood, shaking hands again, and Lloyd departed.

Joe and Johnny sat quietly for a moment, sipping their beers, both reflecting on the big news. Finally Johnny spoke. "How was your trip to the mountains?"

"Interesting to say the least. The fellow was murdered no doubt. We found his helper's body hidden at the mill too and almost got blown up to boot." Joe told the tale of his trip to the mountains and his visit with the Harkins men. "And I even had time to take a gander at the Hotel Fernwood. It looks like quite the place."

"What'd I tell you about those mountain folks, shoot first and ask questions later."

Joe nodded. "You were sure enough right about that. They're damn suspicious of strangers. But I agreed to help Henry so I'll be going back up there on Saturday."

"Just be careful buddy." Johnny finished his beer. "I've got a bit of news too Joe. Looks like your truly is set to become the Connellsville Police Department's first detective. These boom times have brought the crooks to town. We've been hit with a string of breaks-ins and the like. I'll be doing the investigating."

"Congratulations to you Johnny, you deserve the promotion."

"It's worth a couple of bucks a week and no more uniforms. Tomorrow is my first day." He got up from the table. "I'm having supper with Pop tonight. See you tomorrow."

After Johnny left, Joe sat quietly, nursing his beer. *Looks like plenty of changes are in the wind.*

Chapter 11

✳   ✳   ✳

It was 7:30 when Joe, carrying a small leather briefcase, walked through the front door of City Lunch. He waved to Tony, busy taking a table order. "Be right with you Joey." He took his seat at the end of the counter, back to the wall, and looked out the window. The sky was a dull gray, as it was most days. As he watched, a trolley crossed the bridge into town from New Haven, the borough on the other side of the Youghiogheny. A long coal train passed slowly by on the B&O tracks that ran between Water Street and the river, just behind the building.

Tony came over with a cup of coffee. "You back on your old schedule, eh Joe?"

Joe nodded. "On my way to Uniontown to visit Sheriff Miller. I called Mr. Lynch too, going to see him this afternoon."

"See? You a private eye now, just like Sherlock Holmes. What you want for breakfast?"

"A short stack and sausage, if you please. And can you make me a ham sandwich for the road? Don't want to miss lunch."

"Nobody want that. You get grumpy."

Joe smiled as Tony went to the kitchen.

True to his word, Henry's man had delivered several pictures to The Star last night, including close-ups of both tattoos. They were in Joe's briefcase, along with a larger tablet, an appointment book and several pencils. He'd bought the book yesterday, a response to his busier schedule. *When classes start I'll be even busier.*

The bell on the door tinkled and in walked Johnny Davidson, on the job but out of uniform. He joined Joe at the end of the counter. "Morning Joe."

"Hello Detective Davidson. I've something to show you." He retrieved the pictures and spread them on the counter. "This is the fellow that attacked us Wednesday. The next one is of his tattoo. The others are of our victim, Half-moon Harkins."

Johnny examined the photographs. "He doesn't look familiar to me. Never saw any tattoos like these either. Who took the little pictures?"

"Henry has a new box camera. His cousin developed them. The prints are small but still a big help."

Johnny nodded. "I'm going to talk to the chief, see if we can get one, bring our investigations into the modern times."

Tony brought out Joe's meal. He looked Johnny over. "You no work today?"

"Yes but I'm done walking the beat. You're looking at the city's first detective."

"You still gonna start your day with coffee and donuts?"

"If you please."

Joe quickly ate his meal. Tony soon returned with coffee, donuts, and Joe's sandwich, wrapped in brown paper. "Here you go boys."

Joe put the sandwich in his briefcase. "Off to Uniontown. See you tomorrow Tony. And good luck to you Detective Davidson."

Joe walked to the streetcar terminal, one block from City Lunch. Here the lines from South Connellsville, Uniontown, and Greensburg ended, a transfer point that facilitated travel up and down the mines and towns of the Connellsville Seam. The eight o'clock trolley to Uniontown was ready to depart. Joe entered and, instead of taking his usual seat up near the operator, took one in the rear. *Stays a bit warmer back here.* While the little cars were electrically heated, they could still be a bit chilly, especially up front near the door.

The trolley crossed the river and passed through New Haven, the line turning south there toward Uniontown, the Fayette County seat. The 12-mile trip would take about a half hour, with stops at several little towns and mines along the way. Electrically powered, the cars ran smooth and quiet. Joe pulled out his tablet and made a few notes.

Tattoo parlors
Black Widow Boys
Deputy in Ohiopyle

They arrived in Uniontown a little after 8:30. The courthouse was a few blocks from the trolley stop, Sheriff Miller's office on the second floor. An institution in Fayette Count, he'd been sheriff for many years. Joe found him sitting at his desk talking on the telephone.

"Yes, I know. I don't blame them for getting riled up. I've got my best deputy working on it. Yes, I'll let you know." He hung up the telephone, pulled out a handkerchief and wiped his brow. Looking up, he saw Joe standing in the doorway. "Zajac, come on in."

Joe entered the small office, Sheriff Miller's substantial rear end occupying the only seat. "When are you going to get a chair for your guests?"

"I discourage visitors. They prit' near always want something and I'd rather keep it brief." He got up, a holstered revolver hanging low on his hip. "Come on. There's a little room down the hall we can jaw for a bit."

Joe followed him, both soon seated at a small table in a windowless room. "This used to be a store room. I hide out here sometime just so I don't have to answer that damn telephone. It's handy but rings too much. What can I do for you?"

Joe opened his briefcase and took out the pictures, his tablet and a pencil. "Take a look Sheriff. This fellow, now deceased, tried to kill me and a friend up Ohiopyle way on Wednesday. The second picture is of a tattoo on the back of his neck. The third a tattoo on another fellow, murdered on New Year's Eve." Joe proceeded to tell the tale of the murder in the mountains.

"Now Harkins I'm familiar with. He's been our guest here on several occasions."

"Ever hear of a Black Widow gang?"

"Never have, but I swear, as Fayette County grows, more and more criminals are moving in. That's what I was on the telephone about. A gang's been robbing folks in their home, breaking in at night and torturing the residents until they tell them where the valuables are."

"How about this fellow. He look familiar?"

Sheriff Miller picked up the picture, looking closely. "Hard to say from just a head shot, but no, he's unfamiliar to me."

"How about the tattoos? Ever seen one like it?"

He shook his head. "Can't say I have."

Joe gathered up the pictures and put them back in the case. "You know of any place you can get a tattoo in Uniontown?"

"No. The only tattoo parlor I know of in Fayette County is in Brownsville, down along the Monongahela River."

"Who keeps the peace in Ohiopyle?"

"I got a deputy for Stewart Township, name of Edsley, Ernest Edsley. He lives just off of Sugar Loaf Road, outside of Confluence, right near the Somerset County line.

Joe noted the man's name and the location of the tattoo parlor. "Think he could help me out if I need it?"

"Give me a piece of paper and that pencil." The sheriff wrote. "To Ernest Edsley. Render any and all assistance to Joe Zajac in his investigation of two murders that have occurred in your district." He signed the note and pushed it over to Joe. "That should do it. Tell him if he has any questions about it to give me a call."

"There's telephones up there?"

"They just ran a line, not more than a half dozen I'd say. One at the train station, one at the Ohiopyle House, maybe three or four more."

Joe folded the paper in half and put it and the tablet in his case. "Much obliged Sheriff. I'll go to Brownsville next week and see if I can track down Ernest tomorrow."

"He's likely to be at the Laurel Inn, on the main drag downtown. He's got a taste for drink, just like a few other folks I know. Speaking of which, too early for you to tip one?"

Joe smiled. "Much obliged Sheriff but I've got to go to Scottdale. Hear about the Frick payroll robbery over at Standard?"

"I was reading about it at breakfast. Long as they stay in Westmoreland County it's someone else's concern. I thought you were through with Frick."

"I am, but agreed to meet Mr. Lynch. Thanks for all of your help. I'll stay in touch."

The two men shook hands, and Joe headed back to the trolley stop, ready to go see Thomas Lynch.

Chapter 12

✳   ✳   ✳

S cottdale was another small industrial town located along the Connellsville Seam. Located in Westmoreland County, it was also the site of the HC Frick Coke Company headquarters. Joe worked out of there until the events of last August. During those days, he'd developed a close rapport with Thomas Lynch, the president of the company.

During the trolley ride back to Connellsville Joe took out his calendar and made an entry on Saturday. *Track down Ernest Edsley.* The sheriff's letter was tucked away in his book. *I'll likely need some help with these mountain folk.*

It was eleven o'clock when the trolley pulled into the Connellsville terminal, the Scottdale bound car waiting on the other line. Joe boarded it, once again sat in the rear, and ate his sandwich as they travelled up the Main Street hill and out of town. The country between the towns was mostly open farmland. Twenty minutes later they arrived at Scottdale, the trolley stop located near the Pennsylvania Railroad station. Frick headquarters was just across the street in a nondescript three story red brick building. *Mighty plain digs for the biggest coke operation in the world.* Joe crossed the street and walked in. A young red-haired woman sat behind an open window in the wall of the waiting room, head bent toward a big black typewriter.

"Morning Polly."

The woman looked up, a smile on her face.

"I thought I recognized that voice. Hello Joe."

He leaned on the window sill, head stuck through the opening, as he looked around the office. "Not much changed here since my last visit."

"Well, we all got brand new Remington typewriters but besides that, not much has. How about with you? Living on Easy Street with that reward money?"

Joe shook his head. "Still got most of it in the bank. Is Mr. Lynch in? He asked me to stop by."

Polly nodded. "We're expecting you." She rose from her desk and opened the door to the office. "Go on up Joe. He's still in the same place."

With a smile and a tip of his hat, Joe passed through the room, where several other women sat typing, and ascended the stairs in the rear. At the top, a hall led to the office of Mr. Lynch, located at its end. A longtime colleague of H.C. Frick, Lynch worked his way up from a clerk's job at a company store to head of the firm, now a wholly owned subsidiary of Carnegie Steel. The office door open, Joe could see Mr. Lynch sitting at a broad table, plans of some type spread before him. Rapping on the door frame, Joe walked in.

Mr. Lynch looked up, then stood. He was a slim man of medium build, with hair turned prematurely gray at 46. With his frameless spectacles and long thin nose, he'd always reminded Joe of a school teacher he once had.

"Mr. Zajac, thank you for coming. Please have a seat."

Joe took off his coat and hat, then sat at a chair in front of the table. Mr. Lynch rolled up the plans and stuck them into a roll-top desk behind him. "We're planning some big changes at the coke works Joe. There's a machine just invented that can pull the coke from the ovens faster than the hardest working man." He sat back down, pulled out a clean white handkerchief, and took a moment to clean his glasses before speaking again. "Let me bring you up to date on the goings on here. That payroll robbery you read about wasn't the first one we've experienced. As you likely read, one of our competitor's smaller operations outside of Latrobe was robbed just before Christmas. And before that another one of ours was hit on the other side of Uniontown. We were able to keep that one out of the papers though."

Three mines in less than a month! "Sounds like you've got an organized gang at work. Any ideas about who's behind it?"

"Not at first, but there was one clue left behind at Standard." Mr. Lynch turned to the desk and retrieved a folded piece of paper from the center drawer. "Take a look at this."

Joe took the paper and unfolded it. At the top was the silhouette of a man in a long hooded robe holding a scythe. *The Grim reaper!* Below the figure was a note. "Whatever a man sows, that he will also reap." Joe felt goose bumps rising on his arms and had to suppress a chill. It was the same message that Kurt Straub had tried to deliver to him personally last year. He sat the paper down on the table.

Mr. Lynch retrieved the note, staring at it a moment before returning it to the drawer. "As I recall, the body of Mr. Straub was never recovered. There's no mistaking the message though."

"No body was ever recovered, that's true, but I saw him go off the bridge and I know he was shot." Joe recalled that August day on the railroad bridge over the Youghiogheny River. "Maybe some of his boys are still around though. If I were you I'd start sending out armed men with the payrolls."

"We did have one guard with the paymaster at Standard, but he wasn't enough." Mr. Lynch paused a moment, a troubled look on his face. "And as inopportune a moment it was for Mr. Straub to cause us trouble the last time, this moment is even more significant." He took a newspaper from the desk and spread it in front of Joe. It was a recent edition of the *New York Times*. "Ever hear of this fellow?"

The paper was open to a story headlined "J. P. Morgan Makes Deal." Below it was an illustration of man in a top hat, his heavy square head adorned with long sideburns joined to a bushy mustache. Joe studied the picture and read the first few sentences. "Never heard of him. What's a 'financier'?"

"A man with money, and access to more, his family bank one source, well-heeled associates another. Lately he's been buying up small railroads, combining them into a larger corporation and selling it off, always at a big profit."

"Would Mr. Frick be one of those associates?"

Mr. Lynch smiled and nodded. "Your insight is a trait I've always admired Mr. Zajac."

"Just Joe is fine. I did read that Mr. Frick was on the outs with Carnegie. This Morgan fellow, how's he fit in?"

"You are correct Joe. HC no longer wields any authority at Carnegie Steel, although he still owns a sizable part of it. But he's still a well-respected steel man and business manager. He's living in New York City for the most part, and in addition to providing investment funds, helps Morgan evaluate the smaller firms."

"I still don't see what that has to do with your payroll robberies."

Lynch got up, closed the door to his office and returned. "It's more than the robberies. There's been some acts of sabotage at the mines, and even a few suspicious events at the Carnegie mills. Now I'm going to tell you something that must remain between us alone. Morgan's next objective is the steel industry, Carnegie Steel his target. His aim is to make it the centerpiece of the largest company ever to exist in these United States, U.S. Steel. Negotiations are under way, Frick once again in the middle of the action. Any problems or disruptions at the mines or mills could potentially cost Carnegie and Frick millions of dollars."

Joe smiled. "And here I thought I was doing pretty good with my five thousand. I still don't see how I fit in."

"I'd like to engage your services. Look into these events. See what you can find out."

"I'm not looking for a job. I've got one, part-time, and going to college some too. Classes start back up next week."

"Yes, Tony mentioned that you are attending the University of Western Pennsylvania. I applaud your efforts Joe. I once intended on studying there, but life had other plans for me. I thought of becoming a teacher."

He'd make I good one I reckon. "Between the two, I'm fairly busy. What's your offer?"

Lynch stared at Joe for a bit, hands folded quietly on the desk top. "Name your price."

Joe leaned back in his chair, arms folded across his chest, meeting his gaze. *I'll make him an offer he can't accept, then I'm done with it.* "My price is ten thousand dollars, paid in advance. I'll only work on it as my time permits and don't guarantee any results."

Lynch smiled, and stood up, hand extended. "Your terms are accepted Joe. We have a deal."

Joe's mouth dropped open for a moment. Stunned, he also stood, and the two men shook hands. "I'll get started on Monday. Arrange a meeting with your new head of security. And on Tuesday I'll be in Pittsburgh. I'd like to meet Carnegie's man too."

Lynch nodded. "I'll see that Mike McMullen is here Monday first thing, and will have your payment for you. If you think of anything else we need to do to get you started, let me know."

Joe thought for a moment. "I'd like to have an updated list of all of your mines, and their superintendents. Let them know what I'm up to. Make note of the weekly payroll at each, when it's delivered and how. That should get me started."

"I'll let Polly know. She'll have the list for you on Monday. And keep me informed of anything you might turn up."

Joe nodded, picked up his coat and case and departed, Lynch already back at the plans as he went out the door.

Chapter 13

*　❋　　　❋　　　❋*

It was just after dawn on Saturday, heavy gray clouds barely lit by the hidden sun. George "Sky" Harkins was already hard at work walking his trap line. *More snow soon, better get a move on.* At 21 years old, Sky was already the head of his branch of the Harkins family tree. His father was dead, killed five years ago when his still exploded. His grandfather was near 80, and had been ailing for a long time. It had fallen upon Sky to keep the family going.

Sky was a big man, over six feet tall with a thick chest and big arms. His dark brown eyes and long black hair were a testament to the Delaware Indian blood that still marked his line. With crude snowshoes on his feet, he trudged along a ridge line, across the Youghiogheny from the where the John Harkins clan had settled. The land was higher here, not much suited to farming. But the game was abundant, and furs were much in demand. It was hard work, but one of the few ways a man could make some hard cash in the mountains. That and selling whiskey.

A rifle over one shoulder and a pack on his back, the going was slow. He'd yet to find a sprung trap, but had hope for the next one just ahead. As he approached, he could see that it had been sprung, but no animal was in it. Kneeling, he could see some fresh blood and a patch of fox fur on the teeth. A faint trail of snowshoe tracks led down the ridge toward the river.

Son of a bitch! That's three times since Christmas some bastard's jumped my traps. I'm wagering Hawk's behind it. He unshouldered his rifle, took off his pack and followed the tracks. *Time to end this right now, once and for all.*

The ridge dropped off rapidly here, Sky more sliding than walking. As he got nearer to the edge he fell back and slid again. With much effort he dug in his heels and stopped, nearly going over the edge of the cliff. Heart pounding, he sat there for a bit, slowly scanning the ground below. This part of the ridge was heavily wooded, much of the snow blown off the rocky ground. He removed his snow shoes and walked along the cliff edge.

With a muffled crack, a rifle shot rang out. Sky felt the bullet hit his shoulder, spinning him around. Losing his balance, he fell over the cliff, landing ten feet below on a small ledge. His rifle fell from his hands and disappeared toward the bottom. The wind knocked out of him, and in pain, Sky struggled to stay conscious. Rolling toward the cliff, he crawled under a snow covered mountain laurel. A swift kick to the bush dropped the snow onto him. He kept as still as he could, trying to catch his breath.

A few minutes later he heard some voices, two men talking at a distance. Their voices grew louder and more distinct as they approached the cliff. "He went over here. There's his snowshoes." A second voice replied. "I know I shot him." The first voice again: "You weren't supposed to shoot him, you jackass." Sky looked up, and could see the barrel of a rifle. He pulled himself even closer to the cliff, into a recess. "Looks like he bounced off the ledge and kept on going. He's a goner for sure." The men turned and left the cliff, arguing as they walked away, but Sky couldn't hear a word. He'd lost consciousness.

*   *   *

A few miles away, Jewel Harkins, Sky's younger sister, was busy with her morning chores. She'd gotten the fires going, refilled the wood bins from the stacks outside, and fed their livestock. Now it was time to feed her mother and grandfather. A tall and handsome young woman, Jewel was aptly named. And unlike most of the George Harkins clan, her long hair was more brown than black, the same color as her eyes. At the moment, those brown eyes suggested a certain weariness that belied her youth. She paused in her labor and gazed out the small front window. *Work hard every day. Nursemaid to both. Will I ever escape this prison?*

This branch of the Harkins family lived a life quite different from their kin across the river. Their home was a rough-hewn log cabin, made up of two smaller cabins joined together. The main room and kitchen were 75 years old and showed their age. A second cabin joined to it was of more recent vintage and was divided into four bedrooms. Jewel heard voices and turned to see her grandfather and her mother, Pearl, come in and sit at the table. *Momma's got old before her time* Jewel thought. *She's heading round the bend.*

"I'm feeling a bit poorly this morning Jewel. Can you fix your momma a cup of tea?"

Jewel nodded, took the old iron kettle from the stove, and poured hot water over some tea leaves in a small pot. "You want a cup too Poppy?" The old man nodded, his head barely moving. *He's getting weaker every day.* She returned the kettle to the stove, took down two cups from a shelf and placed one in front of each of them. "There's a bit of honey left."

"Where's your brother Jewel?"

"He was gone before I got up, likely running his trap line."

Pearl nodded slowly, and poured the tea. "Is your father with him?"

And she's going round the bend… "Momma, you know he's gone five years now."

Pearl sagged and dropped her head, a single tear slowly sliding down her cheek.

*   *   *

Sky Harkins slowly regained consciousness, at first not knowing where he was. He started to get up, the pain in his shoulder quickly reminding him of his predicament. Sitting with his back against the wall, he brushed the snow off, some reddened from his wound. *Ain't bleeding much anymore. Must of been a small-bore.* Shifting toward the front of the ledge, he looked over. The drop to the bottom was substantial, the ground below heavily wooded. *If I had two good arms I'd maybe be able to climb down*. He moved back toward the cliff wall, pulled his knees to his chest and contemplated his options. *I'm stuck here. If someone don't find me before nightfall I'm a goner.*

Chapter 14

‖   ‖   ‖

Joe arrived at the B&O station at a quarter to nine on Saturday morning. He was dressed for a day in the mountains, long-johns under denim jeans, high-topped boots, and a new winter overcoat. He'd also purchased a small leather backpack. In it were his papers, gloves, hat, a holstered .45 and a roast beef sandwich. *No sense dragging that briefcase around. Better to keep my hands free.* The train was on time. Joe boarded the last car and again sat on the right, watching the river as they left town.

While the sky was overcast, it wasn't snowing, the tracks in good condition. As the train climbed the Alleghenies, Joe took out his calendar and pencil and turned to this week. Tomorrow he was to meet Peggy's Aunt Margaret and on Tuesday he started school. He added to Monday a few notes in pencil: *Scottdale-meet Mike McMullen* and *Pick up check.* He smiled and shook his head. *Ten thousand dollars! I was making twenty dollars a week when I left Frick. And I still have most of the reward money.* Joe found this oddly unsettling. *What's that the bible says? Money is the root of all evil? I've seen men like Frick do wrong in its pursuit. About all I want is a new fishing pole.*

Joe added *Meet Carnegie security man* to Tuesday then returned the calendar to his pack. The trip to Ohiopyle passed quickly, the train pulling into the station shortly after ten. *Got an hour to kill before I meet Henry.* He noticed the Ferncliff Hotel arch across the street. *Maybe Marshall McNutt can show me around*. He crossed the road and followed the boardwalk up the hill. Arriving at the hotel, he walked around back and rang the doorbell Marshall had mentioned. The door opened in a bit, Marshall standing there in his long-johns.

"Morning Joe. Come on in. I thought you were my handyman." Joe entered, the door opening into a short hall. "Follow me." The hall led to a large kitchen with a dining room beyond. "Go on through there. I'll be with you soon as I put some trousers on."

Joe entered the dining room, where several dozen tables, each with four chairs, were laid out in three long rows. He looked around, admiring the fancy brocade wallpaper and polished wood floor. Joe wandered slowly through the room and the arched entry at the far end, which opened into the lobby.

This is one fancy place. The lobby was huge, running from the front to the rear of the building. Rich maroon carpets covered the wood floors here. Sofas and chairs were grouped together in several parts of the room, clustered around low tables. Desks for writing sat on each side wall. Four chandeliers hung from the ceiling. *Looks like electric too.* The rear wall had a fireplace in the middle, currently not in use. *It's nice and warm in here.* Radiators provided the heat. Joe removed his coat and took a seat. In a bit Marshall returned, his long-johns hidden under denim pants and a flannel shirt.

"Welcome to the Ferncliff Joe. There's no resort like it in the Alleghenies."

"I believe that Marshall. Looks like deluxe lodgings to me."

"All of the rooms are outfitted with running water, gas and electric. The hotel and them two big fountains out front are fed from our own little reservoir up the hill, the electric generated from a coal station down by the tannery. And that's not all. Down at the end of the boardwalk, by the river, is the dance pavilion and bowling alleys. You should see the crowds in the summer."

"I've not been to a dance hall for a few years. I'll have to come up and give it a whirl."

The ring of the doorbell interrupted their conversation. "Pardon me Joe, That's likely my handyman." Marshall disappeared through the dining room, returning a minute later, followed by a young man in bib overalls, his eyes downcast. "Joe, say howdy to Elmer Fortney. He helps out around here some, carpentry repairs and the like."

Joe walked toward them, hand outstretched. "How do Elmer."

Elmer looked up briefly and nodded, then turned to Marshall. "I'll get started." He turned away and ascended the broad stirs.

He's a bit of an odd duck. "Elmer's a man of few words."

Marshall chuckled. "Some of these mountain folks are a bit standoffish. Don't pay him no mind."

Joe pulled out his pocket watch. "I'm meeting Henry at eleven. I better get a move on."

"Where you two headed?"

"Going to meet George Harkins."

"This got anything to do with the troubles Henry's been having?"

Not many secrets in these parts. Joe nodded.

"You some kind of policeman?"

"I was, but no longer. Just doing what I can for a friend."

"Give my regards to Jewel Harkins. She helps out around here in the summer, and she's a looker to boot."

"Will do. Thanks for the letting me take a look around."

"Come back any time and come on up next summer." The two men shook hands, Joe bundled up and left by the front door.

It was almost eleven when he arrived at the Ohiopyle House, Henry's sleigh sitting out front. Joe entered to find Henry sitting by the fireplace, his arm in a sling.

"What happened to you?"

Henry rose, shaking his head. "Just a little sprain Joe. Got it helping out at the mill, need to take it easy today." He looked Joe up and down. "Looks like you're ready to ride. Let's get going."

Henry boarded the sleigh with some effort. Joe put his pack behind the seat and climbed up, Henry handing him the reins. "How about you handling the girls today?"

Joe took the reins, holding them loosely. "You sure about this? I'm not much of a teamster."

Henry laughed. "You'll do fine. My arm's not up to it. Now give the reins a little shake, then hold them firm but don't pull too hard. Hyaa!"

At Henry's command, the horses trotted off, heading across the bridge out of town. Joe held the reins as instructed as they crossed the B&O tracks.

"We're taking the river road again Joe. Pull back on the right rein a bit harder and the team will turn."

Joe did as he was told and sure enough, they were soon headed back toward Harkins Hollow. *It's mostly a straight shot from here.*

"Just relax Joe. The girls know the way. We've got a bit longer ride today, about twice as far."

Fifteen minutes later they passed they passed Rock Creek Road. By 11:30 they were coming up on Confluence. "We're in Somerset County now Joe. Once we cross that creek we're in Confluence." A sign at the bridge read "Laurel Creek."

The Laurel Inn must be close by. "You know an Ernest Edsley, Henry?"

"Old Earnest? Sure do. He's been deputy up here for years, knows about my timber thefts."

"I was in Uniontown yesterday, stopped by to see Sheriff Miller. He gave me a letter telling Ernest to help us out. We close to the Laurel Inn?"

"Get ready for another turn. Just past the town square, a left and a right."

Joe tugged the reins, the horses responding. Two turns later they were on what looked like the main street.

"There on the right Joe." A small sign read "Laurel Inn." Several sleighs and a few horses stood in front. "Looks like an early crowd in town today."

"If we have time, I'd like to stop on the way back."

Henry nodded. "Take the next right."

Joe turned the team and they crossed another, somewhat larger stream.

"That's the Casselman River, Joe. Laurel Creek feeds it, then the Casselman empties into the Yough." They crossed a narrow neck of land, and over another bridge. "We're back across the Yough again. They call this neck of the woods Turkeyfoot Valley. From up on that ridge those three streams coming together look just like one. Take the first right off the bridge."

Joe, feeling more comfortable with the team, took the turn smoothly. They were now travelling back downriver on the other side. Another 15 minutes found them at the big bend in the Yough. The sky was clouding over, the wind picking up a bit.

"Pull back on the reins Joe. Whoa. Let's give them a little rest. We'll be heading uphill soon."

Joe climbed down to stretch his legs. "We're across from Harkins Hollow, eh?"

"That's right Joe, but the ground is steeper over here. There's a little road up ahead to the left. The George Harkins clan, what's left of them, are about a mile up it. The old man was in bad shape the last time I saw him in town. They call young George "Sky." He's the one that wrestled Hawk. Sky's sister is still at home. She looks after her mother, Pearl, and old George."

"That's Jewel?"

Henry nodded. "Where'd you hear about her?"

"I made the acquaintance of Marshall McNutt, poking around the Ferncliff on Thursday. He showed me around the place today. I told him what we were up to and he mentioned her. Says she's 'a looker'"

"She is that." Henry looked up at the darkening sky. "Let's get going."

Joe climbed back up, grabbed the reins and gave them a little shake. With a "hyaa" of his own they were off again. The turn came up and they started climbing. The road was lightly travelled and soon became difficult for the horses to navigate.

"Stop here Joe. We're close enough to walk in."

The men climbed down and Joe tied the reins to a tree. He put on his pack and they trudged up the hill, following a path where some horse traffic had beaten down the snow. Ten minutes later they came to a clearing with a dilapidated cabin sitting in the middle. A thin wisp of smoke rose from a pipe at one end.

"The George's never were as well off as the John's, and lately more and more of them have left the mountains." They approached unchallenged. Henry called out a loud "Hello," the cabin door soon opened by a young woman.

"Hello Henry. What brings you up here?"

"I was hoping to speak to Sky."

A worried look crossed her face. "I was hoping you were him. He went out early to check his traps, should have been back an hour ago. Come on in."

Joe and Henry followed her into the cabin. The elder George and Pearl were sitting in front of the fireplace. He looked to be sleeping while she stared vacantly out the window. "Momma, Pap, we've got company."

Pearl turned to them briefly, then back to the window. The old man opened his eyes and, seeing Henry, seemed to perk up. "Henry Brooks. Been a coon's age since you come calling." He rubbed his face with both hands and rose unsteadily.

"Here Pap, use your cane."

He took the cane from Jewel and moved to the table. "Sit a spell. We's worried sick about Sky. Jewel was 'bout to go looking for him." He turned his gaze to Joe. "Who's he?"

"Name's Joe Zajac. He's a friend from down Connellsville way."

"What's your business with us?"

"That can wait. Where's Sky running his traps?"

Jewel approached the table. "Up a little hollow and across the ridge, a mile or so from here. I was about to go looking for him. Can you come?"

"We'd need snowshoes if we're heading up the ridge."

"I've got a pair, and Pop's too."

Henry turned to Joe. "With this arm I'd not be much help. How about you two go. I'll keep Pearl and George company."

Joe nodded, took off his pack and pulled out his holstered .45. He buckled it on under his coat, buttoned up and pulled on his gloves. "Let's go."

Jewel and Joe went out back, where the snowshoes hung on the wall. "Ever worn these before?"

Joe shook his head. He watched as she strapped hers on, then tried to do the same. Jewel bent down and fixed them for him. She handed him two poles and took two for herself. "There you go Joe. Now step high and let's go."

Joe's first few steps were hesitant and clumsy, but after following Jewel for a while, and copying her movements, he was able to keep up. She did most of the work, breaking the trail. A hundred yards later they came to a path through the woods. The snow here already showed signs of traffic.

Jewel stopped for a moment. "This is Sky's path." They trudged on, up a rise then down into a hollow, which the path followed. At the end of it the ground rose steeply. Finally they came to the top of a long ridge, the Yough visible below. They stopped to catch their breath.

Pearl turned all directions, hoping to see some sign of her brother. "This here's been known as George's Ridge for a hundred years. Let's move on. I see one of his traps up ahead." They moved on to the trap the fox had been taken from. Pearl squatted down to inspect it. "Looks like he got a fox out of this one. And there's his pack!" She stood up and called out. "Sky, Sky," but there was no reply.

Joe turned toward the river. *Looks like some tracks heading down that way.* He could see that they led to the edge of a cliff. *What's that?* He spied something on the snow. "Look over there."

Jewel saw the tracks and started down the ridge, struggling to keep her balance, Joe following as best he could. She reached the edge and picked up what Joe had seen. It was a snowshoe. Joe finally caught up.

"These are his. Sky! Sky!"

From below, a weak voice called out. "Down here." Joe took off his snowshoes, laid down on his stomach and looked over the edge of the cliff, seeing Sky laying on a rock shelf below. "I'm Joe, here with your sister. You able to move?" Sky nodded and sat up, his back against the cliff wall.

Jewel flopped down next to Joe. "Sky! What happened to you?"

"Whoever's been jumping my traps shot me. Made me slip and fall over."

"Thank the Lord we found you."

We're going to need some rope to get him up, Joe thought. "Jewel, you need to go back home and get some rope. We'll need 25 feet or so. I'll stay here and keep your brother company."

Jewel got up, put on her snowshoes and departed without a word. Joe got back down on his stomach. "We'll get you up out of there, just hang on. Jewel's gone to get some rope. You still bleeding?"

"No, I think the slug is still in me, didn't come out the back best I can tell."

"Just take it easy best you can then."

"Okay Joe. Much obliged."

Chapter 15

✳   ✳   ✳

It was two hours later when Joe and Jewel, with Sky in tow on an old toboggan, arrived back at the cabin. Jewel was tending to his wound as he sat bare-chested at the table. Pearl and the old man still sat in front of the fireplace.

Pearl finished wrapping a bandage around his shoulder. "It's stopped bleeding but you better go into town and get the slug dug out."

Sky nodded, wincing a bit as Jewel applied some salve to the little hole in his shoulder. "I'll go see Doc Havner tomorrow."

Henry moved closer to inspect the wound. "A bit lower and you'd have been in trouble. Any idea who took a shot at you?"

Sky shook his head. "I been having trouble with someone jumping my traps. I blamed Hawk, but didn't recognize the voices I heard." Sky recounted the conversation he'd picked up while on the rock ledge. "Seems they weren't even trying to hit me. That fella must have been a right poor shot."

Henry sat at the table with Sky and Joe. "I don't think Hawk is to blame. We saw him on Thursday. Someone's been jumping his traps too, thought it might be you."

"Just like him to blame a George for his troubles." Sky stood and pulled on an old woolen shirt. "Put another log on that fire. I'm still bout froze. I could use some grub too." Pearl got up and added wood to the fireplace, while

Jewel went to the kitchen. He sat back down and turned to Henry. "Why'd you come callin?"

"It's about Half-moon. He's dead."

"I've not seen that no-account since he got out of the pokey. How'd it happen? Accident at the mill?"

"He was murdered looks like." Henry told the tale of Half-moon's demise, and the subsequent action at the mill, including the finding of Buck's watch. "His body is on ice at my cousin's house."

"Have him planted in the potter's field. His branch of the family is piss-poor at best."

"We took the watch back to Buck. He claims it was stolen, along with their family book, blamed you for that too."

Sky gave a snort, "I don't give two shits about that God damn book. It's been a hundred years since the Harkins clan had any say about who moved into these parts. The old man is living in the past. And he can stick that fancy watch up his ass sideways for all I care 'bout it."

Henry smiled. "That's good to hear. I'd hate to see you feuding with your relations."

"Ain't no relations of mine that I claim. The Georges been on our own since the beginning. The Johns always did look down on us 'cause of the Indian blood. We's about as different as night and day."

Jewel came to the table carrying a bowl of soup and some bread. "They aren't all bad Sky. You and Hawk got along until last year."

Sky dug into the soup. "He showed his true colors rassling me, fightin dirty. I'll have nothing more to do with him. And you'd better do the same."

Jewel colored slightly and returned to the stove. "There's enough of this possum stew left for two more bowls. Joe, Henry, the least we can do is feed you for your help."

Possum stew? Joe rose from the table. "Much obliged but we've overstayed our welcome. I'm due back in Connellsville tonight." Henry rose, they both bundled up and, after saying their good-byes, departed.

"What did you think of the Georges Joe?"

"I agree with Sky. They and the John's are as different as night and day. One thing is sure. There's no love lost between Sky and Hawk. I don't think that the Georges had anything to do with the watch and book theft though."

"You might be right but I've still got my suspicions." They were in sight of the sleigh, the team waiting patiently. "What's next?"

"Let's stop at the Laurel Inn and see if Ernest is there."

Before boarding the sleigh Joe pulled the roast beef sandwich from his pack. "Every time I come up here I end up missing a meal." He gave Henry half.

"You don't care for possum?"

"Can't say, but I'm in no hurry to try it."

They quickly ate the sandwich, untied the horses and climbed aboard. Henry took off his sling and grabbed the reins. "My arm's feeling better. Let's go." With a shake of the reins and a "Gidup" the sleigh pulled away. In twenty minutes they were back in Confluence. It was almost four o'clock when they pulled up to the Laurel Inn. The street was crowded with sleighs and horses. As they entered, the men at the bar turned as one, a few nodding at Henry. They took a seat at a table, as Henry surveyed the room.

"There's Ernest." Henry pointed to a fellow sitting at another table. "I'll go get him. You ready for a beer?"

Joe nodded. "How's the grub here?"

"Not so good."

In a minute Henry returned with two glasses of beer and Ernest, a tall, slim man with long gray hair and a handlebar mustache. He wore a trooper hat and had a holstered .45 at his side. "Ernest, I'd like you to meet Joe Zajac. Joe, Ernest Edsley."

Joe rose and they shook hands, the old man's grip strong. "How do Ernest."

He nodded and they all sat down. "Zajac. You're the fella that stopped those 'Reaper' boys last year."

Joe nodded. "And made the acquaintance of Sheriff Miller along the way. He's a good man." Joe reached down onto his pack. "I saw him yesterday. He gave me this note to give to you."

Ernest read the note, folded it and put it in his pocket. "What's this about two murders? First I'm hearing about it."

Henry spoke up. "Half-moon Harkins was found dead at one of my mills on New Year's Eve, looked like he done himself in at first. I was a might suspicious, asked my friend Joe to look into it a bit. In the course of that, we've determined that it was a murder, and found the body of a second man." Henry once again told the tale, including their visits with the Johns and the Georges.

When he had finished, Joe dug into his pack again. "Here's a picture of the fellow who tried to blow us up." He handed Ernest the pictures Henry had taken.

Ernest studied them for a moment, then sat them down and started twisting one end of his long mustache. "I recognize Half-moon but the other fellow, he's a stranger to me. But now-a-days there's many up here I don't know. Who took these little pictures?"

"Henry did. Ever see a tattoo like that?"

Ernest picked up a picture and looked at it closely. "Can't say I have. What is it? Some kind of spider?"

Henry took the pictures from Ernest. "It's a black widow. His was nice work. Half-moon had a crude one on his neck too."

Ernest took to twisting his mustache again. "No, it means nothing to me."

Joe took a long drink of beer, emptying his glass in one pull. "Thirsty business this."

Ernest laughed. "I can see why you and Miller get along."

"He says you've got yourself some crime gangs working Fayette County. Any of that made its way up to Stewart Township?"

Ernest stopped smiling. "Had our first incident on New Year's Day, an old woman robbed over off of Kentuck Road. They broke in, tied her up and held a candle to her feet until she told them where her valuables were hidden. Poor old girl only had twenty dollars, her life's savings."

Ernest took a little notebook from his pocket and drew a map. "Here's where I live, just over off of Sugar Loaf Road. I'm either here or there most afternoons, have breakfast at the Ohiopyle House regular. Let me know what I can do to help. Meanwhile I'll keep my ears open."

With a tip of his hat, Ernest returned to his table.

Joe picked up the pictures and returned them to his pack. "At least he knows what's going on, but looks like we're on our own." He pulled out his pocket watch. "We've got time for one more I'd say." Henry smiled and went for their refills. Joe took out his notebook, made a few entries and read over his notes so far.

"Here you go Joe."

Joe took another long pull, wiping his mouth with the back of his hand. "You have a chance to get me a map showing where you've been having your troubles?"

"Sure did." Henry reached into his inside coat pocket, pulled out a folded paper and opened it on the table. "Here you go."

Joe studied the map. Henry had noted where his sawmills were, where he held timber lands and the Harkins' homesteads. Through the middle ran the Yough Valley from Confluence to Ohiopyle. His various trouble spots were marked with a "T" for theft, "S" for spike and "D" for damages to his mills. "Whoever's behind this is doing you some serious harm seems like."

"More than I imagined before I sat down and counted them, almost a dozen attacks."

"Which ones hurt the most?"

"Those thefts of the old growth trees. There's real value in them."

Joe studied the map again. "Looks like the spiking and mill damage is spread all over. But the timber thefts are mostly along the valley."

Henry looked at the map and nodded. "You're right Joe. And I've got good lands all over."

"What do you reckon they do with them?"

Henry stroked his chin, taking a moment to consider the question. "Those trees are big. As I said before, you'd need a four house team and a big crew to move them in one piece. They have to be cutting them up."

Joe nodded. "Who's your competition in the lumber business?"

"They're mostly other smaller family-run operations, known most of them for many years. There is one new concern, go by the name of Mill Valley Lumber. They started over in Saltlick Township, over Indian Head way. They've been expanding, buying out the smaller operations all over. I've tried to find out who's the money man behind it but that's still a mystery to me."

Joe took out his notebook and made a few entries, then checked his watch. "We need to hustle back to Ohiopyle so I can make the six o'clock train. How about I come back up here Wednesday and we go look at some of these spots been hit."

"OK Joe. You've been a big help so far. Let's get you to the station."

Chapter 16

Joe awoke Sunday to sound of a howling wind and the clanking of pipes. He'd gotten back to town just after seven. After a late meal at The Dinner Bell restaurant, across from the train station, he'd gone to The Star to catch up on his work. Johnny Davidson had shown up and they stayed past midnight. Joe checked his alarm clock. *After eight o'clock. Missed early mass.* Getting out of bed, he pulled on a flannel robe, then sat at his desk in the corner.

Joe's two-room apartment was located in a modern building on Pittsburgh Street. The White Front's quarters all had electric lights. A shared modern bathroom with running water and a flush toilet sat at the end of the hall, but the new sewers all emptied directly into the Yough. A big coal furnace in the basement kept the building warm on the coldest of days, and it sounded like today would be a cold one.

Joe emptied out his pack and went through his papers. He spent some time studying Henry's map but no new insights were gained. Moving on to his calendar book, he looked to the week ahead. *Today I meet Aunt Margaret.* He had entries on each day but Friday. There he wrote "Visit Brownsville – Tattoo Parlor."

It was nine thirty when Joe left his apartment, well-dressed in his new suit but wearing his sturdy boots. He walked slowly down Main Street, the sidewalks slick with the remnants of a quick squall that had blown through town.

A stiff wind continued to blow out of the north. *Too damn cold to walk across that bridge.* He turned down Arch Street, heading to the West Penn Terminal. *I'll spend the nickel.*

Joe's destination was St. John's Catholic Church located across the Yough in Connellsville's sister borough of New Haven. One of four Catholic churches in the towns, St. John's catered to the Slovak community, many parishioners recent immigrants that worked the mines and coke ovens. After a brief wait, Joe boarded a Leisenring car for the short ride across the river. He got off at 7th Street, entered the New Haven House and sat at a corner table by the window. City Lunch was closed on Sunday, Tony's only day of rest.

"Hello Joe. Coffee for you?"

"Morning, Mary Catherine. Yes please, and let me look at a menu today." Joe ate here most every Sunday, and Mary Catherine was almost always working then.

"Right away Sweetie." A still attractive widowed woman in her forties, she had long ago lost her shyness. In fact, she'd even invited Joe over to her place for dinner more than once.

"Here you go. And here's a Pittsburgh newspaper someone left behind." It was the Saturday *Pittsburgh Gazette*. She sat down a cup of coffee, a menu and the paper.

Joe opened the menu. *Wonder if there's any specials today?* There was indeed. The Sunday Special was "Oven Baked Home Fries Casserole with Ham & Eggs". *Mmm Mmm* He waved Mary Catherine back over. "I'll have the Sunday Special MC.".

She smiled and nodded. "You'll enjoy it Honey, and I'll save you a cream puff for dessert."

Joe picked up the paper and, right on page one, saw a story that caught his eye. "Another Mine Payroll Robbery." This one was at a competitor of Frick's, a J.C. Rainey mine at Revere near Uniontown. The heist was pulled off similar to the Standard one, a road blocked and armed men pistol whipping the paymasters. *That makes four weeks in a row.* No mention was made of suspects or any notes left at the scene.

"Here you go, guaranteed to stick to your ribs." MC laid a small baking dish in front of him, piled high with golden brown potatoes covered with scrambled eggs and diced ham. "And here's dessert." The cream puff was the size of the small plate it was on, and covered with powdered sugar. "Holler if you need anything else."

Joe sat the paper aside and dug into his breakfast. It was gone in a flash, the cream puff right behind it. By 10:15 Joe had paid his bill and headed up Main Street. St. Johns was a block away. It was a magnificent new church, just opened Thanksgiving of last year. The old, smaller church, just down the street, was now vacant. Joe entered, removed his coat, and took a seat in the rear.

Large stained glass windows at the front of each side wall let in plenty of light. The main altar was flanked by two smaller ones where statues of Mary and John the Baptist sat. Down front, a group of old women dressed in black were reciting the Rosary in Slovak. *Every week the same.* Joe knelt and said a prayer, remembering his mother and father.

The church was filled with miners, cokers and their families. *They make a dollar a day but their pennies built this place.* Some looked like they just got off the boat, recognizable by their "old country" clothing and their limited command of English. Others, here longer, had moved up the ladder at the mine and looked more prosperous. A few of the parishioners had joined the growing merchant class, thanks to skills they'd brought with them. But whether from the coal patch villages or from in town, they all shared a strong religious and ethnic heritage, as did the Italians, Hungarians and Irish that attended the other Catholic churches.

The 10:30 service was a High Mass and it was almost noon when it ended. *Might just as well go to Peggy's. I'll have some time before dinner to visit with Aunt Margaret.* Joe caught the next streetcar into town, transferred to the South Connellsville line and was soon at the Patterson's house, located on Patterson Avenue in the South Side of town. Many new homes were being built here, some full-blown mansions. The Pattersons lived in a more modest two-story home built of yellow bricks, a broad porch in front. Joe took a minute to straighten his jacket and slick down his hair, then knocked on the door. A minute later Peggy appeared.

"Hello Joe." She stepped aside and he entered. "We were just visiting in the parlor." She took his hat and coat and they entered the parlor, which was the front room of the house. As he entered, a tall woman rose from the sofa, her firm gaze sizing Joe up. "Joe, I'd like you to meet my aunt, Margaret Foley. Aunt Margaret, this is Joe Zajac, the man I've been telling you about."

Margaret Foley was a well-dressed woman of advanced years, her hair mostly gray and worn in a tight bun. Her long brown dress was plain, a broach at the high collar her only adornment. She approached Joe with her hand outstretched. "Mr. Zajac."

"How do." Joe was at a loss for words, Aunt Margaret's gaze fixed on him in a firm stare.

Peggy finally broke the long moment of silence. "Why don't you two chat for a bit while I get father ready for dinner." With that, she left the two alone. Aunt Margaret returned to the sofa, Joe taking the chair across from it. A small tea table separated them.

Joe finally broke the silence. "Peggy says you run a girls' school."

"Yes, I'm Headmistress at Miss Ellet's School for Girls in Pittsburgh, a position I've held for seven years."

Joe nodded, trying to think of what to say next. He could feel his palms getting sweaty. *Why am I so nervous? That stare!* "And before that?"

Aunt Margaret sat at the front edge of the sofa, straight of spine and unsmiling, her hands clasped in her lap. "I taught there for 15 years. Peggy says you are a former policeman."

"Yes, in Philadelphia, for five years. Worked for Frick after that until last August."

"And now?"

Joe gave a little nervous chuckle. "I guess you could say I'm a bookkeeper-in-training down at The Star. I've got a good head for numbers."

"How long have you known Peggy?"

"Since August. We met while I was still working for Frick."

Aunt Margaret's cold stare turned into a frown. "He's a vile man, as are his cronies, cold exploiters of their workers."

Joe nodded. "I came to the same understanding ma'am. That's why I quit."

"And now you are studying at the university?"

"Start my second term on Tuesday, taking courses in U.S. History and Philosophy."

Before she could respond, Peggy and Andy Patterson entered the room. Joe was surprised by Andy's weak and unsteady gait. His skin was pale, almost gray. Joe stood as they entered, and led Andy to the chair. "Hello Pap. Thanks for having me to dinner."

Andy collapsed into the chair. "You are always welcome at the Patterson's son. Glad you could join us."

Peggy adjusted a hassock under Andy's legs and offered him an afghan. "Why don't you two catch up. Aunt Margaret, can you help get dinner on the table?"

Alone with Andy, Joe took out his handkerchief and wiped his brow. "Don't know what it is about her but she made me sweat."

Andy gave a weak laugh. "No surprise Joe. She's a tough old bird. But she loves Peggy like a daughter, and Peggy loves her back. How'd you like to have her for a teacher down at college?"

Joe just shook his head. "She was younger than your wife then?"

"The baby of the family, and the smartest of the lot." Andy lowered his voice. "She's a suffragette too, so be warned."

Suffragette? What's that? Before he could ask, Peggy returned. "Dinner is on the table."

Joe helped Andy up and the four of them were soon seated in the dining room. A platter of fried chicken sat in the middle, with a bowl of mashed potatoes and another of green beans on the side. A plate of fresh-baked rolls and a boat of gravy rounded out the meal.

"Enjoy the beans Joe. We've only a few more jars left from what we put up last year."

The platters were passed around and all were soon enjoying the meal. As Joe finished a second helping the women started talking.

"Peggy, I got to meet both Susan B. Anthony and Elizabeth Cady Stanton in Pittsburgh last month. They were in town to meet with the local NAWSA chapter. It was a thrill to finally hear them speak in person."

"Any progress being made?"

"Not in Pennsylvania."

Joe cleaned his plate, and leaned back in his chair. "That was a fine meal Peggy." Turning to Aunt Margaret he smiled. "What's this NAWSA? Some kind of women's society?"

Aunt Margaret's stern stare returned. "I'm surprised an educated man like you hasn't heard of the National American Women's Suffrage Association."

Joe could feel the sweat return. He felt Andy give him a kick under the table. "Sorry, no ma'am. What's it all about?"

"It's about letting women vote. We've grown tired of being second class citizens. What is your position on the issue if I might ask?"

Take care Zajac. "I have heard some about it now that you make mention. I've not thought much of it truth told."

Now Aunt Margaret smiled. "Well then, let's think of it together then shall we? Do you exercise your right to vote Mr. Zajac?"

"I've voted in every president's election since I passed the citizen test."

"And you are a student of Philosophy, so let me ask you this. What are the characteristics of a well-qualified voter?"

Think careful. Joe stroked his jaw, composing his thoughts. "I'd say a man has to know about the matters of the day. Read the paper and such."

Aunt Margaret smiled and nodded. "Very good. I agree. Anything else?"

"Have a good head on their shoulders. Be serious-minded, and cast a sober vote. Don't just vote for the man who's passing out the whiskey."

"Agreed. Now are those traits that only men can have? Let's say a woman like Peggy. Is she informed? Serious-minded? Sober?"

Now Joe was squirming in his seat. "I'd say so."

"Then how is it that she, and tens of thousands other women in this country are denied the right?"

Without thinking Joe spoke. "It's a man's place in America to worry about politics and elections and such. It's a woman's place to keep house, raise children and the like."

Joe looked across the table. Peggy's face was reddening. "Joseph Zajac. I can't believe you hold such old-fashioned ideas. Since the Civil War even uneducated former male slaves can vote." She got up and started clearing the table. "Seems like five months isn't long enough to really learn a man's heart."

Chapter 17

* * *

Joe Zajac was dreaming about his school days in Philadelphia. Standing in front of the class, he was reading a paper he'd written on the US Constitution. When he'd finished, his teacher appeared at his side. It was Aunt Margaret! She fixed Joe with a firm, cold stare. "That's all well and good Mr. Zajac, but where in the Constitution does it say that women are second-class citizens? A woman's place is in the voting booth!"

Joe awoke with a start, sitting up in bed. *That stare... makes me jumpy.* He rubbed his face with both hands and fell back down. *My head hurts.*

Joe left the Patterson's soon after his remarks on the issue of women's suffrage. *She made me look like a horse's ass.* Angry and disappointed, he'd ended up at The Star, sitting alone at his corner table brooding. At some point after his third beer he drank a shot of Old Overholt, then another. What had promised to be an important day deteriorated into a drunken night. He barely remembered staggering home up Pittsburgh Street.

Joe sat back up and kicked off the covers. *Maybe I am a horse's ass.* The clock said 8:10. *Hurting head or not it's time to get a move on. I'll straighten it out with Peggy this afternoon.* After a quick cleanup he was out the door. *No time for breakfast.* Briefcase in hand, he jumped on the Scottdale streetcar as it travelled up Main Street. Before too long he was back at Frick headquarters, where, as usual, Polly was at the front desk.

"Good morning Joe. We're expecting you." She handed him a sheaf of papers. "Here's your list of mines and superintendents. They've all been informed that you are helping out again. I've also noted how the payrolls are delivered and how much they are. Saturday is the usual payday for all of the mines, the money delivered on Friday. Just go on up. Mr. McMullen should be in with Mr. Lynch."

Joe stuffed the papers into his briefcase. "Much obliged Polly." She let Joe in and he was soon at the door to Mr. Lynch's office, where he and a big bald man were deep in conversation. Joe tapped on the door frame and Mr. Lynch looked up.

"Mr. Zajac, please come in." Mr. Lynch rose and pulled a second chair around to the front of his desk. "I'd like you to meet Mike McMullen, our head of security since September."

McMullen rose and extended a big beefy arm in Joe's direction. "How do Mr. Zajac."

McMullen appeared to be in his 40s, his face and arms covered with freckles. A big pot belly hung over his belt. The little hair he had was reddish-gray. He had a broad chest and shoulders, looked like he was strong as a bull. "Hello Mike. Just call me Joe. You another former policeman?"

Mike nodded. "Twenty years with the Pittsburgh PD, the last five as a detective. How about you?"

"Five years with the Philadelphia squad before I came west."

The three sat down and Mr. Lynch took the lead. "I've just given Mr. McMullen the details of your previous work for us, plus the information regarding Carnegie Steel that I shared with you last week. I must emphasize that it be held in the strictest confidence." Both men nodded. Mr. Lynch pulled an envelope out of his desk drawer and handed it to Joe. "This is for you. The fee we agreed to."

The ten thousand bucks! Joe took the envelope and put it in his briefcase. "I'll do my best to earn it." He reached back into his case and pulled out the papers Polly had given him. "Let's see if we can come up with a course of action."

Mr. Lynch pulled out his pocket watch. "I've got a meeting to attend in the board room. You and Mike work out the details. He'll keep me informed. Feel free to call me at any time if need be." He picked up a pile of papers from his desk and departed.

Mike got up. "Let's go down to my office." Joe followed him back down the hall. They entered his office and McMullen closed the door.

My old boss's office. "How's Cliff Sellers making out?"

Mike sat down behind the desk. "He's recovered from his wounds for the most part but he's not likely to ever work again. Were you and Cliff friends?"

Joe laughed. "Not hardly. In fact, I'd say he had a high level of disregard for me, an opinion I shared of him. We about traded blows more than once in here."

Mike smiled back at him. "I knew Cliff on the force. He was a foul-mouthed blowhard. Me, I like to keep a smile on my face." He took out a piece of paper and a pencil. "Mr. Lynch said to follow your lead. What's the plan?"

Joe spread the papers out on the desk. "For starters, we might want to start changing up the way we deliver the payrolls, and the times of delivery."

Mike nodded. "That makes sense, should have done that already."

"But what I really want to do is try to guess where they might hit next." He reviewed the mine list. "Looks like most of the mine superintendents haven't changed. I was good buddies with quite a few of them."

Mike pulled out his own set of papers. "They already hit Standard. The biggest payroll after that would be the one goes out to the three Leisenring mines. It might be bigger with funds for the three Union Supply stores."

Joe nodded. "What did Mr. Lynch tell you about 'The Reapers'?"

"Not many details. I know you ended up stopping them at Leisenring No. 1."

"The head of the outfit was a fellow named Straub, Kurt Straub. He was a violent man. Hated Mr. Frick with a passion. I though he died when he jumped into the Yough. But if he's alive and still running that gang, I'd bet he'd love to hit Leisenring again. And consider this. They've yet to hit a mine close to Connellsville." Joe checked the list again. "Almost $4,000 going out there on Friday, travelling on the streetcar. Jim Thornton is still the superintendent. I could go out and see him this afternoon."

"You going to change up the delivery?"

"No, but we're going to see that two of our men are on the Leisenring car when it leaves Connellsville with the money, and make sure no one else is on it. We'll need to give West Penn Railways notice and make sure the operator knows our plan. Can you do that?"

"I see what you're up to, but let's think this through. First off, let's not tell Jim what we're up to. The fewer that know the better. The two paymasters will come into Connellsville on the Scottdale car. They'll transfer to the Leisenring car, two of our men already aboard. We'd better make sure that operator is prepared for some action, and is armed. Then how do you think they'll pull off the robbery? And how are you going to keep other riders from boarding along the way?"

Good questions. "I guess we just won't stop. And if they are true to form, they'll block the tracks at some point. I'd pick somewhere between Trotter and Leisenring. There's a crossroads close by. And I have an idea about the operator. Ask West Penn if they'd be willing to let me be the operator. I've always wanted to try my hand at it."

"And you think they'll go for it this week?"

"They've been hitting one regular for the last month. If not Leisenring, somewhere else."

"I'll call West Penn first thing."

"I'll be at The Star by early afternoon. We have a telephone. I could go over to West Penn this afternoon."

"I'll try to arrange it."

Joe stuffed his papers away and got up. "Let Mr. Lynch know what we've planned." The two men shook hands and Joe was soon on his way back to town. It was after eleven when he jumped off the streetcar in the middle of downtown Connellsville. *Get this check in the bank, then time for lunch.* He entered the First National Bank where another of his friends, Dave Norton, was the head teller. Dave was sitting at a desk behind a low wrought iron railing and waved to Joe as he came in.

"Morning Dave, can you spare a minute?"

Dave got up and opened a gate in the railing. "Sure Joe. Come on in."

Joe took a seat at Dave's desk with his briefcase in his lap. "I'm looking for some advice." He pulled the envelope out of his briefcase, took out the check from Frick and laid it in front of Dave. He looked at it, eyes widening.

"My goodness. Ten thousand dollars. That's a small fortune Joe. Is it a loan to you?"

Joe shook his head. "Payment in advance for some work I've agreed to do for the Frick Company."

"I thought you were all through with them?"

Joe slumped in his chair. "I did too, and I never expected them to agree to my terms, but here you are."

"I'll deposit it to your account. You know, there's almost enough in there for you to start your own bank."

"It's more than I ever dreamed of having. And you know what buddy? It's…. burdensome. In some ways I was better off broke. Now I'm wondering… what should I do with it?"

Dave nodded. "I understand what you mean Joe. I was serious about the banking business. You could become a shareholder here at First National. Or, if not here, there's a new bank being formed, the Colonial. I know the investors organizing it. Want to meet them?"

Joe shook his head. "I'm no money man, just a dumb Pollock that got lucky."

"Don't sell yourself short. You got a good head on your shoulders. There's plenty of other business prospects in Fayette County. This coal and coke boom will continue for many years. Let me do some thinking about it." Dave went to a teller window and in a moment returned with a deposit receipt. "It's here when you need it. How's Peggy?"

Joe took the receipt and put it in his briefcase. "She's fine, but I made her mad yesterday. Now I've some advice for you Dave. Don't ever discuss politics at a Sunday dinner. I'll stop by next week and we can talk more about the money."

With that, Joe left the bank and was soon at City Lunch. Tony was sitting at the counter, a bowl of stew in front of him. "Who's minding the kitchen Tony?"

"My boy Nicky's helping out."

"No school today?"

Tony frowned. "He decide to quit school. He's 14 now. I try to make him stay but he no listen to me."

Young Nicky Molinari came out of the kitchen. "Hello Joe. You want some lunch? The stew is good, I made it myself. We got fresh biscuits too."

"Sure Nicky. What's this I hear you quit school?"

Nicky glared at his father. "I got a lot of brothers and sisters behind me. Pop, he works as hard as he can but the money, it's always tight at home. I'm just helping here until I can find a job." He returned to the kitchen.

Tony just shook his head. "He's a good boy, wants to help provide for the family, but I tell him, we get by. But he no listen. He good at school work too. I always dream he graduate high school, work with his head, not hands."

Nicky returned with Joe's meal. "Here you go Joe. Enjoy."

Joe ate his meal in silence, a sad Tony at his side.

Chapter 18

*   *   *

After his lunch, Joe left Tony, still brooding at the counter, and headed to The Star. The temperatures had warmed some but the gray ski promised more snow. *Tony hoped for a better life for his children.* It was just after noon when he entered the saloon. He saw that Peggy was in the back office working on the books. *Might as well face the music.* Joe's stomach fluttered a bit. He left his coat and briefcase at a table and joined her. She looked up as he entered.

"Hello Joseph." She turned her head back down to the ledger sheet.

Joseph? "And to you. I was going to catch up on the books this afternoon." It had been several days since he'd had the opportunity to work on them.

She spoke without looking up. "Father is looking stronger today. He can look after himself for a few hours." She sat down her pen and looked up. "Please close the door and sit down. We need to talk."

Oh Lord. Joe closed the door and sat down. They looked at each other in silence for a moment before she spoke.

"Sunday was one of the most unpleasant days I've had in a long time."

"I know Peggy, but..."

She held up her hand. "Hear me out. I love my Aunt Margaret dearly. More than that, I respect her. She's a smart and accomplished **woman**. I wanted her to approve of you, feel that we were a good match. Well, quite the opposite occurred."

"Peggy, I didn't even know what a 'suffragette' was before yesterday, never even thought much about women getting the vote."

"It's a struggle that has been going on for more than 40 years! She and I both feel strongly about it. I even mentioned it to you in November when you went to vote for Sheriff Miller."

Guess I wasn't listening close enough. "Peggy, I'm sorry for what I said, and for upsetting your aunt."

"Joe, it's not what you said, it's what you think that has caused me consternation. It's made me realize that, in the five months since we met, we've really not learned enough about each other."

"I know my feelings for you, and I thought yours for me."

Peggy remained quiet for a bit, her and Joe locked in a stare. *She's reminding me of her aunt now.*

"You've gotten quite busy, helping out Henry. And tomorrow you start back to school. I've decided that I can take on the books again."

"Makes sense I guess. I took on another little job today." He told her of his meeting at Frick and the $10,000 he just put in the bank.

"That's quite a bit of money. What are your plans for it?"

"I'd been thinking maybe I'd build us a new house on the South Side."

Peggy looked at him with pursed lips. "You've never even proposed marriage. I think that would be premature."

Joe could feel his face redden, anger and hurt rising up. Before he could respond the telephone rang. Peggy picked it up.

"Hello. Yes, he's here. Who's calling?" She handed the telephone to Joe. "It's a Mr. McMullen from the Frick Company."

Joe stood up to take the phone from Peggy. She opened the door and went to chat with the bartender. Joe took a deep breath. *Don't blow your stack.*

"Hello, Joe here."

"I just got off the telephone with West Penn. Go see Sam Evans at the terminal this afternoon. I've filled him in on the plan. They're willing to help. He'll show you how to be a motorman, too."

Guess I've got plenty of time. "I'll go see him and call you on Wednesday. Say, I asked to meet the Carnegie Steel security chief tomorrow in Pittsburgh. Does he know I'm coming?"

"He does, name's Charlie Kilpatrick. His office is in the Carnegie Building. Know where that is?"

"Can't say I do. What's the address?"

"It's at 428 Fifth Avenue, thirteen stories tall so it's hard to miss."

"Tell Charlie I'll be by in the afternoon, by four at the latest."

"Will do."

Their conversation ended, Joe sat back down, his head still spinning. *I better just leave before I make matters worse.* He left the office, gathered up his things and, with a nod to Peggy, left the bar and shuffled slowly up Pittsburgh Street. *How can good go bad so fast?*

Ten minutes later, Joe was sitting in the office of Sam Evans, on the second floor of the West Penn Terminal. Sam was a short round man of advancing years, his close-cropped hair a silver gray.

"So Mr. Zajac, please explain to me again exactly how you see this scheme of yours going? Mr. McMullen only went over it briefly."

"You've read about the mine payroll robberies been pulled off over the last month." Evans nodded. "The robbers have struck all over, from Latrobe to Uniontown. We're guessing that this week they might hit Connellsville, go after a large cash delivery heading out to the Leisenring mines. The money is delivered by streetcar."

"That's news to me."

"You'd never know that the men are carrying it. There's two that work together. They'll be coming from Scottdale, and change to a Leisenring car here. I'm guessing the robbers will make their move somewhere past Trotter, likely block the tracks."

"Haven't these fellows proven to be armed and violent?"

"Yes sir, they have. That's why we'll be prepared, with two armed men already on the Leisenring car. We'll need to make sure that no other riders are on board."

Evans had slouched down in his chair, his fingertips pressed together. "That might prove to be difficult. What car do they usually arrive on?"

"The 11:20."

"That run is usually not one of the busy ones."

"We'll have to play it on the fly. And we don't want your operator placed at risk. I'd like to take his place."

"You have any experience as a motorman?"

"No sir, but I've rode your streetcars all over, usually sit up front. I've watched them work many times."

"I started as a motorman, and am responsible for their training and the safe operation of the line. In truth, it's not that difficult for the most part, unless the brakes fail or you run off the tracks."

"Can we start this afternoon? I've got a full week ahead of me."

Evans sat silently for some time, brow furrowed. "I am reluctant to have West Penn involved in this. But seeing as how the Frick Company is doing the asking we'll go along with it." He rose and grabbed his coat from the rack. "Let's hop a car over to the shop at the power plant. We have a short track there we use for training purposes."

Ten minutes later they arrived at the West Penn shops in New Haven. A yard was filled with streetcars in various stages of repair. Behind the shop stood the power plant, its smokestacks billowing. Like everything else in America, it ran on coal. Joe checked out the cars while Evans went inside, returning in a few minutes carrying a motorman's jacket and hat.

"If you're going to run one of my units, you better dress the part."

"I always wanted one of these hats."

"There's a car inside we can work with. Follow me."

Joe followed Evans down a track that led into a big barn-like building. Inside sat car 411, freshly painted and ready to return to service. "It's a might warmer in here Joe." He stood at the controls in the front of the car. "Operation is simple. There are two controls, and you can operate the car from either end. This lever is called the 'controller' and adjusts the power. Push forward to go forward, pull back to reverse. This wheel is the brake. Spin it clockwise to apply. The challenge is knowing your run, and where to speed up and slow down. Running to Leisenring from the terminal is not too difficult as it's mostly uphill. Before you can operate the car you have to unlock the controller and hook the pickup on the live wire." They got out of the car and Joe watched as Evans hung the power pickup on an overhead line using a long pole stored under the car. "Be careful not to touch the wire with the pole. Ready?"

Back in the car, Joe took off his coat and hat, then tried on the West Penn gear. *Coats a mite big but the hat fits fine.* "I'm ready." He unlocked the controller and pushed it forward. The car jumped ahead with a jolt.

Evans grabbed a pole to steady himself. "Easy now. Just a little more at a time."

Joe added a bit more power and the streetcar moved down the line.

"Controller to neutral and apply the brakes."

Joe cut the power and spun the brake wheel. The trolley ground to a halt with a screech.

"Flip the pickup and take us back to the barn. A few more short runs, then we'll go out on the main line."

After flipping the pickup, Joe boarded at the other end of the car and they returned to the barn. "I'll make a right good motorman, I'd say, with a little more practice."

Chapter 19

The gang sat at an improvised table inside of an abandoned coal mine, old black powder barrels for chairs. They were an odd lot, two big blond fellows who looked like farm boys, two swarthy older men with long bushy mustaches, and their apparent leader. He was pale of skin, medium height, slim with close-cropped hair and a short beard. His only distinguishing characteristic was his left arm, which rested in a sling. A kerosene lantern cast a dim, flickering glow around the room. Several crates were visible, stacked against one wall. A small pile of money sat in the middle of the table.

One of the young men was speaking. "Not much of a haul." The speaker's name was Charlie Krouse.

One of the older fellows nodded in agreement. "Charlie's right. Revere's a big mine, should have been more."

After a moment of silence their leader spoke. "Split half among you. The rest we save for the big day. And don't despair. This week's target is a fat one."

Their leader was one Kurt Straub, his injured arm a painful reminder of the events of August, 1900 at Leisenring No. 1. Their hideout was an abandoned slope-entrance mine near the Yough, 10 miles north of Connellsville.

Charlie spoke again. "What do we hit?"

"The delivery to the Leisenring mines. The money men ride the streetcar. Here's the plan."

The gang huddled around the table as their leader laid out the heist.

Chapter 20

Joe sat unsmiling, watching the world go by outside of the train window. *Don't even feel like taking these courses anymore.* After his motorman instruction, he'd eaten an early and solitary dinner at The New Haven House, had a few beers after, and walked the mile or so back to his rooms. At 7:30 Tuesday morning, he was on the way to Pittsburgh and the start of the winter semester.

Thoughts of Peggy crowded his mind. *She's not being fair. She should have warned me. Her aunt is just a bitter old spinster.* Then he thought of Tony, still down at breakfast this morning about his son. *Nothing but grief all around.* He set the thoughts aside, pulled out his calendar book and looked over his day. His first class was US History at 9:00am followed by Philosophy at 1:00pm. He'd go to the Carnegie Building after that, his appointment scheduled at four. The remainder of his week was full, with Wednesday's trip back to Ohiopyle, Thursday classes again and Friday's ride with the Frick payroll. He'd not make it to Brownsville's tattoo parlor until Saturday, it looked like.

An hour later, the train pulled into the B&O station. Joe exited and walked toward a line of carriages. *Better take a cab today. Don't want to be late.* Climbing aboard, he called to the driver. "Western University, Observatory Hill." They were soon headed across the Point Bridge to the City of Allegheny on the north bank of the Allegheny River, arriving just before nine.

The Western University of Pennsylvania occupied two red brick buildings on the grounds of the Allegheny Observatory. The four story Main Building had turrets on each front corner, their tall roofs pointed and castle-like. Joe entered the building, found Room 211 and took a seat in the rear of the already-filled class. He surveyed the room and, as was the case last semester, he was likely the oldest of the 30-odd students. All were young men except for a single young lady sitting up front.

At exactly 9:00am the door opened and a woman walked in, carrying a leather briefcase somewhat like Joe's. She took her place at the podium, pulled some papers and a pair of glasses from her briefcase and addressed the class. "Good morning to all. My name is Miss Grace Hall. I'm your instructor for this United States History course. Let's see if we are all here."

For the next five minutes, she called role. Joe studied her as she did so. She was a tall woman in her 40s he guessed, somewhat plainly dressed in a long black skirt and long sleeved gray blouse with a high collar. Her brown hair, streaked with gray, was in a bun. A large cameo hung from a gold chain around her neck. *I didn't know women were allowed to be instructors.* He shook his head. *She's likely a friend of Aunt Margaret's. Better watch yourself.*

"All present and accounted for. We'll be using 'History of the United States' published by Barnes as our primary text for the course. Although several copies are available at the library, I suggest that, if possible, you purchase one for yourself. There is a supply available at the book store." A young man in the front row raise his hand. "Yes sir?"

"Ma'am, Miss Hall, when did the university start employing women instructors?"

Miss Hall gave the man a tight smile. "You are looking at the first one. After five years of accepting women students here, I'd say it's about time."

"Did you go to college?"

"Graduated from Bryn Mawr in 1889."

"Well, I guess you know more about United States history than I do Miss Hall. Let's get cracking!"

The class, including Miss Hall, laughed and moved on. "The first few classes we will discuss the colonization of what is now the United States, and the subsequent battles to control the continent. Then we'll move on to the American Revolution and our Constitution." Without further ado she began her lecture. Ninety minutes later, the class concluded. Joe took his time and was the last to leave. He stopped by the podium where Miss Hall was packing up her papers. She noticed Joe and looked up.

"May I help you sir?"

"I'm Joe Zajac. Good luck to you."

"Thank you Mr. Zajac. Good luck to us both." She glanced down at her class roster. "You're a special admission student, not yet working on a degree."

"That's right. I'm a late-comer to higher education."

Miss Hall gave a throaty laugh. "As was I, almost 30 when I graduated. Don't let that dissuade you. I think education is frequently wasted on the young."

"That's what I figured when I signed up for these courses."

"I hope you find mine of value." She picked up her briefcase and gloves. "Time to prepare for my afternoon class. Good day Mr. Zajac." With a smile, she left Joe standing there.

*   *   *

At 1:00pm Joe was back in Main Building, this time in an elevated lecture hall in the basement. The student desks ascended in steps up from the podium, ending where a row of low windows admitted a dim light. Having arrived early, Joe sat at the front of the room.

A moment later their instructor arrived, a man of about 60. A long mane of white hair was tucked behind his ears. A bushy mustache and goatee mostly hid his mouth. He stepped to the podium, and with his hands on his hips, turned to the class. "This is a lecture on the subject of Philosophy. I'm Professor Conrad Burnsworth." Pulling a rolled up piece of paper from his jacket pocket, he sat at a small table. "Let's just have you call out your name, starting from the back."

Joe gave the professor a long look, lost in thought. *He reminds me of someone. Some picture I saw. That cowboy.*

"And that leaves you sir." Joe looked up, the professor now standing in front of him.

Shoulda been paying attention. "I'm Joe Zajac." *I know, Buffalo Bill!*

"Thank you." He rolled up the paper and stuck it away. "Now, without further preliminary discussion, we will begin our inquiry. This class is an opportunity for us to think of man's oldest question. 'Why am I here?' And even consider the broader issue. 'What is the nature of my existence?'. No lightweight inquiries these, nor intended for the intellectually faint of heart. So we proceed."

The lecture covered the birth of modern philosophic inquiry in ancient Greece. Joe was introduced to Socrates and Plato. *The only life worth living is a good life...makes sense to me.* The professor was wrapping up his lecture.

"And in the spirit of Socrates, believing that knowledge is the only one good, we'll meet again on Thursday. Aristotle's ideas will occupy us for the next several weeks. Our textbook is Volume 1 of the 'Dissertation on the Philosophy of Aristotle' by Thomas Taylor. I suggest that you purchase it if possible or be prepared to spend several nights a week in the library."

Joe stuck around as several other students exchanged words with the professor until they were alone. Joe stood and extended his hand. "How do Professor Burnsworth. I'm Joe Zajac."

"Good afternoon Mr. Zajac. Did you find the class of interest?"

"More than that. Got my head spinning a bit."

The professor smiled. "That's to be expected. You've perhaps not thought much of these questions."

Joe shook his head. "That's not it. You might say I find them all of present concern."

With a nod, the professor turned to the door. "Sounds like 'Grape' talk to me. See you on Thursday Mr. Zajac."

Grape talk? What the hell's that mean? Joe gathered up his papers. *Might as well go get those books.*

Chapter 21

✳   ✳   ✳

J oe, his new books in hand, stood at the streetcar stop on Perryville Road with several other students. He had enough time to take the trolley, the Perryville line terminating two blocks from the Carnegie Building. The next car was already rolling down the hill toward them. It stopped with a screech and Joe boarded with the others. *Lookey here. This one has a stove.* There in the middle of the car stood a little pot-bellied stove, it's chimney pipe exiting through the middle of the roof. Joe took a seat right across from it. The trolley took off and they were soon crossing back over The Point Bridge to Pittsburgh. The Point was perhaps the poorest neighborhood in the city, the streetcar line passing through for several blocks. A ragged gang of children ran after it, laughing and throwing snowballs. *This place makes those coal-patch towns look pretty good.* Open fires burned at several intersections. Most of the shacks had boards over the windows. Coal smoke filled the air. *No wonder they call it Smokey City.*

The line ended on Liberty Avenue. Joe packed his books away in his briefcase, bundled up and walked to the Carnegie Building, arriving 10 minutes early. Several buggies and cabs were parked at the curb, the drivers standing together. Joe entered the lobby, two stories tall with elaborate hand-carved stonework. He consulted the building directory and was soon on the elevator to the top floor, where Carnegie Steel's main offices were located. As the doors opened he was greeted by a guard.

"You've business to attend to Sir?"

"Joe Zajac, here to see Charlie Kilpatrick."

The guard picked up a clipboard from a nearby table, checked it and nodded. "Take a right, see the receptionist at the end of the hall."

Joe walked down the long hall, its walls covered in oil paintings. A thick Persian carpet covered the floor. The few office doors along the hall were open, the occupants sitting at paper-covered desks. *So this is where the biggest steel company in the world is run from. Fancy place.* He approached the receptionist.

"Joe Zajac here to see Charlie Kilpatrick."

The young woman nodded and arose. "Follow me." About halfway down another hall she stopped at an office. "Mr. Zajac here to see you Mr. Kilpatrick."

Joe entered the office to see a short fellow sitting behind a tall stack of papers. He had red hair and thick sideburns that joined a bushy mustache. *Looks like Lloyd but about half the size.* The man got up and approached Joe. "Mr. Zajac. Pleased to meet you. Let's go down the hall."

Joe offered his hand. "How do Charlie. Lead the way." Joe followed him out the door and further down the hall to a set of double doors at the end.

"Nothing going on in here this late in the day." Charlie opened the doors to a huge room, taking up half the width of the building. A long table stretched toward a window, with a dozen chairs on each side. "This here's the Board of Directors room. They had a meeting earlier. Let's go take it easy." In front of the window sat a sofa and several stuffed chairs, a low table in the midst. Charlie sat in one of the chairs, Joe next to him.

Joe sat his briefcase on the table and pulled out a pencil and paper. "Mike McMullen told me to make your acquaintance. He has me looking into the payroll robberies Frick's been having. He mentioned you've been having some troubles too."

Charlie nodded. "We have. Mike tells me that Mr. Lynch holds you in high regard, and has informed you of the negotiations under way."

"I was employed by the Frick Company for six years, up to last August, and worked closely with Mr. Lynch for a time at the end."

"These incidents I'm going to tell you about—we've managed to keep most of them out of the paper."

"I won't spill the beans."

"There was one that did make the papers. We had a fire on a coke train outside of the Edgar Thomson works. You might have read of it."

Joe shook his head. "Can't say I did. What started it?"

"Best we can tell the fire started at a half dozen places along the line of cars. My guess is they used railroad flares to get them going. We had to let it burn out, all 40 cars destroyed. Even the rails melted."

Joe made some notes. "When did that happen?"

"Mid-December."

"What else?"

"Tampering with equipment. Ever been inside a steel mill?"

"No sir."

"They're dangerous places. Men die in them regularly. There was an accident two weeks ago at Homestead, one man dead, more injured and one of the furnaces shut down for three days. I'm sure it was sabotage."

"Any idea who might be behind it?"

"You've heard of the Battle of Homestead? Your man Frick was at the helm of Carnegie Steel in those days."

"I have, a bit, but it was before my time with Frick. I know some union man tried to kill him."

"Not a union man, an anarchist, and one of the most notorious ones in America. But Frick proved himself a tough old bird then, and still is. That failed strike rang the death knell for the union. Not a single mill in Pennsylvania recognizes unions today. But the old union men have apparently gotten wind of these talks with Morgan and are threatening to strike the new company if it fails to recognize them. They've built up support."

"Why start trouble now? What's their angle?"

"If there's labor trouble at Carnegie Steel, its value drops. It's a good plan. The deal gives the union a moment of advantage."

Joe nodded, and put down his pencil. "But killing one of their own? Don't make sense."

"I doubt it was their intent. Sometimes plans go afoul. There's a second gang causing some trouble too. They've been passing out pamphlets to the laborers, the ones just off the boat that the other union doesn't represent. It's called Barat. That's Hungarian for friend. And it's them, the Slovak's and other Hunkies that's getting the papers."

Hunkies like me if I hadn't been lucky. "What papers?"

"Agitation tracts I'd call them."

"You have one?"

"Back in my office." Charlie got up, Joe did as well. "I mentioned that the Board met today. Morgan is in town, your man Frick with him. Morgan wants the deal finished by February. Carnegie, Frick and the rest will see another big payday when it does, hundreds of millions."

Joe thought about his $10,000, a small fortune to him. "Money squeezed from those Hunkies. Carnegie will likely be building more of his libraries."

Charlie gave Joe a funny smile and the two men returned to his office where Joe collected the pamphlet. "I'll let you know if I can find any connection." It was after five and already dark when Joe boarded the B&O train back to Connellsville.

The engine and cars rolled down the Monongahela River bank, passing first the Homestead Mill on the other side of the river then The Edgar Thomson Works next to the tracks. Even with the windows closed, Joe could hear the noise of the machinery. Dozens of stacks emitted dark streams of smoke, many more belched fire. The scene was cast in a flickering orange glow that extended for miles, from one end of the Monongahela valley to the other. *What did that other conductor say? Hell with the lid off. Sure looks like it tonight.*

Joe pulled the pamphlet from his briefcase, along with a doughnut he'd bought at the station. *Let's see what these Barat boys are up to.* The pamphlet was a printed on rough stock paper, the front a drawing of a man in chains. Above was their name, below a simple message. *Lose Your Chains.* Joe turned it over, on the rear a longer message.

Barat – Friend of the Hunkies
Carnegie and his henchmen lured you to America.
They told lies and made false promises.
The criminals must pay for these crimes.
You are only slaves, chained to the mill. Work or let your family starve.
Unions are worthless. Join with us. We promise justice.
For whatever a man sows, this he will also reap.

Joe felt a shiver and goosebumps. *The same message The Reapers spread. The one I got in person. And this is no union, these boys are looking for revenge.*

Chapter 22

*   *   *

Pack in hand, Joe left the warmth of the train to a stiff wind and snow flurries. He could see Henry Brooks standing just inside the Ohiopyle station door. Joining him there, the two sat down at a bench.

"Right on time Joe."

Joe was dressed for the weather and the terrain in his boots, flop-eared hat and long wool coat. For good measure he had a long wool scarf draped around his neck. "I'm ready to get started. Got any news to report?"

"We buried Half-moon yesterday. None of the family showed up. And the other body disappeared."

"Disappeared?"

"When we went in to get Half-moon, the other fellow was gone. Bob forgets to lock up on occasion."

"At least we have a picture." Joe pulled on the pack and his gloves. "I've got a couple of roast beef sandwiches from The Star in here so we won't starve this trip."

Henry smiled. "I've got a lunch packed too. I promise to keep you fed from here on."

As they left the station, Joe looked across the street at the Fern Cliff entrance. *That's Hawk Harkins going in there looks like.* "Henry, recognize that fellow?"

They stopped for a moment. "Looks like Hawk I'd say. Wonder what business he has at the Fern Cliff?"

Henry's sleigh was parked outside of the station. "We're going to go look at the site of the last tree theft, when they got the big old one. The site is over near George's Ridge." The men climbed aboard and headed out of town along the now-familiar road, past Harkins Hollow, through Confluence and back down the other side of the river. They were soon at the turnoff to the George Harkins' cabin. "We'll keep along the river for another mile or so."

The road here ran along some rolling hills, which soon climbed higher until they were travelling parallel to George's Ridge. Henry stopped the sleigh and pointed up. "I suspect this is close to where you found Sky."

"Hard to tell from this angle. Might be it was that ledge there."

"My lands run from about here for another mile or so. My father bought it from old George 20 years ago, before the demand for lumber really shot up. These old hardwoods are too good for mine use. I'm planning on selling them for furniture making." They continued on a bit, the road running in a narrow cut along the face of a rock wall, just a few feet from the river bank. "The grove is on top of that little cliff." They parked the sleigh and walked to the end of the cliff, where the higher ground rose more gradually. Joe could see the grove of old hardwoods.

"There they are Joe, mostly oaks and poplars, some cherry and maple too. These are about the biggest specimens left in the valley. Look about halfway up the hill. You'll see the stump of the tree that was stolen."

Joe looked where Henry was pointing and saw the stump. The tree was at the edge of the grove, near the top. "Think we can get up there?"

"I'm game if you think you can make it." They started up the hillside, Joe struggling through the snow, at times going in almost waist-deep. *Could use those snowshoes.* It took them a quarter of an hour to climb the hill, Joe breathing heavy at the end. He stood, hands on hips, gazing down at the frozen river, 50 yards or so down the hill. Next to him was a stump, almost six feet across.

"That was a good size. How tall you figure it was?"

"Probably a hundred feet or so."

Six feet across and a 100 feet long. Where'd it go? "Any evidence that they chopped it up here?"

"No. Just some smashed smaller trees where it fell, straight across the hill."

"I'm gathering it took someone with some lumbering skills to take it down."

Henry nodded. "I'd say so. You don't know what you're doing, you end up dead underneath it."

Joe edged his way down the hill a bit, lost his footing and took a slide. "Whoa!" He came to a stop almost at the bottom of the hill.

"You alright?"

Joe got up and brushed the snow from the seat of his pants. *That was some ride.* He stood up, deciding which way to go. "I'm in one piece." He started back toward the way they'd come. *What's this?* He noticed several smaller trees, mostly snow covered, knocked over. "Henry, come on down here."

Henry slid down and joined him and Joe got busy shaking the snow off of the smaller downed trees. "What do you make of this?"

Henry examined the trunks. "Appears they've been smashed, like the tree fell on them. But it's too far away."

Joe looked up the hill. They were about fifty feet to the right of the stump. "I'm thinking they rolled that big old log down the hill."

Henry looked up and nodded. "Then what?" They were very close to the edge of the low cliff.

"Over the side on onto a wagon?"

"Not likely. The road is barely passable with a sleigh, and they'd have had to cut it up."

They walked along the top of the cliff until it met the road and then down the road to a spot just below the stump. Joe walked over to the base of the cliff, stopping to look up and down the roadside. *Look here.* The brush and bushes showed sign of crushing. "Looks like the log came down over here." He crossed the narrow lane, where a small decline led to the shore of the Yough. Henry joined him. "Here too."

Henry examined the damaged bushes, turned and looked to the stump spot. "Damn Joe. You figured it out. They dropped the tree and rolled in onto the river."

The two descended to the river bank, then onto the frozen river. "Then what the hell did they do with it Henry?"

"I suppose that with a good team you could drag it a-ways, make it even further if you could get some skids under it."

Some low gray clouds rolled over the ridge, dropping a quick burst of heavy snow. Henry and Joe climbed back up to the road. "Let's get back to town. I'll come out here better equipped to follow the trail." They boarded the sleigh and returned to Ohiopyle, the snow letting up as they arrived. Henry pulled up at the station. "I'll be in town on Saturday, staying over to Sunday down at the Water Street Hotel. Come by around seven and I'll buy you dinner."

Joe climbed down from the sleigh. "I think Saturday might be stuffed pork chop night. I'll join you." Henry gave the reins a shake and turned the sleigh onto the road out of town. Joe looked at his watch. *Just missed the 1:30 back to town.* He looked across the road at the Fern Wood entrance. *Maybe I'll go see what Marshall is up to, share a sandwich with him.* Crossing the road, he walked up the path toward the hotel. Halfway up, he saw a man and a woman talking close to the hotel. Joe stopped to observe the scene. *Now don't she look familiar too. That's Jewel Harkins. And looks like the man is Elmer Fortney.* Joe watched as she backed up a step, shaking her head, then continued toward Joe, head down. As she approached he called out a hello.

She looked up, recognized Joe, and stopped with a smile. "Surprised to see you up in these mountains today. Thought you'd had enough of them Saturday."

"That was an exciting visit. How's Sky?"

"Oh, that old hardhead will survive. Thank you again for your help." She looked over her shoulder, Elmer still standing and watching. "I need to get back home." Her smile now a frown. she quickly walked away.

Joe stood watching her until she left the grounds. *Now that is peculiar and a mite coincidental.* He shook his head and continued on down the path,

Elmer quickly disappearing down the pathway in the other direction. Joe went around back and rang the bell, the door soon answered by Marshall McNutt.

"Afternoon Joe. Come on in." Joe saw a plate sitting on a little table.

"Sorry to interrupt your lunch Marshall."

"I was just finishing up. Come on and sit down."

Joe took off his pack and extracted one of his sandwiches. "Mind if I join you then?"

Marshall sat back down and finished his meal, while Joe ate his sandwich. In a few moments they were both finished. "So what brings you back up the mountain today?"

"Still looking into some of the troubles Henry's been having."

"Heard about your helping rescue Sky last week."

"Did Miss Jewel tell you? She working the winter now too?"

Marshall's face reddened a bit. "Heard from her, plus I ran into Henry yesterday."

Joe pushed back his chair and leaned forward, arms resting on spread legs. "She here meeting with her boyfriend Hawk?"

Marshall's face reddened even more. He pushed back his chair and jumped up. "How'd you come to know about that?"

Joe got up too. "Take it easy Marshall. You don't have to be Sherlock Holmes to add up one plus one. I saw Hawk coming up here this morning when I got off the train. Plus I heard some remarks up at their cabin on Saturday that got me thinking. It was an easy guess."

"Now what do you intend to do about it?"

Joe sat back down. "None of my business I'd say. Both of them are legal age. They been friends long?"

Marshall also sat back down. "A few months, since last summer I reckon. He started coming around in the evenings, after Jewel was off work. Didn't take me long to figure out what was going on. One day she up and admitted it to me."

"And Sky found out?"

Marshall nodded. "Around the time of the harvest fair. He's dead against it and it kind of spilled over into the rassling match. I been looking the other way as they've been getting together down here."

Joe smiled. "You're a regular St. Valentine."

"Guess you could say that. I've come to love Jewel like a daughter. She and Hawk make a fine twosome. And she's desperate to get out of that cabin. They're talking about leaving and getting hitched down in Cumberland."

Better do it before one of them boys kills the other. "Then I wish them good luck. You think it was Hawk who shot Sky?"

"I don't believe it, wouldn't think either would pull an ambush. They was friends once."

Joe nodded. *More likely he'd want to just give him an ass whooping.* "How about that Elmer fellow."

'That fool's been pestering her for a long time. She'd not give him the time of day."

Chapter 23

Joe took out his notebook as the train rolled down the Alleghenies and back to Connellsville. *Hawk and Jewel. Bringing the family trees back together. If Marshall's right, then who's causing their troubles?* He wrote "Troublemaker, Hawk and Sky." Then his thoughts turned to the missing body. *He's got close friends or family around, wanting to give him a decent burial. Must have knew what he was up to.* He wrote "Accomplices, who took the body."

"Connellsville, next stop Connellsville. Five minutes." The conductor moved slowly down swaying car. "Ten-minute layover."

Joe packed up his papers, buttoned his jacket and, pack in hand, moved to the end of the car. He jumped down as soon as he could, the clock at the station reading four. *I'll get cleaned up and stop by The Star. Maybe Peggy will still be there.* It was a bit after five when he walked in. The door to the office was closed. Hiram was behind the bar.

"Evening Hi. Was Peggy in today?"

"Howdy Joe. She was earlier, left around three. You want a drink?"

"I'll have a beer."

Joe, beer in hand, took a seat at his table. *Probably best to give her a few days to stop being mad at me.* He sat staring at his beer, a jumble of thoughts flashing through his head. His eyes drifted shut. *I'm bushed, all that stomping around in the mountains, and school tomorrow, got to get up early. Gonna be an early night.*

"Wake up Zajac. This is a public house, not your bedroom."

Joe's eyes slowly opened. "I was just resting my eyes Johnny. Glad you came by."

Joe's favorite waitress, Nell, came over to the table. "A round for you boys?"

Joe nodded. "And a bowl of soup if there's any left from lunch."

"Might be two bowls left. Johnny?"

"No thank you Nell. I've got plans for dinner."

Joe finished his beer in one long pull. "Ahh, that's good." He wiped the foam from his lips with the back of his hand. "How're your new duties suiting you?"

Johnny leaned back in his chair, hands laced behind his head. "They suit me just fine. I like the plain clothes deal. Makes getting ready for work a breeze."

Nell returned with their beers and Joe's soup, a big heel of crusty bread on the side. "Here you go boys. Holler if you need anything."

Joe dug into his meal, shoveling it in with a big spoon. When the bowl was mostly empty he tore off chunks of the bread, and used them to mop the sides. Finished, he pushed the bowl aside and took a swig of beer. "That's just what the doctor ordered. You working on Friday?"

"Regular hours, eight to five, hour for lunch."

"I've got some news for you." Joe told him of his new work for Frick and explained the plan for Friday, including his role as streetcar motorman.

"Ten thousand dollars, that's a bundle and hard to pass up. But I thought you were all done working for Frick."

"Yes, that was my intent. I supposed I'd made Mr. Lynch an offer he'd never accept, but he did. And there's this. It looks like those 'Reaper' boys are back. They left a note at the Standard robbery. And with Straub's body never recovered, I'm convinced he's behind this trouble too. I'd like to see justice done." Joe paused for another pull of beer. "And there's more. There's trouble brewing at some of Carnegie's mills, most likely connected." He told Johnny of his meeting with Kilpatrick at Carnegie Steel.

Johnny shook his head slowly. "You'll likely earn that $10,000 if you can stop all of that. But you sure you can operate the streetcar without running off the rails?"

Joe nodded. "I likely can, but I fear we're a man short. I'll not be that much help if I'm driving. I'd be much obliged if you'd ride along."

"Count me in. We should let Sheriff Miller know our plans."

"And Chief Kelly. I'll talk to Miller. The money men will arrive at 11:20. You need to be on the Leisenring car by 11:15. Let's meet at Sam Evans office at the terminal by 11:00."

"And you're not even sure there will be a robbery attempt?"

"Not on this run, but I'm sure there will be one somewhere. And in the long haul Leisenring will be the target. It's a big payday." Joe finished his beer and waved to Nell for another round. "One more thing. Dress like a working man, not so spruced up. Carry a lunch pail, denim trousers. Don't shave that morning. And come well-armed. The robbers will surely be."

Chapter 24

At 8:55am on Thursday, Joe was running up the steps of the Main Building at WUP. *Almost late for class. I'll take a cab next time.* Once inside he kept running, up the broad staircase at the end of the hall, arriving exactly as Miss Hall was closing the classroom door. She looked at her wristwatch as Joe squeezed past her, and into a remaining seat in the first row.

"Please try to schedule your arrival for five minutes before class. That will allow you time to review the assignments written on the board."

Joe pulled out his textbook, notebook and a pencil from his briefcase and noted the assignment. *Read and outline the first three chapters. I'll be at it all weekend.* He leaned back and stretched out his legs. For the next 90 minutes, Joe learned of the early colonies and why those first settlers left Europe. *They wanted to be free to worship as they pleased, willing to risk their lives for it.* He learned of debtors prisons and indentured servants. *Dad and I were not much better off, neither are those mill hunkies. Stop working and starve on the street.*

"Next week we will discuss the Seven Years' War, or the French & Indian War as we knew it in North America. Much of the action took place in western Pennsylvania, the headwaters of the Ohio River much valued for its strategic importance."

With that, Miss Hall closed her folder and the classroom began to empty. Once again Joe dawdled, until only he and she remained. She smiled at Joe as she prepared to leave.

"Mr. Zajac. May I help you?"

Joe gathered up his things and joined her by the door. "Maybe you can. You ever hear of Miss Ellet's School for Girls in Pittsburgh?"

"I have. It's a fine institution for young women, perhaps the best in Allegheny County."

"Where is it?"

"On the west side of town, out toward Wilkinsburg. The Point Breeze area. Why do you ask?"

"I know someone who works there, was going to visit."

"I'm quite familiar with the faculty. My niece attended until last year. Who's your friend?"

Joe looked down for a moment. "Not my friend, the relation of a friend. Margaret Foley. We only met once."

Miss Hall smiled. "The Headmistress herself. I know her well. The school is close to the streetcar line, about a 40-minute ride from here."

"Much obliged Miss Hall."

"My pleasure Mr. Zajac." Then, with another smile, she left Joe standing in the doorway.

She's a different kind of woman. Joe smiled himself and followed her out the door.

For the next hour, Joe sat in a reading room on the top floor of Main, working on his assignment for next week. Stomach growling, he pulled out his pocket watch. *Eleven thirty. Time to grab a bite before Philosophy.* He packed up and went walking down Perryville Road. *I thought there was a joint down here, must have closed up.* He turned down a side street where he saw a few people entering an establishment. A sign hung out from above the door. *Looks like a bunch of grapes. Maybe I can get a bite in there.* On the front door was painted "The Grape."

Joe entered a dark and somewhat smoky room filled with tables, almost all occupied by who he suspected were WUP students and faculty. Almost all of the patrons were men. At least half of them were talking loudly. A small bar stretched across the back wall where a few men stood. Several waitresses wound their way amongst the tables, their trays filled with bowls and bottles. Joe spied a small table for two, tucked in the corner and unoccupied. He made his way to it, took off his coat and sat down. *'Grape talk.' Maybe this is what Burnsworth was talking about.*

"What's your pleasure?" One of the waitresses had found Joe.

"How about a beer. What's on tap?"

The woman laughed. "You want a beer, better go to the joint around the corner. No beer here, no hard liquor either. This is a wine-only operation."

Joe never drank wine, except for a little sip at Communion. The only other wine he's seen was a bottle that Tony kept behind the counter. *What's he call that stuff? Chianti?* "I'll have a glass of Chianti if you please. I need some chow too."

"Special of the day is onion soup." She gave Joe a smile. "You'll like it I wager."

"I'll try it then. Much obliged."

After she left, Joe turned the back of his chair to the wall and observed the room, eyeing each table in turn. The folks at a table in the back was particularly lively, one of them jumping up and gesturing for a waitress. *I was right. There's old Conrad.*

The waitress returned with Joe's glass of wine and a small crock, steam rising from the top. "Be careful, it's hot."

Joe examined the bowl. *Where's the soup?* The top was covered with melted cheese over what looked like chunks of bread. He pushed through the top with his spoon, exposing a dark brown broth loaded with onions. A plume of steam rose. *Smells good. Let's see how it tastes.* He loaded up the spoon with some of the broth and a piece of the cheese covered bread and shoveled it in. *Um um. Tony's minestrone has some competition.* He sat the spoon down and picked up the wine glass, giving it a sniff. *Guess it won't kill me.* He took a sip. *Kind of bitter.* Then another. *Might take a bit of getting used to.* He returned to the soup and finished it off, then drained the wine down. *Feeling warmer already.*

The door opened and a woman walked in alone. One of the waitresses greeted her, surveying the room. Joe saw them eyeing the empty seat at his table, the woman smiling as their eyes met. *It's my history teacher.* She and the waitress exchanged a few words and headed his way.

"Excuse me, but Miss Hall wondered if you'd be willing to let her share your table for lunch. We're all out of seats."

Joe stood up and removed his coat and briefcase from the other chair. "Miss Hall is welcome to join me. Might as well bring another glass of the chianti."

Miss Hall removed her coat and sat down. "Thank you Mr. Zajac. I'm pressed for time this afternoon but hate missing their onion soup special."

"Always willing to help a teacher out. And since we're not in school, just call me Joe."

The waitress returned with another chianti for Joe, a crock of soup for Grace and a small glass of what looked like Joe's wine, but darker red. She took a little sip before starting on the soup. "Just what a body needs on a cold winter's day."

Joe lifted his glass toward her. "May there always be warmth in your house and heart." Grace raised her glass and they toasted. "What's your poison?"

"That is brandy wine. It begins as wine then gets distilled, until it's quite a bit more powerful. One small glass with lunch is my limit." She gave Joe another smile. "For the most part."

Joe smiled back and felt his face redden a bit. *Why am I getting all flummoxed.* "I've never had it, or much of any wine. Mostly it's beer for me."

Joe watched in silence as she ate her soup. *She's a good looking woman, yes.* Grace was finishing up now, tilting the bowl to dig out the last bit.

"My my, nothing better on a cold winter day than Claude's soup." She paused, taking another sip of her brandy. "Did you enjoy yours Joe?"

"Almost ordered another bowl. That's some tasty onion soup." *Her manner and forthrightness, she's no shrinking violet.* "I wish I'd known of this tavern last term."

"Claude runs an interesting establishment." Grace fished a change purse out of her bag and laid a quarter down. "I must hurry back. Thank you again for sharing your table." She rose, gathered up her coat and left, turning to give Joe a final smile as she walked out the door.

Any time Miss Hall.

"Polishing the old apple Mr. Zajac?"

Joe turned to see Conrad Burnsworth standing there. "What's that you say?"

"Never the mind. I saw Grace and wanted to greet her, but alas she has departed."

Sounds like the professor had a few. "Ready for class Professor?"

"Indeed I am, or shall be in a bit." The professor turned and rejoined his companions.

Joe paid his bill, walked back to the campus and took a seat in the rear of the classroom. At barely a minute before 1:00, Professor Burnsworth rushed through the door, coat on his arm and scarf trailing over his shoulders. Tossing them both on a table, he took his place behind the lectern.

"Good afternoon. Shall we begin? How many of you have obtained a copy of Taylor's 'Dissertations'?" Most of the students raised their hands. "For the rest of you, I hear the bookstore is temporarily out of stock. Now, here is your first and only assignment for these first few weeks. Read the book, the sooner the better. We will be discussing all of it." The professor paused for a moment, pulled a few rolled up sheets of paper from his jacket pocket and spread them out on the lectern. "Before we speak of Aristotle proper, let's first speak of the general study of knowledge itself, or to pose the classic question 'How do we know what we know?'."

For the remainder of the class, Burnsworth spoke of the two opposing views in Greek philosophy in 350 BC: Plato's world of universal truths and Aristotle's opinion that all knowledge is gained through experience. As he spoke, Joe took copious notes.

The professor pulled out his pocket watch. "We've come to the end. Read the book. Next week we will discuss what it means to live a good life."

Joe closed his notebook. *I'm with Aristotle. You know what you see, touch, hear. You learn from the experience.* He gathered up his coat and briefcase and was soon on his way back to Connellsville.

Chapter 25

✳   ✳   ✳

It was just after four when Joe got back to town and his first stop was The Star. Peggy was still in the office, a ledger open in front of her. Joe stopped at the open door.

"Hello Peggy, glad to see you're still here. Got the ledger all figured out?"

She looked up, nodded and gestured to the chair. "I've just finished up." She closed the book and put it away. "How is school?"

"I've plenty of work to do already, readings and such." Joe sat down, fidgeting with his hat. "You still cross with me from Sunday?"

"No Joe, not cross anymore. But still upset." She paused for a moment, took some pins out of her hair and shook it loose. "I still believe we don't really know enough about each other though. And I have some other news."

Oh Lord. If that ain't news enough. Joe sat silently. *Let her say her peace.*

"I've decided to start a chapter of the Suffrage Association here in Fayette County."

"Fayette County? Who's going to join? The women in the coal patches, can't even speak English."

Peggy's eyes narrowed. "You might be surprised to learn that many local business and professional women support the cause. You needn't belittle the effort."

Jesus. Why'd I open my mouth? Let's change the subject. "How's Pap?"

"About the same."

"He's another tough old bird."

Peggy let a little smile turn her mouth. "I hope the other you are referring to isn't Aunt Margaret. I received a letter from her yesterday. She offered me a job, teaching bookkeeping in the High School."

I'd been better off not stopping by. "That's a long ride every day."

"I'd likely have to move to Pittsburgh. At any rate I declined her offer. I can't leave father."

Joe sat silently for a moment. *No sense trying to talk about it. I think she's spoiling for a fight.* "You free for dinner tomorrow night?"

"I am. Where did you have in mind?"

"The Dinner Bell."

"Come by at six then." She started to gather up her things. "Oh, and Henry Brooks was by earlier. He had some news but said it could wait until Saturday. He said you two almost got blown up last week."

Joe smiled. "I never expected that would happen when I offered to help Henry. But now that I'm involved I aim to see it through. I've got some tales to tell tomorrow."

"OK Joe. Please be careful." She grabbed her coat and hat from a hook on the door and left the office.

Our first night out was at the Dinner Bell. Maybe we can move on. Joe switched to the desk chair and picked up the telephone. "Operator, I'd like a Scottdale line." In a few moments he was connected to Mike McMullen at Frick.

"Hello Joe. Glad you called. Where do we stand for tomorrow?"

"I'm trained in the basic motorman skills, should be all right in that regard. I was thinking I'd not be much help in a fight if I have to operate the streetcar so I lined us up some support from the Connellsville Police." Joe told him a bit about Johnny Davidson.

"I've got my men set here. One fellow will be wearing a suit, the other a milkman's uniform. Both will be arriving on the 10:40 car from Scottdale."

"I'll be looking out for them, and tell your men about Johnny. He'll be in work clothes and carrying a lunch bucket."

"Give me a call after it's over, one way or the other."

"Will do."

Joe hung up and leaned back in the chair. *Hope I've guessed right. We'll soon know.*

Chapter 26

✳   ✳   ✳

Joe started his Friday, as usual, at City Lunch. By 8:30 he was at the last stool of the lunch counter, a plate full of ham, scrambled eggs and potatoes in front of him. The place was busy, with Tony waiting tables and his son Nicky doing the cooking. As Joe finished up his breakfast, Tony took a break and sat down beside him.

"We busy today. I wish every day was Friday, my best day."

Joe swiveled his stool around, facing Tony. "You ever think of staying open for dinner Tony?"

"This no dinner spot Joey. Look around. My place, she look shabby."

Joe looked around. The walls were grimy, the floorboards worn at the door. The counter needed to be refinished and some of the stool tops had holes in them. The whole place could use a paint job. *He's right.*

"I dream about running a fancy Italian restaurant, not some quick lunch and breakfast joint. You know my spaghetti sauce the best in town. I'd call it 'Tony's Place'. I bet I make a good living from it, not squeak by like now."

And Nicky could stay in school. "Your sauce is the best. In fact, I've never had a bad meal here, and I've had many." *Money's only worth what you do with it.* "I've signed on for some more work for Frick, a special job. And they're paying me well for it. I've been considering what I might invest some of that money in. How much you think it would take to open up 'Tony's Place'?"

Tony looked at Joe, mouth dropped open. "You crazy Joey. Why you want to spend your money on me?"

"I'm just looking for a good investment. How much?"

Tony stroked his chin, taking a moment to consider costs. "I say maybe $1,000. Depends on the location. There's a building in New Haven on Third Street, might work. It gotta be a first class joint and that costs money." A smile crossed Tony's face as he considered the possibilities.

Joe nodded. "That sounds about right I wager. I'm in." He finished his coffee and dropped a quarter on the counter. "I got a busy day ahead but next week, let's go look at the spot. How about Monday afternoon?"

"You no waste time my friend. Your offer, it's a miracle. You answer my prayers. But you better think hard till then. We friends. I like it to stay that way. You take a risk with your money."

"I'd be hard pressed to find a better use for it. No sense letting it sit around the bank." Joe gathered up his coat and hat. "See you tomorrow."

Joe walked down the street to the West Penn Terminal. He went upstairs to find Sam Evans sitting at his desk, a stack of papers in front of him. "Morning Sam."

Sam looked up, frowning. "Zajac. Have a seat. I've become uneasy about your scheme. You sure this is a good notion?"

Joe sat down across from him. "Can't say that, but it's the only one I could think of. What's your concern?"

"Quite honestly, it starts with your ability to safely operate the streetcar. That small bit of practice was likely insufficient."

"Maybe if I was going to be running all over, but I know that Leisenring run, been down that track a hundred times. And for most of the rides I was up front, watching the motorman."

"But what if you damage the car, or worse yet, some hapless pedestrian? West Penn is on the hook for it."

"If that's all you're worried about, give a call over to Scottdale. Ask for Mike McMullen. Frick will cover any loss."

That seemed to satisfy Evans. "Fair enough. Now how shall we keep people from boarding your car?"

"I thought of that. Once Frick's paymasters and my three men are aboard we just put an 'Out of Service' sign on it, say it's headed to the shop."

Evans nodded. "That happens on occasion. I'll see to it. We don't want anyone else on the car." He looked down at his papers. "I've got work to do. I'll see you at eleven."

"Much obliged Sam, and there's a good chance all of this might come to naught." Joe left him to his work. A few minutes later he was at City Hall, looking for Johnny Davidson. He found him sitting at a table in the chief's office. Joe rapped on the door frame.

"Morning Joe. Chief Kelly and I were discussing today's plans. He's got a couple of questions for you."

Joe joined Kelly and Johnny at the table. "Thanks Chief for allowing Johnny to come along for the ride."

"I got a problem Zajac. Johnny's police power ends at the New Haven line. You'll be in Dunbar Township after that, and that's the county sheriff's jurisdiction."

"Johnny helped out at Leisenring last year."

"And I knew nothing of it beforehand. I'd have likely stopped it if I had."

Joe sat for a moment, staring out the rear window at the river. *I need Johnny to make sure the odds stay in our favor.* "How about I get Sheriff Miller to deputize him?"

"In that case I'd have no objection."

"Let's see if he's answering his telephone."

Ten minutes later, Johnny was an official temporary deputy of the Fayette County Sheriff. The three talked over the plan, which Joe had to admit was not very clear-cut. "If they hit us like they did the others, the track will be blocked up ahead. Once they show their hand, we stop and attempt an arrest."

"I doubt those boys will come along willingly. Don't get yourselves shot up."

"We'll let the Frick police decide how far to take it." Joe got up from the table. "I've got one other stop to make. Johnny, I'll see you at the terminal, 11 o'clock."

Joe left City Hall and headed up Main Street, his destination the First National Bank. He entered to find Dave Norton sitting at his desk. He saw Joe walk in and waved him over.

"Good morning Joe. What can I do for one of our best customers?"

Joe sat down in the chair in front of the desk. "I've got plans for some of my money. I'd like you to open up a new account, joint between me and Tony. Put a thousand dollars in it."

Dave pulled a paper out of his desk drawer, and dipped his pen in the inkwell. "One thousand it is. Is this to be a personal or a business account?"

"Business. Tony and I are going to open an Italian restaurant over in New Haven, a fancy dinner joint."

Dave smiled and put down the pen. "I did suggest looking for business opportunities. Restaurants can be a risky investment though."

"Well, I've learned to keep books, thanks to Peggy. I'll be keeping an eye on my money. And you know Tony's spaghetti is the best around. He's made a living out of City Lunch for six years. I bet 'Tony's Place' will prove a popular spot."

"I suspect you're right Joe. Have Tony stop by to see me. He needs to sign these papers too."

Twenty minutes later, Joe left the bank. After a quick stop back at City Lunch to speak with Tony, he hurried down to the terminal. It was almost 11:00. He found Johnny, dressed in denim pants and wearing a red flannel coat, already at Sam's office.

"Ready to go Joe?"

"As soon as I get into uniform." His hat and jacket were hanging on Sam's coat tree. He took of his overcoat and put them on. "How do I look?"

Johnny laughed. "You'll pass I'd say. The jacket is a bit big."

Joe opened his briefcase and pulled out a pistol. "Should help hide this." He tucked the gun into the waistband of his trousers and buttoned the jacket. "Can't even see it. And once we're underway I'll unbutton the jacket."

Johnny picked up his lunch bucket and opened it. Inside sat an .45. "I'm ready. Let's go."

The three went downstairs to the portico at the rear of the building, two sets of tracks running underneath. Their car sat on the outer track, an "Out of Service" sign in the driver's window. Sam said a few words to several folks already standing there, then joined Joe and Johnny at the car steps.

"I told them the brakes were acting up on this one." The two climbed aboard, Joe behind the controls and Johnny taking a seat in the rear, where he slouched down with his cap pulled low. "I'll watch from the door until you get away."

A minute later the car from Scottdale pulled into the terminal. About a dozen people got out. Four of them quickly boarded Joe's car while several of the others pointed to the sign in the window. Joe eased the controller forward and the trolley started rolling, slowly rounding a curve out of the terminal and onto the Yough bridge. Joe pulled the sign from the window and pushed the controller forward as the car climbed a small grade. *So far so good.*

Behind him sat his five passengers, the two Frick paymasters together in a seat in the middle, the older man in the suit up front by Joe and the "milk man" in the rear near Johnny. The car crested the little rise and rolled down into New Haven, picking up speed. Joe's left hand rested on the brake wheel.

The car approached 7th Street, where some riders stood at the stop. Joe rolled past, turning to see several of them waving. Looking forward, he saw that a delivery wagon was blocking the tracks in front of his church at 8th Street. He moved the controller to neutral and applied the brake, bringing the car to a stop. He looked to the rear again. Two men were running up the street toward the car. *Uh oh.* As the wagon cleared the tracks the two men reached the car and jumped aboard.

The first man was a big blond haired fellow. He dropped a token in the fare box. "Say, why didn't you stop?"

Joe looked straight ahead. "Didn't see you."

The man shook his head and moved to the rear of the car, sitting across from the milkman.

The second rider, an older fellow with a big mustache, dropped his token without comment and took the seat behind the Frick men. Joe eased the controller forward and the car moved on, soon climbing a hill out of New Haven, a few miles from Leisenring. Joe took a quick glance over his shoulder.

This looks a might suspicious. The robbers might be taking the streetcar too. The car crested the hill and, on level ground, picked up speed. Joe eased back on the controller and resisted the impulse to take a longer look at his new passengers. *If so, no sense tipping them off.* His left hand searched for the revolver grip.

The trolley line ran straight for a bit, past the Trotter coal mine, then curved toward Leisenring. Joe held the speed steady, eyes focused on the track ahead. The man in the rear moved forward, standing next to Joe. He pulled his jacket back, showing a holstered pistol. Leaning toward Joe, he spoke in a low voice. "After we round the curve be ready to stop."

Joe looked up at him and smiled, responding in a loud voice. "Sure buddy. It's not my regular stop but I'll let you off."

The car turned the corner, where a wagon, two men aboard, blocked the tracks a hundred yards on. Joe, hand on the brake wheel, stole a quick glance over his shoulder. Johnny had opened his lunch pail, his hand inside. The milk man had his coat open, hand at his waist. The man in the suit up front was watching Joe, just a few feet behind.

The second passenger suddenly rose up, pulling a gun from beneath his jacket. He stuck the barrel in the ear of one of the Frick men. "Hand over the pay."

Fifty yards remained between Joe and the wagon. Joe could see that both men there had rifles at the ready. *No sense stopping.* He pushed the controller forward. *Full speed ahead.*

The man in front pulled his gun and turned toward the back. "You heard him. Both of you. Take off those money belts." Turning back to Joe. "I told you to stop. Hit the brakes."

At that moment both Johnny and the milk man pulled their guns. Johnny announced in a loud voice. "Put down your guns. You are under arrest."

The man in front turned and fired, hitting Johnny. The milk man shot twice, dropping him, then turned his gun toward the second passenger. "Drop your weapon."

He grabbed one of the Frick men by the collar and pulled him up. "He'll die first."

Joe looked forward. *Can't stop now if I wanted to.* The car was 10 yards from the wagon. Its occupants leapt from the seat, rolling to the side of the track. With a bang, the trolley crashed into the wagon, jumping the tracks after the collision. With a lurch, it tilted sideways, then fell, coming to rest at an angle against an embankment. All of the riders took a tumble, Joe rising first and climbing from the trolley, gun drawn. He gave the wagon riders chase, both running toward horses tied to a tree just down the line. Before he could catch up they had mounted and were riding toward Leisenring at a fast clip.

Joe returned to the wrecked streetcar. The two Frick men had climbed from the car uninjured. The man in the suit was attending to the wounded robber, whose coat was wet with blood. The milk man had the other robber subdued. Johnny lay across the seat in the back, a red stain building from a wound to his left shoulder. "Hang on buddy. I'll go get some help."

Chapter 27

*　　*　　*

As it turned out, help came to them. Another streetcar was already approaching from the other direction. Joe ran down the line, waving his arms, stopping them just before the wagon wreckage. The motorman jumped out, shaking his fist.

"What in tarnation is going on here?" Looking more closely at Joe's uniform, he frowned. "And who the hell are you? You're no motorman I ever seen."

"Sam Evans can explain it all. I've got two shot men on that car, need to get them to town. Let's get the track clear. Think you can get by the wreck?"

The motorman nodded and returned to his car. "Need a few men out here!"

With the help of his passengers, they soon had the track cleared of wagon pieces. Together, they pulled the others from the wreckage. Johnny was conscious, but in pain. The shot robber was laying on the ground, still bleeding profusely. *Don't think he's going to make it.* Joe kneeled by his side and took his hand. "Just hold on. We'll get you to a doctor."

The man gave him a cold look and coughed. "No doctor gonna patch these holes. I'm a goner."

"Who's your boss?"

He coughed again, grimacing. "Go to hell you Frick bastard." His eyes closed as a final breath whistled from his lips.

Joe helped move Johnny to the other trolley. He was able to sit up on his own. "Looks like the bullet went clean through you. The bleeding has slowed considerable."

Johnny gave him a weak smile. "I'll make it Joe. You go ahead and take care of your business."

"I'm coming back to town with you. One of those Frick boys can stay with the body. That fellow's not likely going anywhere."

The paymasters and the Frick policeman in the suit were already walking toward Leisenring, just down the tracks. The milk man stayed with the body. Joe took custody of the second robber and, after easing past the wreckage, they returned to town, pulling into the terminal at half past noon. With his prisoner leading the way, Joe helped Johnny down and onto a bench in the waiting room. They were soon joined by Sam Evans and the other motorman.

"My worst fears have been realized. A man dead, streetcar off the tracks. This mess will be costing Frick a pretty penny."

"We'll settle up Sam, but first things first. My buddy Johnny needs a doctor."

"I'll send for Doc Colvin."

"Can you stay with him? This fellow needs to go to jail."

Johnny rose shakily from the bench. "I'll just take the next car to the South Side Hospital."

Sam grabbed his arm to steady him. "No you won't. Come with me. There's a cot you can lie down on until the doc gets here." He led Johnny down a short hall and into a room.

Joe marched his prisoner upstairs, retrieved his overcoat and left the motorman's gear on the cloths tree. *I'd like to have that hat.* Then, with his gun to the prisoner's back, they marched to City Hall. The chief was still in his office.

"I've got a prisoner here, need to hold until the sheriff can come get him."

Kelly grabbed a ring of keys from a hook on the wall. "Let's go. Where's Johnny?"

"Got shot." Joe told the tale of their morning shootout. "The robbers 'prit near got the jump on us. Lucky the Frick policeman's aim was true." Together they marched the man to the basement jail cells. "Let's see what he's carrying before we lock him up."

Joe went through the man's pockets. They were empty save for a few coins and a West Penn Transfer. *Dickerson Run line.* "What's your name buddy?"

The man just looked up, droopy eyed. A long mustache mostly hid his mouth, extending past his chin. He was shorter than Joe, and skinny, a narrow belt cinched tightly around a thin waist. "Nein sprecht Englisch."

Joe nodded to the chief. "Lock up our German friend here. I hope he's ready for a long stay in the county jail. I'm guessing that more than one eyewitness can tie him to those other robberies." He turned to the prisoner. "Did you hear that the fellow your crew pistol whipped at Standard died? You might end up in that new electric chair."

The man's face whitened. He shuffled slowly into the cell, the door clanging shut behind him.

He understands English I'd say, likely speaks it too. "Let the chief know if you want to cooperate." The man sat on the edge of the cot, head in his hands. Joe and Kelly returned to his office.

"I'll give the sheriff a call, let him know what happened. Our robber will likely be here until Monday."

"Good. Maybe he'll remember he speaks English. In the meantime, I'm going to catch up with Johnny."

Joe left City Hall and returned to the West Penn terminal. Sam Evans was still in his office.

"Where's Johnny?"

"Doc Colvin decided he needed some hospital attention, admitted him to South Side."

Joe sat down at the desk. "Sorry I wrecked your streetcar. Those fellows surprised us, jumped aboard at 8th Street."

"No sense fretting about it now. I already have a crew out there. It's not the first streetcar that jumped the rails."

Joe looked at the motorman's hat, still hanging on the rack. "Mind if I have that hat as a souvenir?"

Sam smiled. "I'll add it to Frick's bill."

"Much obliged. Send it over to McMullen."

Joe grabbed the hat and, after a trip to the hospital to check on Johnny, headed to The Star. Peggy was still in the office. He went in and flopped onto a chair.

"Glad you're still here."

"What's the matter Joe? You look worn out."

"Could say that. Had an exciting day so far." He told the tale of the attempted robbery.

"How's Johnny?

"They will likely let him leave today. His father was there. He's plenty sore and in need of some recovery."

Peggy shook her head slowly from side to side. "Five months ago you said you were through working for Frick. Now here you are risking your life for them, and getting your best friend shot to boot."

Joe nodded. "I've come to the same conclusion. I should have told Lynch 'no' right from the start. Then he asked me to name my price. I took the lure of the easy money." He paused, and leaned forward, elbows on knees. "You know what that robber said to me right before he died? 'Go to hell you Frick bastard'."

"He's hated for good reasons. You know why."

Joe nodded. "And here's another aspect to consider. There's plenty of evidence to show that Kurt Straub might still be alive, or at least his 'Reapers' gang is still operating."

"What's that to you Joe?"

"He's an escaped murderer is all."

"And you feel duty-bound to track him down?"

"I do."

Polly shook her head again. "You are a hard-headed man."

Joe gave her a little smile. "I admit to it. I've decided I'll keep working on the case. I'll earn that $10,000, and I'll put it to good use."

"All right Joe. You do as you see fit." She got up and prepared to leave. "I need to go home and get ready. See you at six."

Joe rose as she left and took her seat. *Better check in with McMullen.* He placed the call and they were soon connected.

"Hello. McMullen here."

"Hello Mike, Joe Zajac."

"Zajac. I've just finished talking to my two men. Good work today."

"Except for my friend getting shot. Frick needs to cover his bills."

"I agree. Send them over. And here's some news for you. Those two that were on the wagon, they tore past Leisenring hell bent for election and left town on the road to Vanderbilt."

Vanderbilt. That's right next to Dickerson Run. "We've got the other robber in the city jail, found a Dickerson Run transfer in his pocket. The 'Reapers' gang is likely holed up somewhere in that neck of the woods."

"You think they'll hit us again next week?"

"If they do, I'm hard pressed to say where. I'd keep mixing up the delivery times and ways. In the meantime, I'm going to work on our prisoner."

"Anything we can do, let us know."

"Just pay West Penn for the damages. And one more thing. You tell Kilpatrick that his 'Barat' fellows are likely hooked up with these 'Reapers' too. And from the sounds of it, they're looking for revenge, not justice."

Chapter 28

*　　*　　*

It was after 8:00am on Saturday morning when Joe walked through the front door of City Lunch. Only a few tables were occupied, Tony on his way to one with a tray of food. He smiled and nodded to Joe. "Be right with you my friend."

Joe sat at the counter, but wasn't smiling. Last night's dinner with Peggy had not turned out as he'd hoped. *She is one stubborn and hard-headed woman.* The issues between them still unresolved, both were on guard, their conversation oddly formal and unimportant. *But then again, I'm no better.* The evening ended early, Joe not even invited in at the end. *Don't know what else to do about it at this point.*

Tony showed up behind the counter with a cup of coffee, still smiling. "My mind, she still spinning from yesterday. You no change your mind?"

Joe's frown disappeared. *Money well spent already.* "No Tony, in fact I'm convinced it will be the best investment I'll ever make." Another thought popped into his head. "Where's Nicky today?"

Now Tony's frown returned. "He's out looking for work."

"I got more good news for you. Our helper at The Star up and quit on us last week. Old Hiram and I've been handling the chores but with me back in school and working again to boot I need to find a replacement. The pay is five dollars a week but that's for some work every day."

"What he got to do?"

"Clean up the joint for starters, before we open every day. Then some chores again later in the day, some help around the kitchen and such. You think he'd be interested?"

Tony's eyes glistened. "He be crazy not to."

"Send him over Monday morning. I'll meet him at seven. But there's one condition."

"What that?"

"He only gets the job if he stays in school."

Tony leaned forward, hands on the counter, his shoulders slumping. When he looked up there were tears in his eyes. He took out a handkerchief, blew his nose and wiped his eyes. Then he stood up straight, hand out to Joe. "A man have no better friend than you. He no agree I boot his rear-end up to his shoulders."

Joe shook his hand and smiled. "He's going to earn that money. You should see that place at closing time. Now how about you scramble me up some eggs, and throw in some chopped ham."

"You got it boss!" Tony hurried back to the kitchen, whistling as he walked.

The little bell above the door tinkled. Joe looking up to see Johnny walk in, coat draped over his shoulders and left arm in a sling. He saw Joe and joined him at the counter, a slight grin on his face. "Morning buddy."

Joe could feel his own eyes moisten. *Almost got my best friend killed yesterday.* "You are a sight for sore eyes. Glad to see you up and about. How's the shoulder?"

"Still a might sore, but tolerable. I see Doc Colvin on Monday, can likely stop wearing the sling after that. Remind me not to take any more streetcar rides with you at the controls."

"I should have known better than to ask you to help. From now on Frick can put his own men on the line. And if I ever forget and do ask, promise to tell me to take a hike."

Johnny smiled. "I'll do that and I'd not want to see you get killed either buddy. I'd say you need to be more wary yourself. In hindsight, your scheme was hastily planned. These men are cold-blooded so be careful."

As Tony delivered Joe's breakfast, he nodded his assent.

"Here you go Joey, scrambled just the way you like." Then he looked at Johnny. "What happened to you?"

Johnny pointed to Joe. "Ask your buddy."

Joe took a few moments to tell the tale, Tony shaking his head at the end. "You almost get killed the last time you work for Frick. Give back his money before you do."

Joe shook his head. "I'm going to put that money to good use."

Tony smiled as he turned to Johnny. "He tell you the news? We partners in a new restaurant we gonna open in New Haven. And I decide on the name. We gonna call it 'Joey Z's'."

Chapter 29

*　　　*　　　*

Joe left City Lunch shaking his head. *Joey Z's. I thought he said Tony's Place.* Briefcase in hand, he headed to the Pennsylvania Railroad station, Brownsville his destination. *I'll see if I can track down that tattoo parlor.* Brownsville was another of Fayette County's small towns, located on the Monongahela River. The streetcar line didn't serve the town and, as there were only a few Frick mines in the vicinity, Joe had never been there before.

While some mines and other industries were established nearby, its location made it a busy port. Thanks to a series of locks, "The Mon" as it was called, was navigable from its end at the Ohio River headwaters in Pittsburgh 105 miles south to Morgantown, West Virginia.

Joe hopped aboard a Uniontown bound train shortly after 9:00, having to transfer to the Brownsville extension there. It was almost 11:00 by the time he arrived. *Looks like a nice little town.* He walked down Market Street, spying a policeman on the corner.

"How do."

The policeman nodded.

"I heard tell there's a tattoo parlor in town. Know its whereabouts?"

"Not in Brownsville. There's one across Dunlap Creek in Bridgeport as I recollect. Keep on walking, the street turns to the left, then over the creek. The joint you're looking for is on Water Street down by the river."

"Much obliged." The wind rose, Joe turning up his collar. He was soon at the Dunlap Creek bridge. A plaque on the end read "1839 – America's First Cast Iron Bridge." A block later, he turned onto Bridge Street, named for the covered bridge at the end that carried the National Pike over the river. A minute later, he turned onto Water Street. *Same as Connellsville. Guess all these river towns have one.* The Mon was deeper and wider than the Yough, which was a tributary. Mostly ice-free here, Joe stopped to watch as several steamboats passed by. A stern-wheeler pushed a half dozen barges of coal toward Pittsburgh, passing a side-wheeler freight hauler heading toward Morgantown. Both had twin smokestacks, black coal smoke billowing out.

Joe walked past a factory of some sort that filled the first block. For several blocks thereafter, commercial establishments lined the street, bars, hotels and small shops. Almost to the end, he finally passed a small one-story building, set back from the street a bit. A small sign read "Tattoos," barely visible through the grimy front window. *Looks like I found it.*

Joe walked to the front door and found it locked. He twisted the doorbell and waited. Eventually he heard the lock turn, the door opened a few inches. One eye peaked through. "We're closed. Come back after one."

"I'm not looking for a tattoo, just some information." Joe pulled a dollar bill from his pocket and held it up. The one eye widened, and the door opened.

The proprietor was a man of advanced years, tall and gaunt, dressed in denim trousers, the red flannel top of his long underwear visible above them. Mostly bald, a long uncombed fringe of white hair gave him a wild look. He held out his hand and Joe gave him the dollar bill, yellow teeth now visible through a smile. "Come on in then. I'm 'bout to eat."

Joe followed him as they passed through a small front store room. A curtained doorway led into the rear. One big room filled the rest of the building, a potbellied stove to one side, a workbench filled with his tools of the trade to the other. A small table with two chairs sat in the middle, a cot sat against the rear wall. "Much obliged."

"Well state your business then. My stomach's growling." He pointed to a pot sitting on the stove.

Smells like he's coking stew. "Name's Joe Zajac." He held out his hand.

The old man took his hand in a firm grip. "Zachariah Enos, but just call me 'Cap.' Let's grab a seat."

Joe followed him to the table and both men sat down. He opened his briefcase and pulled out the picture of the tattoo. "Recognize this work?"

Cap pulled the picture close. After a quick look, his head nodded. "Damned if I don't. That's my work alright."

Joe showed him the other shot of the man's face. "And this fellow?"

"Yes, I recognize this snake too." Another smile appeared. "He looks a might worse for the wear and tear."

Now it was Joe's turn to smile. "Might say that Cap. He's deader than a doornail. What can you tell me about him?"

"First off, who am I dealing with?"

"The man tried to kill me and a friend, got himself killed in the process. I've reason to believe he, and likely an accomplice, murdered another fellow up Ohiopyle way."

"This one, I think his name was Delbert, was one of three boys came in here one night, early last month, just about closing time. I suspect they was brothers, all got the same tattoo in the same place."

"Did you catch their names?"

"We weren't formally introduced. I do know they was all liquored up, and just off a steamboat from Morgantown. I'm certain their surname was Black though."

"How so?"

"I asked them why they wanted the black widow spider tattoos. One of the other ones, a big lug, puffed up his chest and said 'we're the Black boys and we've made plenty of widows.' Then they all started laughing and howling so loud I thought they'd shit their pants."

Joe chuckled, then frowned. *Drunk and boastful, to my good fortune. Sounds like a dangerous crew.* "Catch any other first names?"

Cap nodded. "The big lug was Merle. The third one, a little feller, they just called 'Squirrely.' And he was the nervous type, giggling and jumpin' around."

Joe got out his pencil and notebook, writing down the names. "Can you describe those boys for me?"

Cap closed his eyes in thought for a moment, finally nodding his head. "The little one was a carrot-top, a full head of red hair all slicked back. The big fellow was bald, hair cut short. He had a tattoo on his left arm, a heart with a knife stabbed in it, 'Mother' written across. There was a few drops of red blood 'neath the wound. I'd say they's from the mountains somewhere too, had a hillbilly twang."

Joe put his notebook away and rose from his seat. "Thank you for your time Cap."

"One last thing. At the end, I asked for my pay, a buck apiece. Squirrely started laughing, pulled out a pistol. Didn't pay and stole one of my old tattoo machines to boot. You catch up with them boys they owe me a tenner. I'd be much obliged if you at least took it out of their hide."

Chapter 30

Joe left the tattoo parlor and returned toward the train station the way he came. As he approached the station, he spotted a lunch counter. *Time to grab a bite to eat.* He entered and took the only open seat at the counter. *The place is popular. That's a good sign.* A waitress came through the kitchen door, carrying a big bowl of beef stew and a plate of bread, delivering it to the fellow on Joe's left. *That looks good to me.* Then she turned to Joe.

"What's your pleasure?"

Joe pointed to the stew. "I'll have what he's having."

The waitress gave Joe a wink and a smile. "That'll be fifteen cents, strangers pay in advance."

Joe pulled a quarter out of his pocket and laid it on the counter. "And a cup of coffee, keep the change."

"Much obliged."

Joe spent the next few minutes thinking about what he'd learned from Cap. *I got lucky today. Now we know who we're looking for. Wonder if Sheriff Miller knows anything about the Black brothers. I'll stop by his office on the way back to town.*

The waitress returned with Joe's food and coffee. "Holler if you need me."

Joe bent over and smelled the steam rising from the bowl of stew, big chunks of meat, potatoes, carrots and onions in a thick brown broth. *Just what a man needs on a cold day.* He shoveled it up in a few minutes, finished by wiping the bowl clean with the last chunk of bread. *Tony needs to add this to the menu.*

The waitress came by again. "Lordy lordy, you polished that off fast."

Joe finished his coffee and smiled. "I was hungrier than I thought, and that was a fine bowl of stew." He picked up his briefcase, tipped his hat to the waitress and headed to the train station. By 1:30 he was on his way back to Uniontown.

After first stopping by Sheriff Miller's office and, not finding him, Joe went around the corner to the little bar he knew the sheriff patronized. Sure enough, Joe found him at a table, an empty shot glass and half a beer in front of him. Miller looked up and waved him over. Joe joined him at the table.

"Zajac, you're like a bad penny, turning up everywhere." The sheriff finished his beer. "You ready?"

One just to be sociable. Joe nodded. "Beer only Sheriff."

"Your turn to buy." He waved to the proprietor who came to the table. "What's your pleasure?"

"Another round for me and a beer for him." In a moment he returned with the drinks. Then Miller turned to Joe. "What brings you to town?"

"I'm on my way back from Brownsville, tracked down the tattoo parlor. I've some good information there, wanted to share it with you." He pulled out his notebook. "Had any dealings with some men last name of Black?"

The sheriff thought for a moment. "Can't say I recall any."

"The dead man's name was Delbert Black, according to the tattoo fellow. He recognized the tattoo and the face." Joe took a few minutes to relate the story, including the description.

"Black Widow boys indeed. And bragging about killing."

"Might have just been the liquor talking but I'm inclined to believe 'em."

The sheriff fired his shot, then lifted his beer toward Joe. "Cheers." They clinked glasses and both chugged half of them.

"And to your health Sheriff."

The sheriff leaned back in his chair, hands clasped across his stomach. After another moment of silence, he leaned forward and snapped his fingers.

"Got it. That 'Squirrely' fellow rings a bell now that I think about it, red hair and all. We had to lock up a drunk, oh about a month back. He was a wild one too, like you said, laughing and jumping around like a crazy man. Took a few of us to subdue him, had to introduce him to my own Mr. Black." The sheriff laughed and fingered the nightstick on his belt. "He carried no identification, said his name was Mr. Jones or some such bullshit."

Now it was Joe's turn to think. He got out his notebook and thumbed through the front. "Henry Brooks mentioned that you had Half-moon Harkins locked up for a bit for thievery, let him out early last month."

Miller nodded. "That was his last stay. And now that you mention it I'd say it was close to when Mr. Jones was visiting. I'll check the records next week but I'm thinking they were cellmates that one night."

Now we're getting somewhere. Joe made more notes and put his book away. "And when did those robberies get started?"

The sheriff nodded. "I see where you're going with this, and you're dead right. It was shortly thereafter."

Joe looked at his watch. *Going on 3:00. Better get moving.* He chugged the rest of his beer and got up. "Let me know what you find out about those two being cellmates."

"Don't do anything reckless if you track the Black boys down. Let me know when you find them and I'll do the arresting. And I'll have my township deputies keep a lookout for them. The little red head should be easy to spot long as he's hatless."

That's good advice. "Will do Tom. They might want to start looking in the drinking establishments." Joe tossed a quarter on the table and hurried out the door.

Chapter 31

✳   ✳   ✳

It was just before 7:00 when Joe arrived at the Water Street Hotel. Located across the street from the B&O Railroad station, the hotel was owned and operated by Mary and Mahlon Gilmore, Johnny's aunt and uncle. The attached Dinner Bell restaurant was where he'd dined last night with Peggy. He found Henry Brooks sitting in a lobby chair reading the Courier.

"Evening Henry. What's new?"

Henry put the paper down and got up. "Same old stories of dead miners and hurt railroaders. And they struck oil down in Texas, a real gusher." Together they walked to the attached restaurant, Mary smiling as she saw them enter.

"Well if it isn't two of my best customers. How about a table over by the fireplace?"

Joe nodded and they followed her to the table. "Just what the doctor ordered on a cold night. Still serving the stuffed pork chops special?"

"I think we've got a few orders left. What can I get you to drink?"

Too cold for beer tonight. What was that my teacher had? "You have any of that brandy wine back there?"

"I think we do. Don't get much call for it but Mahlon's been known to take a sip for medicinal purposes on occasion. And you Henry?"

"I'll have the chops too, and a shot of Canadian Club, water chaser."

Mary nodded and left to get their drinks, returning in a minute. "Here you go boys. Your pork chops will be out shortly."

Joe took a little sip of his brandy, which was served in a fat round goblet. *Not bad. Might could take a liking to this.* He took another, bigger sip. *That'll warm a man up.*

Henry watched Joe, a smile on his face. "I thought you were a shot and a beer man. When did you start on wine?"

"Had lunch at a joint close to school. All they served was wine. I saw someone drinking this, thought I'd give it a try."

Henry drank his shot, took a sip of water and sat back in his chair. "You ready to get down to business?"

Joe nodded. "You track down what happened to your tree?"

"Better than that. I found it. Me and a couple of my boys went back out there yesterday, better equipped with snowshoes. We walked down the river bank for about a quarter mile, no sign of it. A bit further on there's a good size island in the middle. We decided to investigate and there she was, dropped on the ice on the far side."

"All in one piece?"

Henry nodded. "I reckon they dragged it down there with a team. And that's not all. We poked around on the island and what do you think we found?"

"Got me buddy."

"Some of my missing saws and the like. Some signs of a campfire and a few empty jugs."

Mary showed up with their food. Two plates with big thick pork chops slit in the middle, stuffing falling out the side. "Be right back." She returned with two bowls and a plate on a tray, mashed potatoes, green beans and a plate full of fresh bread. "Served family style on Saturday. Holler if you need more."

Been a while since I had that stew. I'm 'bout starved. Joe and Henry ate with gusto. *Telling the tale can keep.* It wasn't too long until the chops and most of the rest were gone.

Joe wiped his lips with his napkin and pushed back. "I think I'll stop there. Don't want to overeat. So what do you think they planned on doing with that big old log?"

"Joe, to be honest, I don't think those thieves are too bright. Even if they used the saws to cut the log into smaller sections I don't know what they planned. You'd still need a team to move them and a lumber mill to turn them into boards. The closest mill is Ohiopyle."

"Those crooks might not be too smart but they are vicious. I've a tale to tell too." Joe told Henry about the trip to Brownsville, the Black brothers and what he learned from Sheriff Miller.

"If the sheriff confirms that Half-moon and this 'Squirrely' fellow were cellmates, that would explain some of it. But we still have some mysteries here, starting with why Delbert Black came back to the sawmill."

"I've been considering that too Henry. Maybe they wanted to make sure the other body was burnt up."

"And you think these are the same fellows doing the torture-robberies?"

"Both got started about the same time. Lucky for us we have a way to identify these boys now."

"Why kill Half-moon?"

"No honor among thieves. Those Black brothers are hot-blooded. Maybe he just pissed them off."

"And who's the other fellow got burnt up?"

Joe just shrugged.

Mary showed back up at the table. "You did right by that pile of vittles. Save room for dessert? I've got some of my chocolate cake left."

Both shook their heads, Henry spoke up. "No thanks Mary. What's the damages?"

"That'll be 95 cents with the drinks."

Henry pulled a dollar bill and a few coins out of his pocket and handed them to Mary. "On me tonight. Much obliged for a fine meal."

The dining room was mostly empty now. Mary pulled out a chair, sat down and turned to Joe. "I didn't want to bring this up last night when you were here with Peggy. Please try not to get Johnny shot up again. He's my favorite nephew."

Joe's face reddened a bit. "I'll not involve him again. Promise."

Mary nodded as she rose. "That's a relief." Gathering up the dirty dishes, she returned to the kitchen.

Henry watched her leave then turned to Joe. "What's that all about?"

Joe told Henry of the attempted robbery, wreck and gunplay. "It's my fault for going off half-cocked on these Reapers. They're another vicious lot. I learned my lesson this time."

The two sat in silence for a bit, then Henry spoke again. "I stopped by The Star this afternoon, found Peggy working on the books. She looked down in the dumps. I finally drug it out of her about you two."

Joe's face reddened again, even more this time. "It's a mess. Might as well feed me oats I'm such a horse's ass sometimes. This whole idea about women voting, I'd never even thought about it."

"Let me tell you a bit about Peggy. After her beau got killed at the locomotive works, it was years before she even had an interest in another man. Then we met, and I courted her hard as I could. She showed some notice but it didn't work out. In those years between I reckon she just got used to being on her own. The role of a mountain wife was not for her."

Joe nodded and pushed back from the table. "I'm beat, all this running around today. And I've got my studies to catch up on tomorrow. I intend to go back up to Confluence on Monday. I've got a couple of hunches to play. You free?"

"If you catch the early train I can spend the morning with you. Got some business to attend to in the afternoon." The two shook hands and headed their separate ways.

"I'll be on the eight o'clock. Meet me at the station."

Chapter 32

✳　　✳　　✳

At about the same time Joe and Henry sat down to dinner, the gang of thieves was once again assembled around the table in the abandoned mine. Kurt Straub, Charlie and the old man, plus two other toughs last seen riding away from the attempted payroll robbery at Leisenring. They had just finished their account of Friday's action and Charlie Krouse was now doing the talking.

"How'd Frick know we'd hit that payroll? I've got another dead relation and old Gus is in the slammer. Hope he keeps his mouth shut."

Kurt got up and paced a bit, lost in thought, then sat back down. "You say the streetcar operator that chased you was a tall slim fellow and armed? I also know a man who fits that description, a Mr. Joe Zajac. Yes, they were well prepared to foil our plan. While I suspect it was just a lucky guess on his part, his involvement complicates our operation. We'll lay off Frick and hit his competitors next. A few more heists and we'll have sufficient funds for the big day. In the interim, I'll do some investigating of my own." They sat in silence for a moment before he added. "And let Gus say what he will. If I find out Mr. Zajac is involved I've got an idea about how to deal with him."

Chapter 33

∗   ∗   ∗

In a similar way and at nearly the same moment, Merle and Squirrely Black were huddled next to a potbellied stove in the middle of a one-room shack. Their whereabouts was a remote part of Maryland known as Pullin Hollow, just over the state line from Pennsylvania. The shack was rented from an old farmer and lumberman, Floyd Pullin. Three generations of Pullins had made their home and living off this land. A jug of moonshine sat between them.

Squirrely grabbed the jug and took a pull. "We's about out of 'shine and cash."

Merle nodded, grabbing the jug and finishing it. Then he turned to his brother. "It's your damn fault Delbert's dead. We should have just plugged both them boys and drug them in the woods. But you had to have your fun."

Squirrely jumped up, waving his arms and pacing around. "Half-moon earned it, lost his nerve he did. Should have never let him in the gang. How was I supposed to know company was coming?"

"That's all well and good but we'd not of had to run off and leave the mess behind. And Delbert wouldn't have had to go back to clean it up."

Squirrely sat back down. "That weren't my idea. It didn't matter none if it was found. And he'd of likely gone back anyhow, just to look for that knife he lost." He took a calming breath. "Regardless, we still ain't got a pot to piss in. Let's find us another cabin to rob."

Merle nodded. "I got a notion on that. Half-moon bought the 'shine from up on the ridge, from them Harkins folk. I reckon there's a few bucks there. We'll go pay us a visit tomorrow. And we got to relocate. Old Floyd's been givin' me the evil eye ever since I asked if wanted to buy that big old log."

Chapter 34

✳   ✳   ✳

I t was late Sunday afternoon, and after his usual morning meal at the New Haven House and Mass at St. John's, Joe was back in his room, lying on the bed. Philosophy text book in hand, he'd been reading for several hours. He sat the book aside with a sigh and closed his eyes.

Lord help me, what have I gotten into here? I've read that first part twice and still don't understand it. Writing down notes as he read, he picked up the tablet to see if that would help him make sense of it. The top of the paper read "Ethics." Then a list:

1. How to live the good life
2. Virtues of character are the way
3. Define the extreme and find the mean
4. Doing the right thing at the right time for the right reason
5. 11 moral virtues
6. Courage

The list went on to identify the others, but he'd not read about them in detail. Joe put the tablet down and rose from the bed. *I just might have been better off staying ignorant of these concerns. Made it 30 years without it. That's enough for now. Think I'll head down the The Star.* But in truth he found the study intriguing. *The unexamined life is not worth living. I did learn that last term and believe it.* Ten minutes later he walked through the front door of The Star, the place mostly empty except for Hiram Kane behind the bar. He'd been working there since before Joe's first visit more than six years ago.

"Hello Hiram. How about a short one and a sandwich?"

"Hello Joe, sure enough." He drew a beer, placed it in front of Joe and hollered toward the kitchen. "Roast beef sandwich for Joe." "What's new?"

"I found us a replacement cleanup man, Nicky Molinari."

"He's kinda young eh?"

"Only 14 but he's a big fellow. Only problem is he'll have to do some before school and some after. But leastwise we're off the hook for it."

Hiram nodded. "I ain't cut out for mopping floors anymore. When does he start?"

"I'm to meet him here tomorrow morning at 7:00. But something's come up and I need to get to Ohiopyle on the eight o'clock train. Can you come by around 7:30 and finish showing him the ropes?"

"Sure Joe, see you then."

"And one more thing. I'm paying him five dollars a week."

"Five? The other fellow was doing it for three fifty."

"I know, and if Peggy squawks tell her I'm making up the difference. Nicky was about to quit school so he could help the family. Better yet, I'll just pay him his first week in advance tomorrow and fix it with Peggy myself."

Hiram smiled as he walked toward the kitchen.

Joe's mind wandered back to his studies, and the virtue of generosity. *The extremes are being wasteful and being stingy, and err to being more liberal in your spending. I'd say this is a good time and a good reason to be generous, and the five bucks isn't going to break me.*

Hiram returned with his sandwich and, after he finished it and another short one, he returned to his studies. *Maybe more of this is sinking in than I thought.*

Chapter 35

Little did Joe know that while he was spending that Sunday morning at church, Satan was on the prowl near Confluence. The Black brothers were on horseback, crude packs tied to the saddles, heading north along the Yough. Merle led the way.

"The old man is gonna be a mite disappointed when he gets home from church to find these fine horses done escaped the barn, saddled and all."

"We left him them swayback nags in trade." Squirrely started snickering. "And ain't it a shame that little shack burnt down."

"Why'd you go and do that?"

He hunched his shoulder. "Hell if I know. I've always been the reckless one in the family."

The two rode up to the turnoff for the Harkins homestead. While there was still snow on the ground, none had fallen recently. A well-worn trail led all the way up the ridge. They were soon at the cabin. Merle dismounted first.

"You hold here until I see who's home." He walked up to the door and knocked loudly. "Anybody home?"

A weak voice called out. "Hold on." A few minutes later old George Harkins opened the door, leaning heavily on his cane. He eyed Merle and stepped back. "State your business stranger."

"Names Merle. I heard tell you got some good 'shine for sale."

"Might we do but not to every swinging dick that shows up on the front porch." George started to close the front door. Merle stuck out his foot to stop him. "Now hold on old-timer. Anyone else here I can ask?"

"No, and get your foot out of the way before I go get my rifle and shoot it off."

Merle waved to Squirrely and pushed the door open. George staggered backward, nearly falling. Both of the Black brothers entered, closing the door behind them. Squirrely was cackling again. "I guess Grandpap told you."

Merle turned and delivered a sharp open-handed blow to the head of his brother. "I ain't in no mood to listen to your bullshit today. Shut the hell up." Then he turned to the old man. "Now where's the God damned moonshine Pap."

Quick as could be George swung his cane up, catching Merle between the legs. "Go straight to hell." As Merle doubled over hollering the old man caught him across the head with another blow, breaking his cane. Merle fell on his side, hands holding his balls.

Energized, George moved toward Squirrely, still stunned from his brother's blow, holding the sharp stub of his cane like a sword. He lunged forward but Squirrely was able to avoid the thrust. George lost his balance and fell to the floor. Squirrely gave him a kick to the ribs and turned to his brother. "You hurt bad?"

Merle moaned and rolled onto his back, still holding his groin. "If my balls didn't hurt so bad I'd slap the shit out of you again for being so stupid."

"Your head is bleeding Merle." A smear of blood showed on the wooden floor.

"Help me up."

Squirrely gave his brother a hand and pulled him up. Merle shuffled to the kitchen table and sat down. "There's got to be a bottle of 'shine in here somewhere. Find it."

Squirrely searched the kitchen, finding a jug in the pantry. He took a swallow.

"It's for me dumbass. Give me the jug."

Squirrely put the jug on the table. Old George was moaning on the floor.

Merle took a big swallow, the color returning to his ashen face. "Get the old man off the floor and sit him down." Squirrely did as he was told, without comment, and soon had George propped up in a chair. He slumped forward, head in his hands. The three were silent for several minutes as Merle recovered. He finally took a deep breath and stood up. Then he walked behind the old man and pulled his head up by the scruff of his neck.

"Old man, you are one mean snake. But you are about to find out that the Blacks ain't nobody to mess around with." He turned to Squirrely. "Go find some rope."

Squirrely went out the back door and returned with horse reins. "These should serve."

"Tie his hands behind his back and to the chair."

George was recovering now, his voice strong. He struggled as Squirrely bound him to the chair. "Took two of you boneheads to beat me. I'd have kicked the tar out of both of you."

Merle just smiled. "You caught me unawares but I got to hand it to you. Now let's get down to business. Where's your 'shine stashed?"

George grinned. "Far from here you lunkheads. You think we's stupid as you boys?"

"Forget the 'shine. Where's the valuables stashed?"

George laughed. "Look around. This look like we's rich?"

"All of you hicks got a stash somewhere's. Squirrely, go heat up the poker."

Doing as he was told, Squirrely stuck the poker into the firebox of the stove, returning with it glowing red. "Time to speak up Gramps."

George hung his head, then looked up slowly, speaking in a weak voice. "Come a bit closer and I'll tell you." Squirrely leaned forward until he was just a few inches from the old man's face. George cleared his throat and spit in Squirrely's eye. "Up your ass."

Squirrely dropped the poker and, in a rage, kicked George in the chest. He and the chair flew backward, his head hitting the floor with a crack. Squirrely commenced to kicking him in the ribs again until George stopped moving, and lay there silently. Panting, he stepped back, wiping his eye with his coat sleeve. Then he turned to Merle, who stood there shaking his head.

"Looks like you kilt another one. Let's toss the joint and get the hell out of here." A few minutes later, a small bag of loot in hand, they left the cabin and rode away.

Chapter 36

At a bit before 7:00 on Monday morning, Joe, pack on his back, arrived at The Star to find Nicky Molinari already waiting there.

"Morning Nicky, glad you're on time. I've a full day planned." He unlocked the front door and the two entered, the inside dark and chilly. "You know how to tend to a coal furnace?"

"Yes Mr. Zajac. I do that for Papa at home."

"Just Joe is fine." He pointed to a door down the hall. "That's the door to the basement. Make it your first chore every morning and your last at night."

Nicky nodded, then took off his cap and stood looking up at Joe. "Thank you from the bottom of my heart for this job. God answered my prayers. Now I can help my family and stay in school like Papa wants."

He's a good kid, like Tony says. Joe pulled some bills out of his pocket, found a fiver and held it out to Nicky. "Here's your first week's pay in advance. I'm paying top dollar for you so get busy."

Nicky, wide-eyed, took the bill and hurried down the hall. Soon Joe could hear the clinks and clunks associated with maintaining a coal-fired furnace. *Guess he knows what he's doing.* As Joe was turning on the lights, Hiram came through the door.

"Morning Hiram. Glad you could make it in early. I've a full day ahead of me."

Hiram nodded as he took off his coat and hat. "Sounds like you have our new helper busy already."

"He knows what he's doing down there, sounds like, and he's anxious to do a good job." Joe looked around the place. "Mondays aren't too bad. Wait until he sees the place on a Sunday morning."

Hiram smiled. "I'll not miss cleaning out those spittoons."

Joe pulled his key out and gave it to Hiram. "Give him this. There's a spare somewhere I'll find later."

"Will do."

Joe left and hurried up the street to City Lunch. *Need something to eat before I head up to Confluence.* He entered to find Tony already attending to several customers. Joe pulled off his pack, took a seat and was soon joined by Tony, cup of coffee in hand. "You get Nicky started his new job?"

Joe nodded. "He's hard at it already. I'm in a hurry, got a train to catch. How about a bacon-and-egg sandwich for the road, and a couple of doughnuts."

"You got it boss."

Joe opened his pack, looking for his notes. On top was his holstered .45. *Better safe than sorry.* He pulled the notepad out and reviewed the whole lot of them before making a new list. *First thing I'd like to find out is who's responsible for stirring up the Harkins clans. And I think I know who.*

Tony returned with his sandwich and donuts, wrapped to go. "Here you go." He saw the open pack on the stool next to Joe and shook his head. "And here we go again. You not so good with the gun. Please be careful. I no want my new partner be killed."

Joe smiled. "That makes two of us. That reminds me. What time are we meeting tonight?"

"I get out of here by six. Any time after."

"Make it seven. See you then."

Joe hustled out the door, the wind picking up again. He could see a line of storm clouds through the smoky haze of the coke ovens, moving in from the northwest. *Looks like we're in for another dose of winter weather.* He made it to the station just as the southbound train approached. By the time he bought his ticket it was at the platform. Joe boarded, and a few minutes later they were heading toward Ohiopyle. He pulled the egg sandwich out of his pack and ate it as they rolled out of town. *I'll save those donuts for later.* The track clear, they arrived at Ohiopyle before 9:00.

Joe got off to find a grim-faced Henry standing on the platform. "Morning Henry. What's the bad news?"

"It's old George Harkins. He's been murdered."

The Black brothers back at it! "What happened?"

"I'm short on the details, just got the news over at the Ohiopyle House. I hear his body's at the Confluence mortuary. Let's get on up there."

Ten minutes later, they were both on horseback, riding down the road along the river toward Confluence. Joe, far from an experienced horseman, road uneasily, the pack on his back making him top-heavy. *Hang on. Won't take long to get there at the rate we're going.* They flew past the road to Harkins Hollow, soon crossed Laurel Creek and slowed down. With Henry leading the way they pulled up to a small frame building on Baxter Street, the Casselman River visible right behind. A sign on the front read "A. Humbert – Mortician, Carpentry, Caskets." They dismounted and knocked on the front door. It was soon opened by a tall, slim man with a long, white beard. Henry extended his hand.

"How do Adam. I heard about George. Is he here?"

Adam nodded. "Him and some family, Deputy Edsley too." He stepped aside as they entered, closing the door behind them. "Through here."

The front room had several caskets on display of various sizes. Henry and Joe followed Mr. Humbert through a curtain to a larger workroom. The covered body of George Harkins lay on a slab. Sky and Jewel Harkins were sitting with Ernest Edsley at a long table. Doffing their hats, Joe and Henry joined them.

Henry extended his hand toward them. "Sky, Jewel, my heartfelt sympathies are offered. If there's anything we can do just ask."

Joe nodded. "And also from me."

Sky stood up and shook hands with both of them. "Help me catch the goldang cowardly rats that killed Pap."

Joe spoke up. "I got an idea about who's responsible. Anything you can tell us about how it happened would help."

Sky sat back down. "Pull up a chair. I was telling Ernest what we know. Best I can tell, it happened yesterday, mid-morning. I was out on the trap line. Jewel took Mamma to church. From the tracks, two riders likely stopped by, intent on robbing us. Pap, bless his heart, resisted. Even in his condition he was a tough piece of work and would never go down without a fight. I came back to find him on the floor, strapped to a chair. He'd been knocked over likely, and kicked around to boot. There was another little bit of blood in the middle of the room and his cane broke in two. The house was ransacked and what little we had of value stolen, including a jug of moonshine, my .45 and a hunting rifle."

Jewel started sobbing into her handkerchief. "What kind of man would do such a thing?"

Joe, who'd been taking notes, spoke up. "I've reason to believe it's the same gang responsible for Half-moon's death, and other similar incidents in the county. Two brothers, last name of Black." He turned to Deputy Edsley. "I talked to the sheriff on Saturday. I'll fill you in at your convenience."

Ernest nodded as there was another knock at the door. Mr. Humbert went to answer it, returning with Hawk Harkins. Jewel moaned and ran to him. Sky jumped up, red-faced, and advanced toward them.

"What the hell are you doing here. This is no concern of yours, you trap-jumping bastard."

Before the conflict could escalate Joe jumped up. "Hold on boys. I think I know who's been behind the troubles between you two." Both turned toward him "Now Hawk, look Sky in the eye swear on the bible. Have you been jumping his traps?"

Hawk fixed Sky with a hard stare. "No, I swear. And I never shot him neither. The bad blood got started over me and Jewel." He put his arm around her.

"Now Sky, swear on the bible: Have you been jumping Hawk's traps?"

He slowly shook his head, holding Hawk's stare. "I swear, and I damned sure didn't break into their house. I'm no thief. But I can't bear to see Jewel with him."

Joe stepped toward them both. "I'd say in this day and time and seeing as she's reached the legal age, that would be her choice to make. Just because she's a woman doesn't give you grounds to run her life. Now why don't you two shake hands and stop the feuding. We got us some killers to track down."

Sky scowled at Joe. "Who the hell are you to order me about?"

Hawk nodded. "That's right. It's none of your concern."

Jewel moved to Joe's side. "Thank you Mr. Zajac." Then turning to the men. "And he's perfectly right. Sky, I either marry Hawk or leave. And Hawk, if we do marry you'll be civil with my brother. Now go ahead, shake hands and stop the fighting."

The two men stepped toward each other, Hawk finally extending his hand. With some reluctance Sky did the same. Jewel started sniffling, then moved to embrace them both. "Thank you Lord."

Mr. Humbert cleared his throat. "I'd ask that you all take your leave. Sky, you need to go get George's Sunday best over here for the funeral on Wednesday. I've got my work to do."

The six of them adjourned to the front room, Joe pulling Ernest to the side. "You got some time this morning?"

"I do. Why do you ask?"

"Know where Elmer Fortney lives?"

Ernest nodded. "Not too far from here, lives with a no-account cousin in a shack outside of town."

"Let's go pay him a visit."

Chapter 37

*   *   *

The three Harkins soon departed together, leaving Deputy Edsley, Joe and Henry standing in front of the building. Henry put his arm around Joe.

"I got to hand it to you. I'd have never thought the two sides of the Harkins clan would ever come together. You played your cards right."

"It was Marshall McNutt down at the Ferncliff who deserves the credit. He's the one gave them a place to get to know one another."

"But you sealed the deal. Now who do you think is behind the troubles?"

"Elmer Fortney. He's sweet on Jewel too but she gave him the cold shoulder. Ernest and I are going to pay him a visit. You're welcome to join us."

Henry shook his head. "I got business to attend to. Just leave my horse at the stable when you're done with him."

"I'll be coming back up on Wednesday for the funeral service. They mention the time?"

Ernest spoke up. "Eleven o'clock at the Christian Church."

Henry mounted up. "See you there."

Joe pulled out his watch It was going on 11:00. "Let's get a move on." He pulled his pistol and holster out of the pack and strapped it on under his coat. "We better take care with this boy. He's a bit of a pinhead best I can tell."

Ernest pulled his coat back, showing he was similarly armed. "Most of them is good people but his branch of the Fortneys tends in that direction."

The two mounted up and rode slowly out of town heading east. Joe filled Ernest in on what he'd learned from the tattoo artist and Sheriff Miller. After a few miles, they turned onto a narrow track heading north.

"Welcome to Jersey Hollow, Joe. Elmer's place isn't far. We'll ride in a bit and approach on foot."

And that's what they did. Ten minutes later they approached a rundown shack, a thin wisp of smoke coming for the chimney. Behind the shack stood an outhouse. Joe could see a skin hanging on its side wall.

Ernest unbuttoned his coat and put his hand on his revolver. "You go on around back." He gave Joe a minute to do so then stepped to the front door. "Elmer. Elmer Fortney. This is Deputy Edsley. You in there?"

Joe stood a few feet from the back door, .45 in hand. Sure enough, the door quietly opened, Elmer backing out slowly with a rifle hung over his shoulder. Joe closed the distance and stuck his gun in Elmer's side. "Hold it." Elmer froze as Joe took his rifle. "Go on inside and open the front door."

Elmer did as he was told, and soon the three of them stood in the middle of the room, Joe still to the rear with his gun in hand. Ernest did the talking.

"How do, Elmer. I see you've got a fox skin hanging out back. I've never known the Fortneys to do much trapping. Where's your trap line?"

Elmer started wringing his hands. "Just up the hollow some. What business is it of yours?"

Joe gazed around the room. *What a dump. Stinks in here too.* On one side stood a table, an old leather-bound book on top. He walked over and opened it to the flyleaf. *Property of John Harkins. Got you.* "Hey, Elmer."

Elmer turned toward Joe, who pointed to the book. "Might as well spill the beans. We're on to you."

Elmer's shoulders slumped. "I need to sit down." Ernest nodded.

"Where's your cousin?"

"Haven't seen Clyde since late December."

Joe stepped toward him. "If Clyde ended up with the fancy pocket watch, he's dead."

"I figured as much. Knew he'd gone out to help at the mill."

"Who shot Sky?"

"Not me. That's another cousin did that. He's run off somewhere."

Joe shook his head. "I'd say you need some lessons in courting."

Ernest came forward and grabbed Clyde by the arm. "You are under arrest for theft. Might be some other charges too. We'll let Sheriff Miller sort it out."

"You can't arrest me. We're in Somerset County."

Ernest smiled. "But you committed the crimes in Fayette County. And besides, I'm cross- deputized over here too. Joe, grab that fox skin off the shithouse for evidence. I guarantee you there ain't one trap to be found up the hollow. You take the book and see it gets back to Buck."

Chapter 38

Joe carefully put the book in his pack and followed Ernest and the prisoner, riding double, back to Confluence. They parted ways in town, Joe turning toward Ohiopyle. When he got to Rock Creek, he decided to go ahead and return the book. *Still got time.* The snow on the trail up Harkins Hollow was well-packed. *Likely can ride in all of the way.*

He approached the clearing where Abner's cabin was with caution, and rode by slowly, unchallenged. *Must not be home.* It was just past noon when he reached the Johns' big house. He called out "hello" and dismounted. As he did, Hawk opened the door and came out. He walked toward Joe, hand extended.

"Mr. Zajac, I am forever in your debt. If there was ever a moment for us to stop the feuding it was then. Much obliged for you seeing that, and bringing it about."

They shook hands, Joe smiling. "That was a spur of the moment deal, glad it worked out. I've got even better news. Buck and John Jr. home?"

Hawk nodded. "And Momma too. Come on in. I just told them about me and Jewel. They's all a might taken aback."

Joe followed to find the three of them sitting at the table, grim-faced, with Mayme Harkins dabbing at her eyes with a hanky. They all eyed Joe silently as he joined them. Hawk broke the ice. "Momma, meet Joe Zajac.

He's the friend of Henry Brooks I just told you about. Says he has some good news to tell."

John Jr. spoke up. "We could damn sure use some after what this fool boy just told us."

Joe took the pack off his back and opened it. Without comment, he laid the family book on the table.

Buck was the first to react. "Whoopee! Never thought I'd see this again." He picked it up, carefully opening it to the first page. "Much obliged for its return Joe. Where'd you get it?"

"In the possession of one Elmer Fortney. He's the one been stirring the pot of hatred between you two families." Joe went on to recount the action at Elmer's cabin and his arrest. "All because he was also sweet on Jewel Harkins, can't say I blame him. She's a fine woman and a lucky catch for any man."

John Jr. scowled. "But not a John Harkins."

Hawk moved toward his father. "That's my call and I say I'm a lucky man."

Buck went to the cupboard, returning with the whiskey jug. "This calls for a drink." He took a big slug and passed it to his son.

John Jr. shook his head. "Nothing to celebrate for me."

Joe took the jug. "Then you're a damn fool." He took a swallow and put the jug on the table.

John's face reddened as he rose from the table. "You watch your mouth. Friend of Henry's or not, this is family business."

Hawk grabbed the jug, took a swig and turned to Joe. "Thanks to you, the feud between us is over. It's time to end the division too. We share a common ancestor." He turned to his father. "When Jewel and I marry, and I'm determined to do so, the split ends with our children."

With that Mayme started bawling. Then she grabbed the jug and took a swallow. Calming some, she handed it to her husband. "Jewel is a fine woman. You know that, you hardhead."

John sat back down, jug in his lap. Finally, he took a deep breath, then raised the jug to his lips. After taking a long draw he sat it back down and looked at Hawk. "Just going to take some getting used to I reckon. You have my blessing."

Hawk came around the table and, hands on his father's shoulders, intoned. "The Harkins are one family from now on."

Buck grabbed the jug and took another swig. "Hooray!" Then he turned to Joe. "I'm in your debt Joe. How can I repay you?"

This should seal the deal. "By coming to George's funeral on Wednesday, you all and as many of your clan as you can round up."

Buck nodded. "I'll be there. Me and George were friends as kids, and hunting buddies later on until things got out of hand."

"And one more thing. We need to run down his killers."

John Jr. spoke up. "If they're still in the valley somewhere, we'll track them down."

Joe grabbed his pack. *Time to quit while I'm ahead.* "I'll leave you to it then. See you Wednesday."

Hawk followed him out the door. "I never thought I'd see this day. You showed true courage in there. The old man was never one to take much lip, particularly from a stranger. Seen him fight men for less."

Joe smiled. "There's times my mouth gets going before my head." They shook hands again then Joe mounted up and rode off.

Chapter 39

As Joe rode back to Ohiopyle, it started snowing. By the time he arrived, it had picked up, the big, wet flakes falling fast. He dropped Henry's horse at the stable, unbuckled his holster and stashed it in his pack. *Glad I didn't have to use it. Lord knows I'm not a sure shot.* It was just past 2:00, the next train to Connellsville not due until 3:00. *Time for a bite to eat.* He walked up the street to the Ohiopyle House dining room. Marshall McNutt was at a corner table, just finished his lunch. He saw Joe enter and waved him over.

"Joe, you heard old George Harkins got murdered?"

"Henry told me soon as I got off the train this morning. He's laid out at Humbert's. We've been there already." He sat down at the table. "I've good news for you about our lovebirds." Joe went on to recount his day, including the end of the feud, the arrest of Elmer and his visit with the Johns. "All in all, a good morning's work I'd say."

Marshall's eyes glistened. "And you called me Cupid. It's the end of an era here in the Yough Valley."

"Spread the word then. Let's give George a big sendoff."

Marshall rose from the table. "I'll do that. And come summer you give us a visit. There's a room for you at the Ferncliff any time you want one, on me."

After Marshall's departure, Joe ate a quick lunch, the two donuts still in his pack for dessert. *A bit worse for the wear and tear, but still good.* By then it was time to catch the train. He arrived back in town and headed to The Star to check up on Nicky. When he arrived, he saw Peggy at work. *Been since Friday. Let's see where we stand.* He joined her, flopping into a chair across the desk. She looked up with a smile.

"Hello Joe."

Good to see her smile. "Hello to you. Working on the books?"

She shook her head. "Working on getting our local chapter of the NAWSA organized. The response from the women I've talked to has been very positive. We're having our first meeting next Monday and I'm working on an advertisement for this week's Courier. They've promised a story too."

Think before you speak. Joe took a deep breath before responding. "Good luck to you then." He got up and closed the door to the office, then turned, still standing. "Peggy, speaking for yours truly, there will be no more quarrels with you. Hell, I know you're smarter than me, and admire you for it. I regret what I said to Aunt Margaret and apologize for spoiling the day. No matter what happens between us from this point, I want us to be friends."

Peggy looked up at Joe, eyebrows knitted. Then she stood, locking him in a stare. "Apology accepted. What's done is done, and we are friends. I'm willing to move forward on those terms."

Joe held out his hand and they shook on it. *That's good progress. Let's let it sit there.* "Did you meet our new helper?"

The smile returned to her face. "I did. He's a sweet young man, and the spittoons have never been cleaner. I guess he's worth that extra dollar and a half."

"I told Hiram not to mention it to you. I plan on paying him out of my own pocket."

"Nicky told me himself, not Hiram. The Star can afford it. I closed the books on last year and we made a tidy profit."

"No shortage of drinkers in this town. I hope we do as well at the restaurant."

"What restaurant?"

"I guess with all that's been going on I forgot to mention it. Tony and I are going partners in a new place across the river. He wants to call it 'Joey Z's.'" Joe looked at his watch. "In fact we're looking at a spot this evening. I need to get cleaned up." He turned to leave. "And I've got that murder solved for Henry, but too late to prevent another one. I'll tell you about it next time we're together."

"Joe, I almost forgot. Sheriff Miller called, said he'd just heard from the sheriff of Garrett County, Maryland. He says the Black brothers were likely behind some crimes just across the state line."

Not far from Confluence. "Much obliged Peggy." With that, Joe hurried out the door and up Pittsburgh Street to his rooms. After a quick cleanup and a little nap, he left to meet with Tony. By now it was snowing very hard, a stiff wind behind it. *Already half a foot on the ground.* He arrived at the proposed location on the corner of Third and Main just before 7:00. He could see Tony inside through a big front window, talking to another fellow. He stomped the snow off of his boots and joined them.

Tony turned to him as he entered. "Joey, you right on time. Say hello to Mr. Morton. He the owner."

The fellow stepped forward, hand extended. "Walter Morton here. My pleasure Mr. Zajac."

"How do Mr. Morton." Joe surveyed the space, the first floor of a two-story brick building, recently constructed. The front wall was mostly two big windows. A row of smaller ones lined the side. The other side abutted against the building next door. Other than several radiators and some temporary electric ceiling lights, the room was unfinished. "You just finish the construction?"

"Yes indeed. Tony tells me a restaurant is planned. This is a prime location, the space ready to be finished as your plans require."

Joe walked the space. *Nice size. Plenty of light. Should do fine.* "What's upstairs?"

"There's plans for three apartments but it's also mostly unfinished."

Joe nodded, then an idea popped into his head. "How much you want for the whole shooting match?"

Mr. Morton's eyes widened. "Tony said you were planning on renting."

"He's right. That was our plan. But I've changed my mind. You interested in selling?"

Joe could see the wheels spinning in Mr. Morton's head. After a few minutes he nodded. "If we can come to terms that return me a profit, I'd consider it. I'll work up a number for you by tomorrow."

Joe smiled. "You deserve your profit. You've built a sound building in a good location. Just let Tony know."

At that moment the door blew open, a gust of wind following a big man into the room. Tony went to greet him. "Franco. I thought you not make it. Come meet my partner. Joey, meet my cousin, Franco Sabatini. He just come to visit from New York City."

Franco was about Joe's height and bigger than Lloyd. He removed his hat to expose a full head of black hair, slicked back tight. "Hello Joe, whadda you know?"

Joe smiled. *He's a funny one.* "Ciao Franco. You here for a visit?"

Tony spoke up. "He maybe stay on. I tell you in a minute."

Mr. Morton cleared his throat. "Well gentlemen, I'll let you to it. I need to go work up my costs. Tony, I'll drop by your place tomorrow with my offer to sell." Without further ado, he departed.

"Joey, you crazy. Now you gonna buy the place?"

"Why pay rent? I bet he'll offer it at a fair price. There's plenty of vacant lots in New Haven. He can take his profits and build another one." Tony scanned the space again. *Room for plenty of tables, maybe a short bar on the side.* "And Dave Norton will know what's a reasonable deal. Then I'm the landlord, the restaurant can pay me the rent."

Tony nodded. "You smart Joey."

"Now tell me about Franco here."

"He's my mother's sister's boy. He got lots of smarts too. I figure he could run City Lunch while we're busy getting this place going. He's a good cook. Then maybe we decide to sell that business and I get some money to throw in the pot."

Joe turned to Franco. "Why's a big city fella like you want to move to a little town like this?"

Franco looked down, spinning his hat in his hands. He looked at Tony, who nodded his head. "Tell him the truth Franco. No secrets between partners."

"I like New York but I make some mistakes there. I fall in with a bad crowd, do some things I'm not proud of. The best way to change that was to get out of town."

Joe nodded. "How bad?"

"I was a, how you say, debt collector. I always was a good fighter, used my muscles to collect."

"You kill anyone?"

Franco shook his head. "No, and I repent those ways. I make a true confession and God forgives me. Now I want to make an honest living, and I'm not afraid of hard work."

"Tony, you decide. If you say so, we'll find a place for him in our plans."

"I say yes then. If he screw up though, we send him packing."

"Okay Franco, you got yourself a job."

A big smile spread across his face. He rushed forward, grabbing Joe in a bear hug and almost lifting him off the floor. "Many thanks Mr. Zajac. And I'll earn my pay. You never regret giving Franco a chance."

"Just call me Joe." He turned to Tony. "Tomorrow's a school day for me. I'll see you in the afternoon."

Tony slapped his forehead with the palm of his hand. "Wait, I almost forget to tell you. A big young guy stop by the place today, wants to know if you still eat here. I think he maybe your friend? I tell him, 'sure, most every day.' Then he smile kinda funny and leave. I watch through the window, see him cross the street and talk to another fella. I no get a good look but his left arm was in a sling. Then the two of them jump on the Dickerson Run streetcar as it turned the corner."

Arm in a sling? Dickerson Run? "Thanks Tony." *Someone's trying to catch my attention.*

Chapter 40

✳   ✳   ✳

While George Harkins lay cold on the slab at Humbert's and peace came to the Harkins clan, the Black brothers continued their evil and violent flight up the Yough Valley. After the killing, they rode south along the river until, saddle sore and weary, they came across the cabin of one Joshua Sechler. Tucked almost out of sight midway between Confluence and Somerfield, they'd stopped there to rest and decide on a future course.

The two brothers sat at a crude table, tin plates in front of them, while Joshua worked at the stove. In his 60s, and a near hermit, he'd been surprised by the two and was now their captive. They'd roughed him up and proceeded to get drunk on the stolen 'shine.

Merle leaned back, rubbing his face. "Make it snappy old man. My stomach's growling."

Joshua turned and glared at the two. *Lord please give me the chance to send these devils to hell.* "You's some toughs, sure enough." He took the skillet to the table and deposited a slab of fried mush on each plate.

Squirrelly looked at it with disgust. "This the best you got to eat around here?"

"Slim pickins this time of the year. Tell you what, I'll go check my rabbit traps."

"Just stay put old-timer. We'll be on our way soon enough."

The two ate what was offered without further comment. Then Merle got up. "I need to use the privy. Keep an eye on the old man." He walked out the back door. A heavy, wet snow was falling. *Where's the God damned horses?* They weren't where Squirrely had tied them last night. *That dumb bastard. Ain't nothing he can't fuck up. Now we's stuck here.* He used the privy, returned to the cabin and delivered another sharp blow to his brother's head, knocking him off his chair.

Squirrely rose slowly, backing away from Merle. "What the hell was that for?"

"The horses run off you lunkhead." He turned to Joshua. "How far to the Pike?⁴"

The old man laughed. "Bout three miles or so to Somerfield. I got some snowshoes if you's ready to take a hike."

"Not in this weather." He turned to Squirrely. "We're stuck here until the snow lets up."

---

4 The National Road which passed through Somerset and Fayette Counties

Chapter 41

*   *   *

Meanwhile, back at the abandoned mine, Kurt Straub and Charlie Krouse sat alone at the table. A map of Pennsylvania was spread out in front of them. Kurt was tracing the route of the Pennsylvania Railroad from Pittsburgh to Philadelphia. "Somewhere near here." He marked a spot near Altoona. "On the uphill run after the Horseshoe Curve."

Charlie nodded. "We've stockpiled enough explosives and weapons to blow them straight to hell. We'll need more manpower though."

"That will be provided by our friend Istvan. His efforts have built Barat into a potent force. He claims over a hundred followers, many army veterans from time spent in their service to the Empire[5]."

"Any idea when we move?"

"Mr. Bako has a man inside at Carnegie. He will let us know of an opportune moment."

"What about Zajac? Think our plan will work?"

Kurt nodded. "I'm sure of it. My source inside of Frick confirms he's been there twice and met with Lynch both times."

"You're sure Gus will talk?"

---

5   The Austro-Hungarian Empire

"Reasonably certain. We will learn soon enough. Our man is keeping an eye on him." Kurt rolled up the map awkwardly using his one good arm. "I'm looking forward to us meeting again."

Chapter 42

✳   ✳   ✳

Joe was up early on Tuesday, at City Lunch when it opened at 7:00. Franco was wiping off tables when he entered.

"Buongiorno Joe. See, I'm on the job already. What do you want for breakfast?"

"Coffee for starters, pancakes and sausage if you please."

"You got it boss."

Sounds just like Tony. Joe took his seat at the end of the counter. A few minutes later Johnny Davidson walked in, his sling gone. He saw Joe and joined him.

"Morning Joe. What's new?"

"It would take an hour to tell you. I've got school today and a train to catch. How about we have a beer tonight?"

"My pleasure."

"I'm due back by five. See you at The Star around six. How's the shoulder?"

Johnny held out his arm and rotated it in a circle. "Healing fast. It's still stiff but I don't need the sling anymore."

Franco came out with his coffee and breakfast. "Here you go Joe, enjoy."

"Franco, meet Johnny Davidson. He's a detective on the city police force, and as steady a customer as I am."

Franco's face reddened a bit. "Don't worry about me. I'm no troublemaker."

"Johnny, Franco is Tony's cousin from New York. He's new to town, going to be helping Tony out around here."

"Welcome to Connellsville." They shook hands. "I'll have two doughnuts and a coffee."

"Right away." He returned to the kitchen.

"What's with him? Got a guilty conscience?"

Joe smile. "No comment buddy. Say, what happened to our German friend? He up at Uniontown?"

"No, as of yesterday he was still across the street. The sheriff hasn't had time to send a deputy down."

"I want to see him." Joe ate hurriedly as Franco delivered Johnny's order. "I get you coffee."

Joe shook his head. "Don't bother. Pack those donuts for him. We have to run."

"Sure thing boss."

A minute later Johnny and Joe were in City Hall, standing outside of the German's cell. He was sitting on the side of his cot, head still in his hands. *Looks even more worried than the last time. Let's see if he's more willing to talk.*

"Good morning. Enjoying your stay?"

"Nein sprecht...."

Joe interrupted him. "Don't give me that horse shit. You speak English. I'll give you one chance this morning to get off the bullseye for the trouble you're in—and I'm in a hurry. I know you're in with Kurt Straub and his Reapers. I know he's holed up somewhere down Dickerson Run way. You tell me what you know and if it's enough to help track him down, I'll work with my friend Sheriff Miller to see that's taken into consideration."

The man sat there silently.

Joe turned to Johnny. "Send him up to Uniontown. He'll go down for murder."

The German jumped up. "It wasn't me that pistol whipped that fellow. It was Charlie."

Charlie Krouse? The fellow that visited City Lunch.. I thought he was locked up. "What's your name?"

"Gus Stein."

"Go on Gus."

"Straub is holed up in an abandoned coal mine north of Dawson. The entrance is on a hillside, well-hidden. We always met there. Where else he might be staying, he kept secret."

"How'd you get there?"

"Go out River Road until it turns away from the Yough. Then you cross over a small stream, follow the railroad tracks for maybe a quarter mile. Then go up the hill, about 50 yards."

"What's he doing with the money?"

"Some the gang gets. The rest he's saving for later. He just called it 'The Big Day.' That's all I know."

Joe tipped his hat. "Much obliged Gus. I'll talk to the sheriff after we check out your story." He looked at his watch. "See you tonight Johnny."

Fifteen minutes later, he was Pittsburgh bound. But the train was delayed, and despite his best efforts, he was a few minutes late for class. Miss Hall frowned as he entered, her lecture already begun. "Mr. Zajac. Seems your punctuality is not improving but getting worse. I must warn you that another late arrival may well jeopardize your continued attendance in this class."

"Yes Miss Hall. It won't happen again." He slunk to the rear of the classroom and opened his notebook.

"As I was saying, near here was where much of the early action in the French and Indian War took place, and young George Washington's first military experience. Has everyone read their assignment?"

Joe had just read it on the way down on the train. It was still fresh in his mind. Everyone in class raised their hand.

"Very good. Now who can tell us a bit about it to get our discussion started?"

Joe's hand shot up first.

"Mr. Zajac?"

"The war here was a part of a larger conflict between France and England called 'The Seven Year War.' The fight was between the North American colonies of both countries and their Indian allies. Control of the Ohio River and its commerce was the goal of both. The death of Jumonville and a later battle at Fort Necessity sparked the larger conflict." *Listen to me. I sound like a professor.*

"Very good Mr. Zajac." She gave him a smile. "You've apparently done your homework. With that as a preface, let's continue." For the next hour and a half, she alternately lectured and had her students respond. Joe took copious notes. *So much history right around here, including Fayette County.*

"And that's how the English drove the French into Canada and came to control the Ohio River. Thursday we will discuss the period from the end of that war to our Declaration of Independence. Class dismissed."

Joe once again dawdled until he and Miss Hall were the only two left in the room. He approached her as she was packing up her bag. "I apologize for my tardiness and it won't happen again."

She looked up with a smile. "I'm sure you have a good reason. You can explain it to me over lunch. I can meet you at The Grape in an hour if you are able to do so."

And I was getting the shy's about asking her. "I am able, and willing. I'll make sure we get a table."

"Adieu, until then." She gathered up her things and swept out of the room.

She's a different kind of woman, that's for sure. Joe went upstairs to a study lounge to finish preparing for his afternoon class. At 11:15 he packed up and walked over to The Grape, which wasn't quite half-full. He took the same table for two where they'd sat together the first time. A waitress appeared with a menu.

"The special of the day is Beef Bourguignonne. Can I get you a drink?"

"A glass of Chianti if you please. I'll wait to order." He gestured to the empty chair. The waitress nodded and went to get his wine.

By 11:30, Joe had sipped half of his wine and the place was filling up. A few minutes later, Miss Hall came in, saw Joe and joined him.

"Hello Mr. Zajac. Thank you for saving us a table." She took off her coat and sat down at the empty seat.

"This is a popular joint, seems most every day of the week." *How to say this?* "Would it be breaking a school rule if we were on a first-name basis when not in class?"

She tilted her head, lips pursed as in thought, then smiled. "Perhaps, but let's through caution to the wind Joe."

The waitress reappeared. "Hello Grace. The usual?"

"If you please. Serving your traditional Tuesday special?"

She nodded. "Been simmering away all morning."

"I'll have a bowl then." She looked at Joe. "It's very good."

"Make it two then." After she left Joe turned to Grace. "Never heard of Beef Boryone before. What is it?"

"It's pronounced 'boor-gee nyawn', a fancy French name for beef stew. It's made with Burgundy wine, another red I prefer to chianti."

Not reluctant to straighten me out. Grace had pronounced the word with a distinctly French accent. "You speak French?"

"Oui monsieur. I lived in Paris for several years after I graduated from college, in Montmartre."

A woman of the world. "I grew up in Poland before we came to America. Moved from Philadelphia to Fayette County going on seven years ago. I've not seen much of the world outside of that."

The waitress delivered their food, two big bowls of the stew and a small thin loaf of bread. "I'll get your drink." She looked at Joe's near empty glass "Another for you?"

Joe finished his chianti and handed her the glass. "Have any of that burgundy? I'll give that a try."

She nodded and left to get them. Joe picked up his spoon, sampled a taste and nodded. *Like regular beef stew but different. Must be the wine.* "Tasty."

Grace sampled hers and smiled. "Claude is an excellent chef." She pulled a heel off of the loaf of bread. "And his French bread is wonderful."

The waitress returned with their drinks. "Holler if you need anything else."

The two ate in silence, their meal soon gone. Joe picked up his wine and raised it toward Grace. "Here's to France, home to some mighty fine stew."

Grace raised hers. "To France." They both took a drink, then Grace spoke. "So tell me Joe. What caused your tardiness this morning?"

"It's a long story."

She checked her watch, hanging from a thin chain around her neck. "We've some time."

Where to start? "I was a cop in Philadelphia, came west to work for the H, C. Frick Coke Company, as a plainclothes member of their police force. Last August I got tangled up with this fellow, a Mr. Kurt Straub. He was intent on blowing up some of Frick's mines. We managed to foil his plans. I thought he'd met his maker then." Joe paused for a moment for a sip of wine. "I quit working for Frick after that, come to not abide his dealings with the workers. Some reward money I got for stopping Straub gave me the means to do it. Then I decided I'd give college a try. Well, as it turns out, Straub is likely still around, and behind some payroll robberies along the Connellsville Seam. I'd gotten to know the man running Frick, Mr. Thomas Lynch. He talked me into getting involved, not working for them but on my own." Joe paused again to take another drink. *Umm... that's good. Better than the chianti.*

"So you're a private detective now?"

"I guess you could say that, but I'm no Sherlock Holmes. Anyway, we managed to stop another payroll robbery last Friday, with a robber killed and my best friend shot, luckily not serious. The other robber is in the Connellsville jail. I stopped by to grill him this morning. I was intending to take an earlier train and will from now in."

"My, my, you live an exciting life. Learn anything from the prisoner?"

Joe nodded. "I did, and come Friday I'll be trying to track Mr. Straub down."

"Well, that's some story Joe. We'll count it as an approved tardiness." She took a sip of wine. "And how are you enjoying your studies?"

"The history is right up my alley. I've learned a lot. The philosophy classes are harder. Got me thinking about things never crossed my mind before. Might be I was better off being ignorant in that regard."

Grace smiled and nodded. "You've opened Pandora's box, Joe. Life can get complicated after that, but there's no turning back."

Pandora's box? Enough about me. "I'd like to hear more about Paris." *In for a dime, in for a dollar.* "Any school rules about sharing a dinner with a student?"

"Might be, but I've never let the social conventions keep me from enjoying myself." She finished her drink. "And I enjoy your company."

Joe felt a flush creeping up his neck. "Thursday then. You pick the place."

At that moment a man approached their table, a white apron cinched high on his waist. His black hair hung long over his ears, a long waxed mustache twisted up and into circles at the end. "Bonjour Grace. Como se va?"

"Tres bon Claude, the meal excellent as usual." She gestured toward Joe. "Say hello to Joe. He's quickly becoming a regular here."

"Bonjour Joe. Pleased to make your acquaintance." A waitress called from the bar. "Gottta run, just stop to say hello."

Grace looked at her watch again. "As do I. See you Thursday." She quickly gathered up her things and left a quarter on the table. "Au revoir." Turning with a swirl, she hurried out the door.

She's quite the woman. Joe finished his wine, dropped another quarter on the table and headed to his afternoon classroom. As usual, Professor Burns rushed in at the last minute.

"Good afternoon all, shall we begin? Today we shall discuss what it means to live a good life, in accordance with the beliefs of Aristotle. Where do we start? Anyone?"

A hand shot up in the first row. "Aristotle believed that the goal of a good life was happiness."

Burnsworth nodded. "Yes, but let's remember that 'happiness' is a somewhat imprecise translation of the Greek word 'eudaimonia.' A better understanding will ensue if we think of it more precisely as 'human flourishing.' How does one live in a way that encourages a growing and thriving human spirit?"

Joe raised his hand and the professor nodded. "I'd say Aristotle saw a duty to righteous living as the key. Live prudently, practice temperance, show courage and act justly for starters. Know what those words mean and keep them in mind every day."

"And that's what we will talk about today, the four Cardinal Virtues."

Joe's mind whirled as the professor spoke. *Temperance. I've come to an understanding of that without Aristotle's help. There's more to life than devotion to pleasure.* Before long the class was ending.

"We will continue this discussion on Thursday, focusing on a proper understanding of the extremes and the mean for each virtue. And remember, living the good life is not possible without the development of the daily habits associated with it. As Aristotle said, 'one swallow does not make a spring.'"

Joe wrote that down as a final note, quickly packed up and was soon on his way back to Connellsville. *Need to stop and see Tony, then meet up with Johnny.* It was almost 5:00 when he walked in the door at City Lunch. The place was empty, with Franco busy mopping the floor and Tony sitting at the counter looking at some papers. He waved Joe over.

"Joey, Mr. Morton just stopped by. He left these papers."

Joe sat down and took a look. The first was a lease for the first floor only, three years at $50.00 a month. The second was an offer to sell the entire building as is. The asking price was $4,500.

"What you think? Fifty a month seem high to me. I only pay $20 here."

"I don't know Tony. I'll take these to Dave over at the bank. He's got a head for business. First thing I have to figure out is how much it's going to cost to finish the construction of the insides."

Franco joined them. "When I was 15, I quit school and worked for my uncle. He was a good carpenter. I learned plenty. I need to see the second floor. Then we make up a bill of materials we need to do the job."

"Tony, you talk to Morton. I'm going to Confluence tomorrow, likely not make it by the bank until Friday. I'll see you then."

After a quick stop at his place, Joe arrived at The Star just after 6:00. Johnny was already there, standing at the end of the bar. Joe waved and pointed to the corner table. Johnny joined him carrying two mugs of beer. Joe raised his mug toward him. "Friends as long as we are able to lift theses glasses from the table." They touched mugs and both drank deep.

"That's a good one Joe. You've been a good friend and may it always be so. Now catch me up on the payroll robbers."

"For starters, I was lying to Gus this morning. The payroll man didn't die. But I'm sure Kurt Straub is back and behind it." He recounted Tony's story of his Monday visitors. "The big fellow, Charlie, I figured he'd be still locked up."

"Best I recollect he did 60 days for disturbing the peace. That's all they could pin on him."

"I'm going to go down to Dawson and see if I can find the mine Gus described."

"Want some company?"

Joe smiled and shook his head. "No more action for you, at least until the shoulder heals. Let's plan on meeting here again on Saturday night. I'll let you know what I find out."

Chapter 43

*　　*　　*

Tuesday morning found Sky sitting with Hawk, John and Buck at their home. After some minor arguments, they'd succeeded in putting the past behind them and agreed to join forces in search of old George's killers. Hawk was doing the talking.

"Between the two sides of the family, we can likely muster two dozen strong men to hunt these dogs down."

Buck stood up and took his rifle from the rack. "Include me in that number. Thank the Lord I'm still able to get around. And between us, we's likely to know every cabin and shack in the valley on both sides 'tween Ohiopyle and Somerfield."

Now John spoke up. "You say they got some 'shine. I reckon they found a place to drink it. And with the big snow yesterday, they're likely still in the vicinity."

The storm had stalled over the valley, dropping a foot or better. The winds picked up after, piling up some drifts. Hawk continued with his plan.

"First off, we need to have a man at both the Confluence and Ohiopyle railroad stations, more watching the roads out of both towns heading east and west. Then we start checking cabins, at least four teams of three men together, starting from Somerfield and Ohiopyle working toward Confluence, and four more teams starting from Confluence north and south, on both sides of the river. It's bound to be a slow slog, so let's get to it. Sky, go get your men gathered, we'll do the same. You got anything to add?"

"No. Your plan is solid. If they're still in the valley, we'll find them."

Chapter 44

*   *   *

Just past noon on Tuesday finds the Black Brothers still holed up at Joshua Sechler's cabin. Merle sat at the little table while Squirrely paced the floor, four steps one way, four steps back across. Joshua tended to the fire in the stove. Merle stuck out his arm to block Squirrely's way.

"Your pacing ain't gonna change the facts. We's stuck here. No way we'd make it far on foot."

Squirrely stopped pacing but didn't sit down. "I'm 'bout sick of mush, and I never did like being confined. Reminds me of jail."

Joshua turned from the stove. "Want to make yourself useful, go get an armful of wood."

"Go get it yourself old man."

Joshua nodded, and put on his coat, hat and gloves. "Might as well take a crap while I'm out there. That mush always gets me moving."

Squirrely finally sat down at the table. "You sure you ain't got no liquor in here?"

"Gave up my drinking habit some time ago. You boys would might consider it."

Joshua shuffled slowly out the back door, the Black brothers paying him no mind. As soon as it closed he straightened up and plowed through the snow to the outhouse, but instead of going inside, went around to the rear, where a pair of snowshoes hung on the wall. *I'm not about to give these shady fellas a chance to do me harm. Time to skedaddle.* He strapped on the snowshoes and moved slowly up a narrow path away from the cabin, a steep uphill climb. *Old man eh? Lord give me a five-minute start and they're not likely to catch up.*

Five minutes later Merle spoke up. "Go see what's keeping gramps."

Squirrely got up and walked out the back door, returning a minute later. "He's done lit out of here. Ain't no sign of him, just some kinda tracks heading up the mountain."

Merle rushed outside and inspected the tracks. *That old son of a bitch has snowshoes on.* He took a few steps to follow, sinking into the snow past his knees. Shaking his head, he returned to the shack. "Let him go. He's likely to run out of gas and freeze to death. I'm not about to go chasing after him."

Meanwhile, a hundred yards up hill, Joshua turned north along a low ridge, following another faint trail. *A half a mile or so then back down to the valley. Slow and steady should get me to Confluence in a couple of hours.* He tightened the snowshoe straps, turned up the collar of his coat and trudged on.

But the going was tough. The decent to the river proved treacherous, his way often blocked by drifts taller than he. Near exhaustion, it was mid-afternoon until he made it to the river, *Lord help me. At least I can walk along the side.* He turned north toward Confluence. *Two more miles.*

About the time Joshua left the cabin, Hawk and his neighbor Abner left Confluence, travelling south along the east bank of the Yough. They'd already visited a half dozen cabins, some close and some further up the many little hollows that lined the valley. Often needing snowshoes, the going was slow and strenuous Now both men were panting some.

Abner stopped and pulled his pack off. "Let's take a little blow." He pulled some venison jerky from the pack, grabbed a chunk and passed the little bundle to Hawk. They spent the next few minutes chewing in silence as their breathing calmed.

Hawk checked his pocket watch. "We got time to check a few more before heading home. Let's keep moving before we stiffen up." As they rounded a small bend in the river Hawk stopped suddenly. *Who's that?* "Hold up. Look up river." A small bent figure was walking toward them, head down and moving slow. *That's not our outlaws.* He cupped his hands to his mouth. "Who goes there?"

The old man raised his head and, seeing the two, waved. "Joshua Sechler." He continued his slow trek. Abner and Hawk rushed to meet him. *What's old Josh doing out on the river this time of day?"*

They finally came together, Joshua grabbing Hawk by the arms. "Ain't you two a sight for sore eyes. I'm 'bout tuckered out."

Abner took his pack off and dug out the jerky. Joshua took a piece and gnawed it ravenously. "I was running out of steam."

Hawk pulled out his canteen. "Have a drink. What are you doing out here Josh? Ain't fit conditions for man or beast."

Josh grabbed it and took a big swallow. "Much obliged. Some fellas stumbled into my place late Sunday. They's a couple of no-goods, struck me as dangerous. So I took a chance and lit out of there, figured I could make it to town. Not so sure I would have." He took another drink. "The big guy's Merle, called the little fellow 'Squirrely' and he sure was." Joshua told his tale of the two days he'd spent with the Blacks "Now what brings you two out?"

Grim-faced, Hawk told of the murder of old George. "It's surely them that done it. We've got men out searching up and down the valley." He turned to Abner. "You go on up and stand watch at the turnoff to Josh's place. I'll get him to town and send some men out on horseback to relieve you. We might need to wait to go in on them."

Joshua nodded. "They's armed and dangerous for sure, and stuck there for a while. I'd send some men in from behind, back the way I come."

With that, the men split up and went their separate ways.

Chapter 45

Homestead Pennsylvania was a mill town, had been since 1881. The Homestead Steel Works was constructed then, along the south bank of the Monongahela River. Purchased by Carnegie Steel in 1883, its sprawl of buildings and smokestacks dominated the town. More than half of Homestead's 12,000 residents worked at the mill, most of them immigrants. Hungarians, Poles, Slovaks and Slavs lived together, a mélange of nationalities lumped together as "Hunkies." They were the human fodder that powered the plant, working the most perilous jobs for the lowest wages. And they often payed the biggest price. In the next year one of four would be hurt or die.

Homestead was also a name destined to live forever in American labor history due to one event: the Homestead Strike of 1892. H.C. Frick, then President of Carnegie Steel, cut wages. When the workers refused to accept the wage cuts, Frick responded. He shut down the mill on June 28th of that year. The workers soon surrounded it, stopping Frick from reopening it with non-union workers. In a subsequent battle between the workers and armed Pinkerton agents hired by Frick, a dozen were killed, including 10 workers. Anarchy reigned, the state militia called in. After an failed attempt to assassinate Frick on July 23rd, the strike was ended and the union broken. Frick was the most despised man in America, Andrew Carnegie close behind.

Nowhere was that hatred stronger than in Homestead. Wounds there had never healed.

Nine years after the strike, the evening of Tuesday, January 15th, Kurt Straub was walking down Second Avenue. Dozens of smokestacks spewed their black discharge into the air. Yesterday's snow was already covered with a dark crust. He stopped at the last building on the block, the last one in a row of identical small homes. An old woman in a long black dress answered his knock, a shawl around her stooped shoulders. She nodded and stood aside as Kurt entered the small front parlor.

"Bako is expecting me."

Another nod. "In kitchen." She shuffled over to a small sofa, sat and returned to her mending.

Kurt entered the kitchen, where a man sat alone at a small table, some papers spread in front of him. He was perhaps 50 years old, a few white streaks in his jet black hair. A long bushy mustache, mostly gray, drooped down his face. His most distinguishing characteristic was a black patch over the right eye. Kurt took off his coat and joined him at the table.

"We've run into some problems. Our Friday operation did not turn out well. One of our men was killed, another now jailed. And the man responsible for this is likely behind it." Kurt pointed to his left arm, no longer in a sling but hanging limply at his side.

Bako locked Kurt in a stare with his one good eye, black as the night. "You're sure of this?"

"I am. My agent at Frick headquarters confirms two visits by Mr. Zajac."

"How much money you have in the pot?"

"Two thousand. We plan another raid for this week."

Istvan Bako hated H.C. Frick, perhaps even more than Kurt Straub. The patch he wore covered an eye blinded during the 1892 battle. His only son was killed last year in an accident at the mill. Since then he thought only of revenge. *Kill the capitalists. Destroy the mills. Bring down the government.* "If you want Barat to help with your plot you need twice that. And we'll need even more for delivering my final blow."

"But you have your other resources for the mill plan."

"And all for that only. I have men to help but you must pay the price. That was our agreement." Bako rose and pulled a bottle from a cupboard. "Already it's costing me money."

He sat the bottle on the table along with two small glasses. "You have a plan to deal with this Zajac?" He poured some whiskey into each.

Kurt nodded. "He will be dispensed with on Saturday."

"To his poor health then." The two clinked glasses and drank.

Chapter 46

Wednesday, January 16th was a bitter cold day in Confluence. Arctic winds drove temperatures to zero, but the morning dawned to a clear blue sky. The sun rose and reflected off the fresh snow, producing a blinding light.

Joe Zajac's train pulled into Confluence station near 9:30. Backpack on one shoulder, he crossed the street, boots crunching on hard-frozen snow. The Christian Church was his destination. *Glad I wore my snow shoes.* He would be early for the 11:00 funeral. *Hope the doors are unlocked.* Climbing the front steps, he hauled on an iron ring and the big door dragged open. *See if I'm the first one here.*

Joe was not the first arrival. George Harkins was already there, his closed coffin perched on two wooden horses. Joe sat on a bench in the rear, removed his boots and replaced them with good shoes from the pack. As he was stowing the pack and boots under the bench, a side door opened. In walked Adam Humbert, carrying a black bunting. Joe watched in silence as Humbert affixed the skirt to the front of the coffin. Then he removed the lid and stood, examining the contents. After straightening George's jacket, he bowed his head for a moment, then turned and left the way he'd come in.

Joe removed his cap and walked to the coffin. *Old George. We'll track down the murderers.* With a sign of the cross, Joe said his prayer. *Rest in peace.*

He took a seat midway back. A few minutes later he heard voices and turned to see Deputy Edsley, with Sky and Hawk Harkins right behind, come in. The deputy was talking.

"Boys, you sure it's the same ones that murdered George?"

Hawk nodded. "Sure as we can be until we grab them. Joshua Sechler said they was wild, and had a jug of whiskey when they showed up."

"And you're sure they're still at the cabin?"

"We checked yesterday, saw smoke from a fire. They've lost their horses, we been watching the path out since yesterday."

Sky spoke. "I was up half the night, 'bout froze. Nobody left Josh's place."

"We'll move on them after the services."

Joe jumped up and joined them. "What's this all about? You found the Black Brothers?"

Edsley nodded. "Mayhaps we did. We'll know soon enough."

As Hawk caught Joe up on the events of yesterday, Sky noticed the casket and walked slowly to it. "Don't worry Pop. We'll send your killers to hell." He turned away and rejoined the others. "I want to lead the men in."

More people entered the church as Joe sat back down. Henry Brooks soon joined him. By 11:00 the pews were nearly filled, save for the first ones. Organ music began to play lowly. Joe turned to see Buck, John and Hawk Harkins standing with George, Jewel and Pearl. They filed down the aisle and filled the front pew, Hawk and Jewel together in the middle, she dabbing her eyes.

From beside the altar a preacher entered the chapel and walked to the pulpit. He was young, clean shaven and wore a stiff white collar. After affixing a pair of reading glasses to his nose, he spoke to the crowd. "It is with heavy hearts we gather here this morning to mourn the passing of our friend and brother George Harkins. Let's join today in song as we commit his soul to its heavenly repose."

The music got louder, Joe now recognizing the song. The preacher belted out the first words, most of the congregation joining in. "Nearer, my God, to Thee, nearer to Thee! even though it be a cross that raiseth me, still all my song shall be, nearer, my God, to Thee."

The service was a testimony to the life of George, and to his breed of self-sufficient men who had settled the Youghiogheny valley. In turn, George and Buck delivered their own heartfelt memories of a caring grandfather and life-long friend. Then many others, unknown to Joe and mostly anonymous, rose to do the same, until all who wanted to speak were heard from. After a final blessing, Adam Humbert came from the rear and closed the coffin lid. "Folks, there will be no burial service at this time. The family invites you to join them in the church hall for further fellowship and remembrance."

With that, the organ again played as people left the service. Joe and Henry stayed behind, along with the Harkins men. Together they carried George's coffin out the door onto a waiting sled, a single horse hitched in front. They watched as Humbert led the rig away, then went to the church hall. Inside, small groups mingled, in turn offering condolences to Pearl and Jewel. They all joined Deputy Edsley, who was standing in the rear with two young men.

"Plenty of time to grieve for George after we round up those that done it. Here's my idea. We'll travel up river in one of Groff's wagons. He'll meet us at the bridge at noon. These two can come in from the back, the way Joshua got out. The rest of us will move in from the river. Now let's get organized."

As the men dispersed, Deputy Edsel turned to Buck. "We've got a wagon full. I've a room at the Hotel Dodds. Use it if you wish. We'll be back by three I figure."

Buck shook his head. "I'll follow on my horse then. You'll not leave me behind."

The deputy considered this for a moment, then nodded. "We'll squeeze you in."

At just after noon, the men reassembled at the river bank. A large delivery wagon sat there mounted on two sets of iron runners. "Groff's Transfer" was painted on the side. Two draft horses were harnessed to the front, Mr. Groff holding the reins. The men climbed in and huddled together.

Joe was ready, wearing recently purchased hat, gloves and heavy coat. *Glad I brought the .45.* All of the others were similarly attired, only the deputy standing out in a Stetson hat and long coat, a scarf wound tightly around his neck and ears. With a "hiya" and a shake of the reins the teamster urged on the horses, the heavy sled finally jerking into motion. They headed south along the bank of the river for about a mile, then stopped. The two cousins got off and climbed up the bank, then followed a faint trail up the hillside. The rig moved on, about another mile up stream, where two men were huddled around a campfire. The four Harkins men, along with Henry and Joe, followed Deputy Edsley to them.

"Any sign of them?"

Both men shook their heads. "No sign of them. They's still in there though. Smoke's coming from the chimney."

"We'll give the boys some time to get into position before we move in." The men huddled closer to the fire and waited.

Chapter 47

*   *   *

Inside Josh Sechler's cabin, the mood of the Black Brothers was foul. Squirrely was again pacing the floor. "We've got to try and get out. Food's gone and I'm 'bout crazy. Going on three days now."

Merle shook his head. "It's still too cold out. We'd freeze before we made the pike."

"What about the old man?"

"What about him? He likely froze trying to get away."

Squirrely just shook his head and kept pacing. "Tomorrow I'm leaving, first thing. We need to get."

"All right then. Now stop that pacing around. It's getting on my nerves. Go get some wood."

Squirrely's shoulders slumped as he walked out the back door.

Meanwhile, 20 yards or so up the hill, the two Harkins cousins were in place, watching as Squirrely walked to the wood pile. Both had rifles trained on him.

"We could drop him now."

"The deputy said wait."

The men held fire as he returned to the cabin.

On the river side, the posse was climbing up the path. As they crested a small rise, the cabin sat 100 yards away at the bottom of a low gulch. The hillside rose again behind it. They stopped for a moment to deliberate. Buck spoke first.

"I'm a bit winded. How 'bout I stay up here in reserve."

Edsley nodded. "Hold your fire until we see if we can take them out alive. I'd like to see them stand trial for their crimes."

"Sure deputy." Buck left the trail and moved along the ridge line to a spot where he had a clear view of the cabin.

"Let's the rest of us move to the bottom and fan out. Once we're in place, I'll call them out. Just watch the front door."

The six men moved slowly down the hill and spread out, John Harkins with Joe and Henry on the left, the others in front. Deputy Edsley stood, hands cupped to his mouth. "You men in the cabin. This is Deputy Edsley. Come on out."

Inside, the two brothers looked at each other across the table. Then Squirrelly jumped up. "I told you we should have got out of here. The old man made it to town."

Merle got up and pulled a pistol from his pack, along with a box of bullets. He stuck the gun in his belt and retrieved a rifle from the corner. "Let me do the talking." He went to the front door and cracked it open a few inches. "What's your interest in us? We's just friends of Joshua."

"That's not the way he tells it. Come on out now boys or face the consequences."

Merle closed the door. "Go look out back, see what you can see."

Squirrelly, rifle in hand, crept out the door. Peaking around the side of the cabin, he spied John Harkins, standing toward the front of the tree line. He levelled his rifle and fired a shot, the round striking a tree just behind John. Pulling his revolver, he fired several more times, then retreated. Several rifle rounds slammed into the door frame as he returned to the cabin. Merle looked at him, shaking his head.

"You at least hit one of them?"

"Not that I saw. There's men up the hill behind, at least one on the side."

"And more out front. We's surrounded and pinned down."

"What're we gonna do Merle?"

"Either go out shooting or surrender, and I'm not ready to die yet. All they can pin on us is some robberies."

"Easy for you. I'm the one that killed Half-moon and the old man."

At that moment the deputy called out again. "Any more shooting and we'll blow that shack up. Now come on out."

Merle propped his rifle in the corner and lay his pistol down. "I'm coming out unarmed." He opened the door and stepped onto the porch. Deputy Edsley came out from the trees. "Where's the other one?"

In an instant Squirrelly jumped through the door and fired at Edsley, the shot hitting him in the thigh. A second later a shot rang out from a distance and Merle fell to the ground, as his brother returned to the cabin.

Simultaneous gunfire erupted from three sides of the shack, rounds breaking out one window and penetrating the door. Hawk and Sky retrieved Edsley and pulled him back to the woods. He was bleeding heavily from the leg wound. "Better tie me off. I think he clipped a vein." Hawk pulled off his belt and used it as a tourniquet, the blood flow in due course slowing. By then the shooting had stopped.

Joe could see Merle from where he stood. He lay motionless on the porch, a red stain spreading under him. *Looks like he's a goner. Old Buck got him with a long shot.*

John Harkins called out. "Your brother is dead. Either come out or join him." In reply several shots were fired in his direction from the side window. He crept up to Joe and Henry. "Start firing at the window. I'll move in." They returned fire as John crouched and ran toward the building. Once close by he moved to the rear, revolver in hand. There he saw the young cousins, now in position, one behind the outhouse, the other crouched near the wood pile. John spoke loudly. "Let's burn the place down. We'll make it right by old Josh and build him a better one." In reply several shots were fired through the rear door from inside. More shots came from the front and side.

"Hold your fire. We're going to burn him out." The cousins piled wood against the rear wall as John stood with his pistol aimed at the door. Using a safety match, one of them soon had it started. Within a few minutes, flames were licking at the wall. The three backed away, taking positions across the rear. Five minutes later, the entire rear wall was engaged. Coughing could be heard from inside over the flames.

Around front, Sky and Hawk stood, rifles shouldered. Flames now spread along both side walls toward the front. Still the door remained closed. Finally a voice screamed out. "You think I'm afraid of fire? I'm heading to hell anyways." The door finally opened and Squirrelly ran out, hair burning and pants smoking. Both men fired and he fell back as the fire enveloped the front wall and porch. Ten minutes later, only a smoldering pile of ruins remained. The men moved in to find Squirrelly mostly burnt up but Merle still identifiable. Joe and Henry rolled him over, his black widow spider tattoo still visible. "There you see it. The Black Widow Gang is finished."

Joe nodded. "An end suitable for their violent ways. Maybe now your troubles at the mill are finished."

Henry shook his head. "We ran into more spiked trees yesterday."

Chapter 48

It was almost 4:00 by the time the group returned to Confluence. They'd had to haul Deputy Edsley out on a small sled they found out back of Sechler's former home. Edsley was at Doc Havner's office being attended to. Joe and Henry were sitting in the dining room at the Hotel Gilchrist, along with John Harkins Jr. Joshua Sechler sat with them and had just been informed of the afternoon's events.

"So my cabin is gone, and all my belongings as well?"

John nodded. "Sorry to say, yes Josh. We can go out there tomorrow and pick around."

"Well, I suppose it's lucky I was piss poor to begin with. That old shack wasn't much, but it was home."

"Well, I got a place up Harkins Hollow sitting empty. What say you move in up there until spring? Me and the boys will get you a better cabin built soon as we can."

Josh perked up. "Say, that's right neighborly of you John. I'll earn my keep too."

"Let's go then, while there's still some light."

The two departed, Henry and Joe remaining at the table.

"What's this about more spiking?"

"In my farthest holdings, over in Salt Lick Township, almost in Westmoreland County along Champion Creek. It's one of my father's original holdings, cut once 50 years or so ago. The timber on it now is good-sized, furniture quality hardwoods."

"When do you think it happened?"

"Hard to tell. We just sat a mill up last month. One spike we caught before the saw. The spike wasn't rusty yet. We missed the other and it destroyed the saw. The mill is down now."

"You've got more than one enemy then. It's unlikely the Blacks had a hand in it."

A waitress approached them. "The kitchen just opened for dinner. You men interested in a meal?"

Joe nodded. "Yes ma'am, I am. Seems like every visit I make up this way, I miss lunch."

"We've got a chicken pot pie—should go good on a cold day like today."

'I'll have it, and a cup of coffee."

"Make it two." Henry continued. "As the demand for lumber has increased, and prices with it, the whole business up here has changed. Used to be mostly small operators working family owned plots. My father was one of the first bigger operators, buying up land all over. Now its outsiders coming in and buying timber rights. They clean cut and leave a mess behind."

"You mentioned one before. What was their name?"

"Mill Valley Lumber. There's few others. Indian Creek Mills and Highlands Timber are both growing concerns, all big as or bigger than my operation."

Joe dug his notebook out and made a few entries. "I'll see what I can find out about them. My banker friend might would know something."

"Much obliged. Dinner is on me."

By 5:30, Joe was on a train back to Connellsville. *What a day, and school tomorrow.* He drifted off as the car rocked side to side.

Chapter 49

It was 8:30 a.m. on Thursday the 17th and Joe was already seated in his history classroom. He'd taken an earlier train and even had time for a quick breakfast near the station. The first one there, he was going over some notes he'd made last night. *Ten years of commotion after the French war. Battles over tax collections. Colonists wanted independence.* Other students arrived, as did Miss Hall. She surveyed the room, giving Joe a nod of approval. Precisely at nine she started her lecture.

"The years between 1763 and 1775 were tumultuous times in the English colonies of North America, after England's victory over France in the Seven Years War. In debt from the campaign, the colonies were looked upon as sources of commerce and levies, the colonists held as lesser citizens of the British Empire. These, and other events, helped to sow the seeds of independence." Miss Hall lectured and questioned the students for the remainder of the class, Joe taking more notes.

"And that brings us to April of 1775. Mr. Zajac, can you tell us what happened then?"

Joe had done his homework. "That's when the British soldiers moved to destroy the colonists' guns and powder. First at Lexington, later at Concord. First blood was drawn on both sides and the revolution was on."

"Very good Mr. Zajac. Next, we will examine the conduct of the war itself, and early attempts to unify the colonies. Class dismissed."

Joe dawdled as usual until the other students left. Miss Hall was sitting at a table, organizing her papers. "Good morning Miss Hall."

She looked up with a smile. "And a good morning to you Mr. Zajac."

"Where are we going for dinner?"

She thought for a moment. "Ever been to the Lawrenceville neighborhood?"

"Not that I recall."

"I live there. My favorite local restaurant is Rothman's. It's on the corner of 39th and Butler. The streetcar line runs close by."

"I'll find it. What time?"

"Around 6. If you get there early, I'll look for you in the bar room." She packed up the papers and grabbed her coat. "I've an appointment with the dean. See you then."

Joe followed her out and left for the library, where he spent the next hour preparing for his afternoon class. Looking up at the clock on the wall, he noticed it was almost noon. *Better go grab some lunch.* Five minutes later he was walking through the door of The Grape. Looking around, he saw that all of the tables were filled. *Guess I'll go stand at the bar.* As he approached it, he noticed Professor Burns standing at one end. Joe slid in beside him.

"Mind if I squeeze in here Professor? The joint is jam packed today."

"Ah, Mr. Zajac. It always is on Thursdays. Be my guest."

"Much obliged." A waitress showed up with a bowl of onion soup for the professor and a glass of wine.

"Here you go Conrad." She turned to Joe. "What's your pleasure?"

"I'll have the soup and a cup of coffee."

"Coming right up."

A few minutes later, she returned with his order. Conrad had already finished eating, and turned to Joe. "Where's your dining companion today?"

He's talking about Grace. "My companion?"

The professor smiled. "Come, come Mr. Zajac. Are you familiar with the word 'coy'?"

Joe's face reddened a bit. "Miss Hall and I shared a table is all. I'd not refer to her as my 'companion.'"

Conrad nodded, a serious look on his face. "Of course. The University would frown on such familiarity. And for your information I am quite fond of her myself, in an avuncular sort of way."

Avuncular? I need a dictionary to talk with this fellow. Joe finished up his soup in silence as the professor sipped his wine. He pushed the empty bowl away and turned to the professor.

"You're a well-educated fellow. I've got a question for you."

"About our coursework?"

"Not exactly, more about current affairs. Politics."

"Ask away then."

"What's your opinion about women being given the vote?"

Conrad paused for a moment before answering with his own question. "Let me ask you this. Although we've not gotten to it, Aristotle, and many other philosophers, have delved into the concept of justice. Have you made it that far in your reading?"

"I have, at least I've read it over once. I'm still working to understand some of it."

"I'd say that the idea of not permitting women to vote challenges the very notion of distributive justice he espouses. That is, equal shares for equals. Now, in Aristotle's time, and to a large degree still, women are not looked upon as being the equal of men. Do you agree with that?"

There's another thought I've not considered. "The Bible says a woman should be obedient to her husband. I never thought about it much beyond that."

"The Bible also says that a slave should be obedient to its master. But the world has moved beyond that idea. Other than the obvious physical differences, do you think women are intellectually inferior to men?"

"Some are, but some aren't I'd say."

"Just as all men are not equal intellectually. So the sexes are really the same in that regard."

Joe nodded. *I know Peggy is smarter than I am, I've admitted as much. Grace too now that I consider it.* "But women have always kept house and such."

"Yes, that's true, a biologically driven imperative when we humans all still lived in tribes, just as it was the more robust men who did the hunting. But, once again, our modern world is quite a different place. In my opinion there is only one reason men have come to dominate women. They are physically stronger."

Joe thought about that for a moment. *I see what he's driving at.* "And men are accustomed to running our politics and business. I don't figure they'd give that up freely."

"And that's where women like Susan B. Anthony and Elizabeth Cady Stanton come in. Women are willing to fight for the right. In the end they will not be denied. We've freed the slaves, let's free the women from their masters, too." The professor looked at his watch. "Come man, decide. We've class to attend. Are men and women equal as humans or not?"

Hard to deny that as true. "Yes we are."

"Then justice demands they get the vote." With that, the professor rose to depart. "See you in class Mr. Zajac."

Joe rose to follow. *Conrad has a good head on his shoulders. I'll do what I can to help Peggy.*

Joe's afternoon class passed quickly, Joe still somewhat distracted. *Don't feel much like studying. Wonder if I could catch up with Charlie Kilpatrick down at Carnegie. Got some time to kill.* It was almost four when he arrived at the Carnegie Building. The same security guard greeted him as he exited the elevator.

"Yes sir? May I help you?"

"Name's Joe Zajac. I was wanting to see Charlie Kilpatrick. He's not expecting me."

"You the same fellow was here last week?"

"I am."

"He's back there. I'll check and see."

A few minutes later he returned, Charlie right behind him.

"Mr. Zajac. What can I do for you?"

"I had a few more questions regarding what we discussed last week."

"Come on back then." Joe followed him back to his office. "The conference room is in use."

Joe sat down across the desk from Charlie and pulled the Barat pamphlet from his briefcase. "I'm sure these fellows are tied up with the payroll robbers. They called themselves "The Reapers" and used the same bible passage in their tracts."

"That doesn't surprise me. I've come to the same conclusion. Barat has continued to court the Hunkies. They've started having regular meetings, even have a place in Homestead they say is a social club. According to my men it's crowded at all hours, but I've not been able to get a man inside."

"You heard about last Friday's action?"

"I did."

"The man we captured gave us some information. The gang has a hideout near Connellsville I'm going to stake out. Any more acts of sabotage?"

Charlie shook his head. "Nothing too suspicious."

"I wonder if they'd let me inside of a meeting."

"You're too long off the boat buddy. You still speak Polish?"

"Still remember a bit. You're likely right though. How's the wheeling and dealing going?"

"Getting down to the end looks like. There's a big meeting planned for next Friday afternoon. Frick and Morgan will be coming down from New York to meet with Carnegie."

"If Barat and the union men know that, next week should see more violence. How about I stop by again on Tuesday?"

"Sure Joe. I'm here most afternoons. And as for the unions, Carnegie has likely bought them off. He's quietly raised wages for those jobs, a move likely to forestall any trouble from them, at least in the short run."

Their business concluded, Joe packed up and left Carnegie Steel headquarters just before five. *Don't feel like riding the streetcar.* He approached one of the cabs parked outside. "Looking for a ride to 39th and Butler in Lawrenceville."

The driver nodded. "Twenty-five cents, paid in advance." Joe paid up and climbed aboard the cab, which was more like a two-seat carriage. The inside was well appointed, with leather seats. The cabin walls were covered in what looked like brocaded silk. *Pretty fancy.* They arrived at Rothman's Restaurant at 5:30. The two-story brick building had a main entrance on the corner for the dining room and a separate bar entrance just up the street. *Grace said meet in the tavern.* Boisterous chatter greeted him as he entered, the long bar mostly filled. Joe found a spot to squeeze into near the middle. *Kind of a fancy place. Makes The Star look shabby.* The bar top was made of white marble with a polished wooden front. *Looks like cherry.* The foot rail and spittoons were similarly gleaming. *Our new place needs to look this good.* The bartender, a big fellow with a handlebar mustache, approached.

"What's your pleasure?"

Joe looked at the taps. "I'll try a glass of that Iron City lager if you please."

The bartender nodded. "Lawrenceville's finest, brewed just up the street." He drew a glass and sat it in front of Joe. "Want a shot?"

"No thanks, just the beer."

"Five cents."

Joe put a dime on the bar and took his beer to the other side of the room, where a long and less-crowded counter ran the length of the wall. Lifting his glass, he took a long pull. *Got a bit of a bite to it.* He passed the time thinking of nothing in particular, content to watch the other patrons. *Been a long day.* Just before six he saw Grace Hall come in and survey the room. He gave her a wave, she noticed and joined him.

"Hello Joe. I've reserved us a table in the dining room." Several of the men at the bar had turned her way, staring silently. "I'm afraid this is sacred ground, reserved only for the male of the species." Joe finished his beer and followed her through a short passage to the restaurant. She waved to a fellow standing near the front door. "That's Hans Rothman, the proprietor." He pointed toward an empty booth on the far wall. He met them there and set two menus on the table.

"Guten abend Miss Grace. A pleasure to see you as always."

"And you Hans. Say hello to my dining companion, Joe Zajac."

Hans extended his hand. "Willkommen Mr. Zajac. A drink for you?"

"A glass of Iron City if you please."

"And the usual for you Miss Grace?"

"I think I'll join Joe in a beer tonight Hans."

He gave them a nod and a small bow as he departed.

Grace smiled at Joe. "Hans is a dear man, his food authentic and delicious."

"You've been to Germany?"

Grace nodded. "I toured all of Europe after college. I enjoyed Germany but loved Paris most of all."

Hans returned with their drinks. "Ready to order?"

Grace gave the menu a glance. "Any specials tonight Hans?"

"Oh yes. Hilde made a big batch of jaeger schnitzel. And there's a sausage sampler, the best wurst in town. Ha-ha."

"I'll have the schnitzel. Joe?"

"Make mine the sausage."

"Coming right up."

Grace raised her glass. "Prost."

Joe raised his in return. "Sto lat." They both took a drink.

"You can still speak Polish then?"

"I can, but I'm out of practice. I was 15 when we came to America."

"You said you lived in Philadelphia?"

"Yes, after my father was killed in a coal mine explosion up near Scranton. I was a lucky boy, my uncle Stan able to take me in. Thanks to his kindness I was able to finish high school. You could say I've had an easy time of it."

"Then I'm a very lucky girl. My father made a small fortune off of some family land in Ohio when they discovered oil on it. He sold to Rockefeller around 1880 and then went to work for him, eventually managing refineries here in Pittsburgh. He is gone now, as is my mother. As their only child I was left quite well-off."

Well-to-do. Wouldn't have guessed it. "How long did you live in Paris?"

"Three wild and care-free years."

Hans returned carrying a tray with their meals on it. He served Grace first, her plate filled with small slices of breaded meat served over a bed of noodles and covered with a creamy mushroom gravy. Joe's plate held three fat sausages, with a mound of potatoes on the side. "That's a bratwurst, a knack-wurst and a liverwurst, with warm German potato salad." He added a basket of dark rye bread and a jar of mustard to the table. "Aufessen. Eat and enjoy!"

Joe's mouth watered. *Smells good.* "What's jaeger schnitzel?"

"It roughly translates into 'hunter's cutlet'. The meat is venison."

"I had that for the first time two weeks ago, up in Ohiopyle."

"Oh I love it there, my family visited many times in summer."

The two ate in silence for a few minutes, Joe sampling each of the sausages. *All three are delicious.* "Don't know what's in them but they sure are good." In no time his plate was clean.

Grace smiled, her plate still half full. "Glad to see you enjoyed your meal. For some, German food is an acquired taste." She put a few pieces of her schnitzel on his plate. "I'm finished. Care for a sample?"

"Sure, I'm game." He ate the small portion in two bites. "That's tasty too." He sat his fork down and pushed the plate back. "This is as good a meal as I've had in some time."

Hans returned and spoke to Joe. "And how was it Mein Herr?"

Joe nodded and smiled. "You were right Hans. That was the best wurst I've ever had."

"And Mein Fraulein?"

"Wonderful as always Hans."

"Room for some dessert?"

Joe shook his head. "None for me."

"Nor for me Hans. We'll finish with some Kirschwasser."

"Excellent." He cleared the table and gave it a wipe.

"What's this you've ordered us?"

"Oh, just a little libation. It's a German style of liquor, 'Cherry Water' is the translation."

Hans returned with a bottle and two small glasses, filling each in turn. "The perfect end to a meal." He left the bottle on the table.

Grace lifted her glass again. "Now start with a little sip. It's potent stuff. To a fine meal and good company."

I guess a little cherry water won't hurt me. Joe touched his glass to hers. "To my favorite teacher." Despite her warning he fired it down in one swallow. *Damn, that is strong, but sweet too.* "Tell me about your time in Paris."

Grace took a little sip of her drink and sat it down, staring into space for a bit. "It was a beautiful time to live there, the 'Belle Époque.' Peace and prosperity reigned, the arts flourished. I was just the right age to enjoy it. I'd travelled enough to have become world-wise but was still young enough to enjoy the adventure."

"What sort of adventures?"

"Visiting the museums, lunch at the cafes, watching the artists working along the river. And the night life was fantastic."

"You were there alone?"

"Yes, a small set of rooms all to myself. But I made many French friends."

On her own in Paris. "I had my good times in Philadelphia but I doubt it compared."

"There is a big difference between Paris and American cities. Women may go wherever they wish, alone or in groups of other women, including to saloons and nightclubs. And some of those were unbelievably wild."

Joe took the bottle and poured himself another glass, taking just a sip this time. "Wild as in rough joints?"

"Wild as in outrageous and bizarre. Places like the 'Cabaret of Death' where the tables were coffins and 'Cabaret of the Inferno' where she-devils served the drinks. They made the Moulin Rouge look like a church picnic."

Joe finished his drink and poured another. *I thought those waterfront saloons in Philadelphia were bad. And this cherry water sure goes down smooth.* "I'm not world-wise, not by a long shot. But you don't strike me as a wild woman."

"And what do I strike you as Joe?"

Uh oh. I'm on the spot. "That's hard to say as I've never met a woman quite like you before."

Grace held her hands together in front of her, fingers interlaced, and smiled sweetly. "Pray tell me more."

She has a quick wit. "You're no shrinking violet, that's for sure, and better educated than anyone I've known, man or woman. Except for maybe Conrad Burns. He's a smart cookie."

"I'm not the wild young woman I was in Paris. The night life became a bore once the initial fascination wore off. But I was never a shy person, you are right about that." Now it was her turn to take a drink, draining her glass. "And now shall I tell you how you strike me?"

Joe took another drink. "I'm game."

"I've not met a man quite like you either. No one even close since I left Paris. You are genuine, unpretentious and also a 'smart cookie', whether you realize it yet or not."

Joe finished his drink and poured them both another. *No more after this. I'm feeling it.* "I'm going to need a dictionary to understand all of that, but I'll take it as a compliment."

"As it was intended."

They sat in silence for a while. Then Joe spoke again. "How'd an attractive woman like you stay single?"

Grace leaned forward, closing the distance between them. "I've had my suitors. But I'll not be any man's property. The closest I came was with a man in Paris. We were quite the couple, even lived together for a time. But in the end we were too much alike." She took another sip. "Now I'll ask you the same. How is it a smart and handsome man like you isn't married?"

We're moving at a fast clip here. "After reading a bit of Aristotle, I'd say that my life was, until of late, one devoted to pleasure. I had no interest in marriage or family life. I've come to appreciate that's not enough for me in the long haul." Joe paused, staring at his drink, then met Grace's eyes. "There's only been one woman of consequence in my life, and she reminds me some of you."

"And what became of her?"

"We met in August, her father the owner of a bar I patronize. We saw quite a bit of each other over the last four months but we've grown apart of late. Peggy's a fine woman but I don't know what the future holds for us." *I'm damn near drunk. Time to shut up.* "Beg pardon, be right back."

Joe walked unsteadily to the men's restroom. Inside, he stood at the urinal, swaying slowly back and forth. *I am drunk. Grace was right. That's some potent stuff! Time to head home.* He finished up and returned to the table.

"I've had a fine time tonight, best in quite a while. But that cherry water has hit me hard. Time to hit the road before the road hits me."

"All right Joe. I feel the same way. Let's do it again on Tuesday."

Chapter 50

Joe was dreaming about Paris. He and Grace Hall were strolling arm-in-arm along a wide boulevard, the Eiffel Tower visible in the distance. Stopping to watch a painter at work, she wrapped her arm around his waist. Turning, they kissed.

Somewhere in the distance, Joe heard a bell ringing rapidly, the sound getting louder and louder. Paris and Grace faded away as Joe awoke with a start. He silenced the alarm and fell back, smiling. *That was a strong dream.* He lay there, recalling last night. *Barely remember the ride to the station. Slept the whole way back.* Grace had accompanied him in the cab to see that he made the train. *And the kiss, not a dream.*

Joe got up with a grunt. *Dry mouth, headache. I remember why I gave up the liquor.*

An hour later he was finished his breakfast, a heavy and soothing plate of biscuits and gravy. Tony came and sat beside him.

"You talk about those papers with Mr. Norton yet Joey?"

Joe shook his head. "Not yet, but my next stop is the bank."

"Mr. Morton stop by yesterday. He says someone else looked at the spot."

"I'll go see him then after I talk to Dave. Did Franco go look at the second floor?"

"We both go last night. Franco says the finish is an easy job. He making a list of what he needs."

"Good work buddy. We'll be in business before you know it."

"I trust you to do the smart thing." Tony left as Joe finished his coffee. Just as he was getting up, Johnny came in.

"Stick around for a minute."

"What's up?"

"First off, a deputy came to pick up Gus. I got him to check on Charlie Krouse and I was right. He did his time and was released. And old Gus was plenty mad when he heard the fellow over at Standard was still alive."

Joe smiled. "Too bad for him. And now I'm sure of it. Our boy Charlie and Kurt are still around and holed up down Dawson way. I've some business to attend to, then I'm going down there to see what I can see."

"Sure you don't want some company?"

"I'm sure. Let's meet here tomorrow for breakfast, say around 8:00. I'll let you know what I find out."

Joe moved up Main to the First National Bank. Dave Norton was at his desk. He saw Joe and waved him over.

"Morning Joe. Come by to visit your money?"

Joe shook his head. "I know you'll keep an eye out for it. I have some papers for you to look at, need some advice." Joe pulled the lease and offer to sell out of his briefcase. "Tony found us a spot for our restaurant over in New Haven on the corner of Third and Main. You know Walter Morton?"

"I do. He's a local real estate investor and builder. His brother-in-law has a construction company. They are both solid fellows."

"You familiar with the building?"

"I am. It's well-constructed and in a good location."

Joe handed Norton the papers. "We talked of renting the first floor. Then I got the idea to just buy the place, pay myself the rent."

Norton took the papers and looked them over briefly. "I can offer my opinion regarding the price. The space is unfinished?"

"Neither floor is finished. The upstairs could be made into three apartments according to Morton. I'm working up a bill of materials."

"Knowing Morton was working with his brother-in-law, and unfinished, I'd say his price is certainly negotiable. You'll need an attorney to help with negotiations and the papers."

"I figured on that. Got one in mind?"

"I do, one of the fellows that started up this bank is a fine one, name of Porter Newmyer. He's got an office upstairs."

"The fellow that built the opera house?"

"One and the same. If you want, I'll make the introduction."

"I'd appreciate that Dave. Pass on the papers. How's these lawyer fellows work? Pay in advance?"

"In a way Joe. He's require something called a 'retainer,' an advance payment he will work against. I'd say $50 should be sufficient."

"Take $100 out of my account. I need some pocket money."

Norton smiled. "I'm enjoying this Joe, watching a former Frick cop turning into a local businessman."

"Just make sure I don't do anything stupid buddy. See if Newmyer can meet at one. I'll stop by then. Meanwhile I'll go tell Morton we're working on a deal."

By 2:00, Joe's business was attended to. *Newmyer's a sharp fellow.* He'd met with Morton, stopped by The Star and spoke with Peggy briefly. *She's calmed down considerable. We'll let nature take its course.* He'd stopped by his rooms and changed into his cold weather gear. Remembering Johnny's advice, he took his revolver. Pack by his side, he was on a streetcar heading for Dawson. *Ready for a little walk in the woods.*

The streetcar line ended at Dickerson Run, just across the Yough. Close by was a stable where he was able to hire a small sleigh. By 3:00 he was travelling out River Road. When it turned away from the river, he led the horse up a rough lane next to the railroad tracks until it ended at the stream Gus had mentioned. He tied the reins to a tree and, pack on his back, headed down the tracks. After walking for about 10 minutes, he stopped, examining the hillside. *That's better than a quarter mile I've walked. He said the entrance was well-hidden. I'll head up the hill and see what I can see.*

The uphill walk was a struggle, Joe pushing through snow and brush. Eventually, the slope evened out a bit, running flatter along a small rock face. *Looky here. There's a little coal seam in that rock.* Joe turned and headed back the way he came. After a bit, he spied a spot where dead limbs and brush were heaped against the rock. Further on, he noticed what looked like evidence of recent foot traffic. *This might be the place.* He took off his pack and began pulling the brush away. Eventually a small opening was revealed. After rolling a few rocks aside the mine manway was fully exposed. *Found it!*

"Looks like that Pollock is as stupid as you thought." Joe turned to see Charlie Krouse, pistol in hand, standing behind him, a Mr. Kurt Straub at his side. "Turn around, hands up."

I am a dumb ass for coming out here alone. Joe did as he was told.

Charlie moved in behind him. "Say goodnight you piece of shit." He hit Joe's head with the butt of the gun, laughing as Joe crumpled to the ground.

Chapter 51

✳   ✳   ✳

Joe gradually regained consciousness to find himself trussed up and put down on cold stone, back against a wall. After a bit, he became aware of voices, barely audible through the ringing in his ears. In due course he was able to make out the words. *It's Straub doing the talking.* He stayed still. *Like to crack my skull. Damn, my head hurts.*

"Bako says next Friday. Once we finish with Mr. Zajac, we'll clear out of Dawson."

Joe moved his head a little. A sharp pain shot down his neck. Moaning, he squirmed in spite of himself. Joe opened his eyes to see Charlie and Straub sitting at the makeshift table, a kerosene lantern turned low casting a dull glow. Straub stood, a smile on his face.

"Looks like our guest is awake. Hello Mr. Zajac. It's a pleasure to finally meet up with you again. I've had my eye on you since last week."

Joe struggled at his restraints, hands tied behind him, legs bound together at the knees and feet. With some effort, he was able to rise to a seated position. After moving his neck around some, the sharp pain faded to a dull ache. *Least my neck's not broken.* Joe recognized Straub easily, even with the beard, and noticed his left arm hung limply at the side. In spite of his pain, he smiled.

"Wish I could say the same. You're lucky I'm a bad shot." His smile became a grin. "Say, looks like you've got a broken wing there, buddy."

Straub took a few steps closer, squatting until he looked Joe in the eye. "Still the wise fellow. Yes, it's a little souvenir of our last encounter. None the less, I survive. You won't be as fortunate."

Charlie joined them. "Can I kill him now? He's cost me a brother and a cousin."

"I've a better plan for his end. However, I will let you inflict a bit more pain on our Polish friend." Straub picked up a short piece of board and handed it to Charlie. "Give him a good wallop on the left shoulder."

Charlie smiled and took the board. "My pleasure." He swung, connecting with Joe's shoulder and arm. The blow sent him tumbling to the side.

Joe saw stars, and passed out again. He came to, terrible pain radiating from his shoulder and into his chest and arm. *He must of broke something.* He didn't even try to rise. Straub and Charlie were still standing beside him. *Couldn't have been out long.* Another moan escaped his lips.

"He's back. Now we can proceed." Straub produced a short fat candle and sat it on the floor in front of Joe. "Light it please Charlie, then go prepare the fireworks."

Charlie gave one final kick to Joe's midsection, turned and left. Straub squatted back down toward Joe.

"Here is what the future holds for you, my friend of Frick and the rest of the robber-barons. Do you know why they stopped working this little mine? Ran into a pocket of fire-damp. While much of it has dissipated, it's still here, especially further back. One has to be very careful with an open flame." He stood back up. "We'll be leaving you now. On our way out we'll be blowing up the entrance. If you are fortunate enough, the roof won't fall on you. Or maybe you would be lucky if it does. Lacking a front entrance, the mine should fill up with methane long before the candle burns out. Then there will be an explosion. Perhaps before then you will pass out from lack of oxygen, but I hope not." Straub turned and walked away, still talking. "For whatsoever a man soweth, that shall he also reap."

Joe lay in the dim light of the candle, slowly regaining his senses. The sound of Straub's feet receded, the room now absolutely silent. *Looks like the end of the line.* He was able to squirm around until, facing the wall, he prepared to meet his maker. *God, I am sorry for having offended you.* Joe's confession was cut short with a boom. The floor shook. Pieces of roof fell to the ground. Joe felt the wind from one landing close to his head. A cloud of dust rolled back from the entrance, filling the room. Eventually, the room became quiet again. Coughing and gagging from the dust, Joe again struggled to a seated position. *I'm alive.!*

Alive, but in rough shape. As the dust settled, Joe took inventory of his injuries. *Head hurts. Stomach sore. Arm aches like the devil.* He surveyed the room. One big piece of rock had fallen in the middle, a few smaller ones here and there. *But they all missed me.* Legs extended, he strained to loosen the ropes. *A bit of give, but strong knots. Got to get out of these bonds.* He sat staring at the candle. *My only hope.* He inched forward until his bent legs were as close to the flame as he could get, then leaned back until his hands rested on the ground. Spreading his feet as far apart as the ropes would permit, he was able to expose a short length to the flame. Then, very carefully, he extended his legs until the rope was just above the flame. His left arm throbbed. *Can't hold this long.* Just as he was about to drop, the rope smoldered, then caught fire. Pushing his feet apart as hard as he could, it burned through. Now able to spread his feet further apart, he rested one on each side of the candle.

Joe's face was covered in sweat, more from the pain in his arm than the effort. He sat quietly for a while, taking slow, deep breaths. Then he inched forward again, until his legs were bent over the flame. *Hope I don't catch my pants on fire.* Slowly he inched backward, knees dropping closer to the flame. *This one's a bit looser.* He was able to separate his legs several inches. *Got it.* The ropes once again smoked, then caught, Joe straining to push both legs outward. The rope broke with a snap and caused him to fall backward, landing again on his injured arm. "Owwwwww.".

Joe lay still until the pain subsided. *Think I'm gonna puke.* After a few dry heaves, his stomach calmed. Somewhat renewed, he again sat up. *One more to go. Be working blind on this one.* He was able to spin around until his hands were close enough to the flame that he could feel the heat. *Lucky I wore this wool shirt.* Using the heat as a guide, he maneuvered his arms until he could feel it on his wrists. *These are still tight. Just have to let it go.* He could feel the heat build. Holding steady, he pushed his arms apart, the pain in his arm worsening. *I'm catching fire!* He could smell smoke. *Come on!.* With jerk, the rope let go. Joe hauled his arms around front. His shirt cuffs were smoldering. He put both wrists between his legs, smothering out the flames. *Praise the Lord. I'm free.*

Yes, he was free, but exhausted. Slumping forward, he let out a groan. *Now what?* Able to stand finally on unsteady legs, he leaned back against the wall. Then he picked up the candle and slowly walked the perimeter of the room. In the rear was a passage but other than that the walls were solid. He moved to the table, placed the candle on it and sat down. His feet struck something. *What's this?.* Under it sat his jacket and, beneath that, his pack. He pulled it out and examined the contents. *Took my gun of course. What's this?* At the bottom lay a small paper sack. Inside was a sweet roll he'd bought on the way out of town. *Shoulda packed a sandwich.* He pulled the bag out. Underneath was a container of matches and a small penknife. Both went in his pocket. Then he looked at the candle. *Methane building up.* Joe started shivering, although it wasn't very cold in the mine. *Too tired to think.* He cleared the table and lay on his good right side, using his jacket as a blanket and pack as a pillow. Then he blew out the candle and fell asleep.

Chapter 52

Saturday morning, Johnny had just left City Lunch. Joe had not shown up. *I warned him.* His next stop was Joe's place, where his knocks were unanswered. He'd moved on to The Star. Nicky was at work mopping the floor.

"Morning Nicky. Joe happen to be around?"

He shook his head. "No sir Mr. Davidson. I'm the only one here."

Something happened to him down at Dawson I'll wager. He returned to City Lunch. Franco was clearing some tables. *I need to take someone with me, but it's not police business.* Tony emerged from the kitchen.

"You find Joey?"

"No. He was doing some investigating yesterday afternoon, down Dawson way. We had a lead on those payroll robbers."

Tony shook his head. "I tell him so many times. Be careful. He never listen."

"I told him the same. I know about where he was headed but don't want to go after him alone."

Tony grabbed his coat off the rack. "I go with you."

"No, let me Tony." Franco had been listening. "Be right back." He sat his tray on the counter and disappeared into the kitchen, returning in a minute, coat on. "Let's go."

As they walked to the streetcar terminal, Johnny told Franco about the events of last week and what they learned from Gus. "So I've already been shot once by these fellows. I've got my pistol."

Franco opened his coat where the butt end of a .45 showed above his belt. "I'm no stranger to gun play. Joe tell you about me?"

"No."

"I'll tell you on the way. You picked a good compagno."

It was almost 10:00 when the two arrived at Dickerson Run. Franco had talked almost the entire way, Johnny intrigued by the tales of his life on the streets of New York. *Makes Fayette County look peaceful.* Franco was indeed the right man to bring along.

"I know where he was going and doubt he'd set out on foot." Johnny looked around and saw the stable across the street. "Let's go get us a ride." They entered the building to find the proprietor feeding his horses. "How do. You have a little sleigh to rent?"

The man nodded toward. "I do. One dollar for the day, be back by five or it's another dollar."

"You rent one to a tall, slim fellow yesterday?"

"I did, the same one."

"He return it?"

"No, but some other feller did. And returned it late to boot."

"My name's Johnny Davidson. I'm a detective with the Connellsville Police. What did the fellow that returned it look like?"

"Big blond youngster. Paid the extra, no squawking."

Charlie Krouse. "Much obliged. We'll take it."

A few minutes later, Johnny and Franco were on their way across the bridge to Dawson.

*   *   *

At the time Johnny and Franco were heading out on the sleigh, Joe was just waking up. *Can't believe I slept so long.* He lay on the table, stomach rumbling. *Damn I'm hungry.* Sitting up, his hand found the candle. *Hungry and stiff but still kicking. Let's check this place out again.* He pulled out a match and, hesitating for a moment, struck it. *Phew.* Lighting the candle, he got up. His left arm swung, the pain of his injury still sharp. *Wish I had a sling.* He looked at his pack and, slinging both straps over his right shoulder, he was able to lay his arm across it, taking some of the weight off. *That's better.* Then he returned to the entryway. As he approached, he detected a bit of daylight at the top of the rock pile. *Not wholly sealed up.* Carefully climbing, he was able to get to it, an opening but just a few inches wide. He pressed his face closer. *Can't really see anything, just sky. But what's this? There's some air moving.*

Now, Joe was no mine engineer, but he did have some common sense. *If it's coming in here, it's going out somewhere. Must be a ventilation shaft in back, like at Leisenring.* He descended with care and headed back down the manway. *What's this?* Laying on the floor by the side was a roll of paper. Joe picked it up and returned to the table. When unrolled, a map of Pennsylvania was revealed. He sat the candle in the middle for a better look. *Someone's marked it.* Head bent close, Joe examined the tracing. *That's the Pennsylvania Railroad mainline, from Philadelphia to Pittsburgh.* Tracing the route with his finger, Joe crossed the state. Just outside of Altoona he noticed a dot. *Made on purpose.* With a shake of his head, he rolled the map back up and stuffed it inside of his jacket. *Does me no good in here. Where's that air moving to?* Candle in hand, Joe returned to the rear room. He blew out the candle and, after his eyes adjusted back to the darkness, was able to detect a faint light, high in the back corner. Relighting the candle, he moved toward it. Holding it high, he was able to identify the source. *Had to be an air shaft in here.* He maneuvered under it and could make out a sliver of light, the top of the shaft not far from the roof. *Might be I could work my way up it, bad arm and all.* He returned to the first room, sat at the table and thought about his predicament. *With some effort I could haul this table back, maybe reach the roof.* Upon closer inspection, the table was made of three wide wooden planks sitting on two big barrels. The seats were smaller kegs. *It's all I got to work with. What if Johnny missed breakfast?* He pulled off one of the top planks and, with his one good arm, pulled it toward the back.

*　　*　　*

Franco and Johnny were at the turn on River Road. "We keep going North." He pointed up the railroad tracks. "There. Runner trails." They followed the trail until it stopped at the creek. "We walk in from here." Other footprints were visible in the snow. "Come on." The two broke into a trot, following until they turned up hill. Both men stopped to catch their breath. Franco looked up the hillside and pointed. "There."

About halfway up, a brown patch of dirt and a pile of rocks was visible on the field of white. "Looks like a blast site." Again, they hurried up the hill. Arriving at the spot, Johnny nodded.

"Right where Gus said the entrance would be." He climbed the rock pile. "Joe! Joe!' No reply was received. He pulled out his gun and fired a shot into the air. "Maybe he'll hear that."

Inside, Joe was standing where the table had been. Only the two big barrels remained. *Moving the boards was hard enough. I'm played out.* At that moment he heard the shot. *What's that?* He hurried back up the manway, climbed the rock pile and shouted out the little crevasse. "In here. In here." A moment later Johnny called back.

"You okay Joe?"

"Alive but hurt. Only got one good arm."

"We need to get more men and equipment."

"No time for that. There's gas building up in here. I found an air shaft though."

"What in Sam Hill is going on here?" Johnny turned to see an old man standing behind Franco, rifle in hand.

"Easy there, buddy. I'm Johnny Davidson, Connellsville Police. We've got a man in there."

"What in tarnation? That's a dangerous spot. I should know, it's my old mine."

"Who are you?"

"Raymond Keffer. My place is just over the hill. I heard this blow yesterday, come out to have a look-see. Then I heard your shot."

"Know where the air shaft is?"

Raymond nodded and pointed up hill. "Sure do. It's on top of the hill there."

Johnny turned back toward the rock pile. "We got lucky Joe. There's a man out here says he knows where the shaft is. Go on back there."

"Will do. Hurry up. I'm getting hungry."

Johnny smiled and climbed down. "What's the best way up there Raymond?"

"Follow me. We'll go around and come up from the other side, toward my place. Ain't as steep." He strode off. "And we better stop by there first and get some rope."

Twenty minutes later, the three stood next to a big wooden box, the lid slightly askew. "I covered it up. Looks like someone's been fiddling with it You boys pull it all the way off."

"I got it." Franco grabbed one edge and yanked it free. Johnny leaned over the side. "Joe. You there?"

A face appeared at the bottom, visible in the noon sun. "Johnny. Thank the Lord."

"Can you tie a rope?"

"Not likely. My left arm is in bad shape."

Johnny thought for a minute, then lashed one end of the rope around his chest, running under his arms. "Franco. Think you can do the dropping and lifting?"

He just nodded, wrapped the rope around his chest and tied the other end to a nearby tree. Then he braced himself next to the box. "Go ahead."

Johnny climbed over the side and started his decent, feet pressed to the side wall. He could hear Franco grunting as the rope lengthened. "Almost there." It wasn't long until he touched bottom. *Maybe 50 feet.* He turned to see Joe sitting on a keg. His left arm was still cradled in the makeshift pack-sling. Joe was barely recognizable through the black grime on his face. His pants and jacket were torn and filthy. Johnny shook his head. "You are in rough shape."

Joe rose, with obvious stiffness, from his seat. "Don't I know it. Get me out of here."

Johnny untied himself and hitched Joe to the rope. "You ready for a ride?"

"Let her rip."

"Franco. Pull." With a jerk, the rope went taut. Joe yelped as he started rising. Length by length, he disappeared up the shaft. A few moments later, the rope reappeared, and soon Johnny joined the others on the surface. They got untied and, after re-covering the vent, all hiked toward the Keffer cabin. As they approached, a low rumble shook the earth.

Raymond shook his head. "Wonder what sat it off? Got you out in the nick of time."

The candle. Joe shrugged. "I'd say."

Chapter 53

✳ ✳ ✳

Later that day, Joe and Johnny were in The Star, beers in hand. Joe was cleaned up, well-fed and patched up, his left arm in a real sling. "Doc says he thinks the collar bone is just cracked."

"Lucky they didn't kill you outright. Now what?"

"We get the sheriff to make some inquiries down Dawson way, though its likely they've cleared out."

"Another payroll was hit yesterday morning, a Rainey operation this time."

Joe pulled the map out of his jacket. "They've something bigger planned. I remember Straub saying something, just as I was coming to, about 'Bako says next Friday'. You ever been to Altoona?"

"Yes indeed. Rode around Horseshoe Curve many times. Mother and I would ride up there just for fun."

"What's the lay of the land?"

"Hilly. Isolated. About five miles west of Altoona. The railroad follows a long climb out of town, toward the highest ridge on the main line. The curve turns around a reservoir. Higher ground rises to the outside."

"I know one thing of Straub. His actions spring from a hatred of H.C. Frick more so than efforts to help the working class. Maybe Frick himself is the target this time instead of his holdings. It wouldn't be the first attempt." Joe knew of the Homestead Strike and subsequent events.

"Frick spends most of his time in New York now. He's not just a steel man. He's a 'financier,' like his friend J.P. Morgan."

And they're both coming to Pittsburgh this Friday. "One reason I got brought on by Carnegie Steel is there's a big deal's in the works. The two of them are coming to town." Joe told him a bit about the deal making and negotiations.

"And you think Straub is planning something?"

"Don't see him robbing payrolls for a living in the long term." Joe finished his beer. "I'm done for the day, need to go sleep on it."

*   *   *

Later on that evening Kurt Straub was back in Homestead. He, Charlie and two other men were sitting at the kitchen table in a duplex a few blocks away from Bako's. Straub was smiling.

"You say you could hear the explosion?"

"And felt it half way to Dawson."

"I hope the end was slow and painful for Mr. Zajac. Now let's get some rest. It's a busy week ahead."

Chapter 54

✳   ✳   ✳

Joe was up and at it on Sunday, going to an early Mass and grabbing a late breakfast before heading to The Star. Although still closed, Nicky was cleaning up. Joe sat in the office, notebook and calendar open in front of him. The notebook page was headed "Frick & Morgan Attack." Under that, he'd started a list:

1. Call Scottdale
2. Call Charlie at Carnegie
3. Security on train – layout

The private car is usually the last one, after the baggage car. We'll need a contact at the railroad. The crew needs to be on alert. He'd been thinking about the likely plan of attack all morning. *They'd have to stop the train. Something on the tracks. High ground to the outside means they'd come from the inside. We can surprise them. But who?*

The front door opened and in walked Peggy, dressed in her Sunday best. Her church was just around the corner. As she walked toward the office, Joe was glad to see a smile on her face. That turned to a frown as she walked in and looked at his arm.

"Now what Joe. This week it's you?"

"It's not as bad as it looks. I'll likely be out of the sling in a day or two."

She took of her coat, hung it up and sat down. "Tell me what happened."

For the next few minutes, Joe told her of his visit to Dawson and reunion with Kurt Straub and company. He did not tell about the mine explosion. At the end she just shook her head.

"What good will the money do when you are dead? I don't know what your police work amounted to while in Philadelphia, but from what I see, your work here often ends up with personal injuries."

Joe's face reddened. *Can't argue with that.* "I admit, I'm no Sherlock Holmes at detecting, nor a sure shot. But I am on the trail of Straub. I know what he's up to and I'm duty bound to stop him." *Time to change the subject.* "How are the meeting plans coming?"

Peggy brightened up. "Very well. Did you see the ad in the Courier?"

"No. And there's a story too?"

"Indeed, and a complimentary one as it turns out. Not every man sees women's suffrage as a challenge. The response has been so great that we're having it at Newmyer's"

My attorney's place. "He's a supporter?"

"With three daughters, indeed." The two sat in silence for a moment, locked in a stare that Joe finally broke.

Now's not the time and place. "You need the office?"

"I do. Oh, and Henry Brooks is in town. He took me to dinner last night, told me all about your mountain adventure. That's even more gun play you're involved in."

Joe got up from the desk. "I was not in danger. The Harkins men did the work. Old Buck, he's some sure shot."

"Henry's at the hotel. Said to tell you to stop by if I saw you." Peggy got up and they stood close together. "He also said you stopped a family feud and brought a young couple together. You are a good man Joseph."

He smiled and nodded, packing his briefcase. "On occasion." Squeezing by, he left the office. *At least no harsh words today. And I'm back to being a good man.*

A bit later, Joe found Henry having his lunch at the hotel dining room. Joe joined him at the table.

"Henry. Glad to see you're still in town."

"I've got business tomorrow. Came down early so I could see you." He pointed at Joe's arm. "What happened?"

"I made mention of the work I've taken on for Carnegie Steel. It continues to prove riskier than I'd foreseen." Joe told him some of what was going on. "I need to figure out how to hide a small band of men on the train out of Altoona, ready to respond if Straub tries something."

"Best way might be to hide them in plain sight."

"That's a good notion. Just have them sit among the passengers. But they also need to be sure shots. My own accuracy is limited at best. Can't imagine how Buck hit that man from 100 yards uphill."

"He's a lifetime of practice on the white-tails. All of the Harkins men are good with firearms, both rifles and pistols."

Maybe they'd help. Sit them in the coach, some mountain men travelling to the city. "Maybe I could enlist them. What time are you going back tomorrow?"

"The noon train if I get my business finished."

"I'll go with you, see if I can talk them in to it."

"Imagine they will. They feel in your debt."

Joe dug his calendar out and made note of the plan. "You said you looking to see me? What's on your mind."

"The tree spiking. I'm not the only Stewart Township lumberman having trouble over Salt Lick way. Two other fellows, friendly competitors, told me the same has been happening to them."

"Anything else?"

"Mill Valley Lumber approached me, interested in buying some or all of my holdings."

I forgot about them. "I've yet to see what I could find out about those fellows. I'll do so tomorrow morning."

"Thanks Joe. I'll see you at the station tomorrow."

Chapter 55

*   *   *

By 8:00 Monday morning, Joe was at The Star and had Tom Lynch on the telephone. He'd just told him of his run-in with Straub.

"I remember hearing him say something about 'Bako on Friday.' Put that together with the map evidence, and with Morgan and Frick likely coming to Pittsburgh that day. I would take some extra precautions."

"I can confirm those plans. Work through Kilpatrick. He'll advise Carnegie. Frick and Morgan will be informed. They never travel without a contingent of armed Pinkertons."

"I'm planning on riding that train with a small force of men. Get word to Kilpatrick and tell him I'll see him tomorrow afternoon."

Joe finished up his work and was at his bank when it opened. He caught Dave Norton as he walked toward his desk.

"You're up and at 'em early again today Joe. What can I do for you?"

"What do you know of Mill Valley Lumber? According to what I hear, they're a big and growing concern up in the mountains."

"Mill Valley. Nothing I know of. No accounts here in that name."

"Thanks in any case." Joe saw Porter Newmyer transacting business at a teller window. "There's my lawyer." Joe waited for Mr. Newmyer to finish his business, then approached. "Morning to you. I was wondering, did you see Mr. Morton on Friday?"

"I did indeed. Come on upstairs."

Joe followed to the rear of the building, where an elevator waited. Newmyer's office was on the top floor. From the window, Joe could see the busy Main Street scene below. He waited as Newmyer pulled some papers out of a drawer.

"Here we are." Newmyer was almost Joe's height but with a full beard and mustache that almost joined his bushy sideburns. From the gray streaks, Joe guessed him 50-plus years. "Yes, I met with Walter Friday. When I explained that we were coming with an all-cash proposal, his ears perked up. I offered him $3,750. He called his partner, then countered to $4,000. What do you think?"

"I think you earned your $50. That leaves me plenty to finish off the insides and outfit the restaurant. Draw up the papers. The sooner we can get to work the better." He began to leave then had an idea. "Say, you do legal business with mountain folks?"

"I do, some. My mother's family is from Springfield Township."

"Ever hear of Mill Valley Lumber? I hear they're a big outfit up that way."

"I might have, now you mention it. I'll ask my uncle. He still owns some timber land up that way."

"Much obliged."

Joe stopped back by Norton's desk. "Looks like we made a deal. I'll need a check for Mr. Morton."

"I'll talk to Porter. We'll draw up a bank check." He stood up, hand outstretched. "Congratulations Joe, and best of luck to you and your ventures."

"I thank you for the help Dave." Joe left, in a hurry to tell Tony the news. He entered City Lunch to find both he and Franco, drinking a cup of coffee. Only one table was occupied. Joe sat down with them.

"Good news today boys. Looks like I've struck a deal with Morton. We have us a restaurant and apartments to build."

Tony jumped up, grabbing and pumping Joe's good arm. "I no believe it. Joey, you crazy and I love you. When we get started?"

"Maybe as soon as Wednesday."

Franco pulled a sheet of paper from his pocket. "Here's your bill of materials. I figure maybe $1,000 to do the apartments up nice. Another $1,500 to do the restaurant, including furniture and china. That's with first class materials."

Joe did some quick math in his head. If the restaurant made money he'd earn that back after a few years, and still own the building. "I want a white marble bar."

Tony was called away by the other table. Joe turned to Franco. "I need some help later on this week. Might be early Friday."

"What kind of help?"

"The kind where you bring your gun."

"For you boss, whatever you need. Just let me know."

After having breakfast, Joe walked to the B&O station, bought his ticket and settled on a bench to read the Saturday *Courier*. Toward the rear was the article about Peggy. It mentioned her management of The Star and her looking after her father's "other interests." *Wonder what those are?* The article was fair, presenting both sides of the issue. Joe was well familiar with the topic by this time. Once again was mentioned the links between the Suffragettes and the temperance movement. *That's a big part of it. Men thinking that women will outlaw alcohol.* On the page next to the article was a small advertisement for the meeting and mention of the NAWSA organizers. The announced start time was 7:00pm. *I'm going to stop by after I get back.*

Joe continued his reading until he heard the whistle of the approaching train. As the arrival was announced, Henry came through the door from his hotel just across the street.

"Morning to you Joe."

"And to you." Joe followed Henry out to the platform and, a bit later, they were riding up the hills to the south of town. Joe pulled the Pennsylvania map out of his briefcase. "I've been thinking about this, was able to verify a few facts this morning with a fellow at Frick. Private cars are hauled to the rear, after the baggage car. They have two doors and two smaller windows on each side."

"What sort of attack do you suppose they'll do?"

"A rapid advance, not a large force. Get close enough to blow up the car. They're not interested in taking prisoners. Then a quick escape back the way they came."

"And your men would drive them off from the baggage car?"

"Something like that. I've not worked out all of the details yet."

Henry looked at Joe, nodding. "You better."

The trip to Ohiopyle was uneventful and the two were soon on their way to Harkins Hollow. Upon arrival, they found Hawk and Buck at home. Joe had just finished telling them of his work for Carnegie and his plan for Friday.

"I'm not positive there will be an attack, but if so we need to plan a surprise. All that is required is a few stout defenders. I'd see Carnegie pays you well for your time and efforts."

Hawk responded. "That's not necessary. I'm personally in your debt. Hell, I bet Buck would enjoy a train ride."

Buck jumped up and took his rifle down from the rack. "Damn sure would."

"And your father and Sky if they're willing. Come on down to town Thursday evening I'll have rooms for you at the Water Street Hotel, across from the station. We can meet for dinner, say at seven."

"We'll all be there."

The men shook hands all around, then Joe and Henry headed back to Ohiopyle.

"Henry, these other lumbermen having troubles, have they received offers from Mill Valley?"

"I didn't ask them. I will next time I see them."

"And ask around again about the Mill Valley operation. I'd like to know who are the men behind it."

Henry soon dropped Joe at the B&O station and by 4:00 he was riding down the mountain toward town.

Chapter 56

*   *   *

Joe went to The Star upon his arrival and was in the office. He had Sheriff Miller's deputy on the telephone, relating the weekend's events.

"If you could get your deputy down that way to check around some, they weren't staying in the mine."

"Will do. Call back Wednesday morning."

Business concluded for the day, Joe went home to catch up on his homework. At a bit before 7:00, he closed his books. *Time for Peggy's meeting.* He got cleaned up and arrived at Newmyer's Opera House a few minutes before. The seats were half full. *Big crowd.* He took a seat in the rear. *A few other men.* Joe noticed a fellow up front, pad and pencil in hand. *Maybe a reporter.* Looking further, he noticed Porter Newmyer a few rows forward. There were three young women seated next to him. *His daughters.* Promptly at 7:00, Peggy walked out from the side curtain and stood at a lectern, center stage.

"Good evening women, and you few brave men, of Connellsville and Fayette County. Thank you for coming out tonight to show your support for women's suffrage." Peggy gave those two words a throaty emphasis, causing an echo. The assembled women applauded and cheered. 'Without further ado, I'd like to introduce Miss Catherine Johnson, director of the Pennsylvania chapter of the National American Woman Suffrage Association." A small slim woman of middle years joined Peggy, her black hair worn in a bun. Warm applause and more cheers rose from the crowd.

"Thank you Miss Patterson, and thanks to all of you for attending. This is a battle that has gone on too long. I for one am getting tired of asking for my political rights. It puts the man as the grantor, the woman as the applicant. I'm through with it."

The woman's voice was firm and strong, its volume belying her small stature. She'd moved from the lectern, walking back and forth in front. "I'm through with asking. I stand here tonight demanding them! For myself and every other woman in America. We demand them!" She continued to stalk the stage, arms held behind her back. "And it's time to take the battle to the home front. Time to make the men who say they love us explain where they stand. Time to let the fathers and husbands out there know that we will not be denied."

Joe could feel his own pulse rise. *Damn. That little woman has the power.* The room was rocking its assent. *I see some of what's behind my troubles with Peggy.* Miss Johnson continued speaking, and by the end the crowd was standing on its feet. She stepped back and, as the room quieted, Peggy returned to the lectern.

"The purpose of tonight's meeting is to organize the Fayette County lodge of our state chapter. To do so, we need 25 signatures on a petition to them. I have the papers laid out on the table. Those interested in signing up please do so. Help yourself to a pamphlet after."

A line immediately formed at the table. *More than 25 already. Looks like Peggy is in business.* Joe saw the three young Newmyer women join the line. He went to say hello to their father.

"Evening Porter."

"Joe, you a suffragette supporter too?"

"Might say. I've at least come around to an understanding of the issue."

"Say, I happened to see my uncle today, asked him about the Mill Valley operation. He says there's whiskey money behind it. Mentioned a family up there, the Prinkeys. They've been making whiskey in Salt Lick and Springfield for close to 100 years. I never could see how they got away with it, as big as the operation got. They're going legitimate though, just got one of their distillery operations certified by the state."

Joe took out his little book and made note. "Much obliged. You get back to Morton?"

"Yes and he accepted the offer. We can close the deal at my office on Wednesday morning, say 9:30."

"I'll be there." The men shook hands and Joe returned to his seat. The signup line was still long. Groups of women stood talking, others sat reading the pamphlet. He saw Peggy chatting with one of the groups. *And look who's with her. Miss Margaret Foley.* Joe hitched up his trousers, smoothed down his hair and joined them, standing next to her. The talking stopped as Joe approached.

"Good evening ladies. Best of luck to you in your efforts." Then he turned and walked back the aisle, Peggy catching up with him halfway.

"Joe, you are a man of mystery. What caused you to attend?"

"I've changed my thinking on the matter. Women and men are equal. They deserve to be treated equally."

Peggy looked at him with knitted eyebrows. "What's brought this about?"

"You can thank my Philosophy professor for explaining it to me."

"It warms my heart to hear that Joe."

"Are you busy Wednesday evening?"

"Having dinner with father."

"I'll stop by after, say around seven."

"Come at six and join us."

Joe nodded and smiled, leaving Peggy standing, chin in hand. *We'll get this resolved one way or the other come Wednesday.*

Chapter 57

Joe was on the early train to Pittsburgh and the first to arrive at his U.S. History class. He sat in the rear and reviewed the chapters as the other students trickled in. His injured shoulder, though still painful, no longer required the sling. Miss Hall came in at five of nine, closing the door behind her. "Good morning class." Taking a few minutes to organize her notes, her lecture started soon thereafter.

The class period, as usual, passed quickly. As was her habit at the end, Miss Hall asked questions of her students. "And what were the weaknesses of the Articles of Confederation?" Joe raised his hand. "Mr. Zajac?"

"The general government was very weak. The organization was unwieldy and raising funds from the states difficult."

"Very good. That takes us to the United States Constitution. We will devote the next two class sessions to it. Please read the relevant textbook chapters and the Constitution itself prior to our next meeting. Class dismissed."

Joe, of course, held back and was the last to leave. He joined Grace at her desk. "That was an excellent lecture Miss Hall."

"I bet you say that to all of your instructors, Mr. Zajac. Have you recovered from the Kirschwasser?"

"It took the next day, but yes. You did warn me. It was a timely reminder of why I stopped drinking the hard liquor."

"We spoke of another dinner. If you are still interested, I'd like to invite you over to my home this evening."

Her place? "Yes, I'm surely interested. But I don't want to put you out. We can go back to Rothman's."

"I won't be put out. I have a woman who helps out around the house. She's a wonderful cook too." Grace dug in her purse, pulling out a card. "Here's the address. Come any time after six."

"I'll be punctual Miss Hall. I know your opinion of tardiness."

Grace smiled. "You do. See you then."

The remainder of the school day passed quickly. By 4:00, he was once again at the Carnegie Steel building, waiting for Charlie Kilpatrick, who was coming down the hall.

"Mr. Zajac. Good to see you. Come on back." Joe followed him, past his office, to the conference room. Inside, several other men sat at the table. Joe and Charlie sat down and the men were introduced. "Bill here is with the Pennsylvania Railroad. These two gents are with Pinkerton."

"Men, as Charlie has likely told you, I've reason to believe that a Mr. Kurt Straub and others are planning an attack on Mr. Frick. It's likely to come this Friday, and to occur near the Horseshoe Curve." He told the tale of The Reapers from the start, including the events in the mine. At the end he pulled out the map. "In our favor, Straub thinks I'm dead and doesn't know I heard him talking or that I found the map. He will figure on there being Pinkerton men on board and be prepared to fight it out with them."

One of the Pinkerton fellows spoke up. "And we'll be ready for them. I'd rather the amateurs stay out of this Charlie."

"I've talked directly with Morgan and Frick about this. They say let Mr. Zajac do what he suggests."

The man shrugged. "All right. Go over your set-up again."

"They'd have to stop the train to attack. It won't be going very fast here." He pointed to the dot on the map. "I'd send a track inspector out to give it the once-over in the morning."

The railroad man was taking notes. "I'll need the names of your men. You'll need to identify them to the conductor."

Joe nodded. "The attackers are crude and violent. Like as not, they'll detonate a charge at some point. If anything happens, we'll make for the baggage car. Our rifles will be packed in a crate there. And make sure the windows will open."

"Will do. And if the train is stopped or comes under any form of attack, the engineer will be instructed to reverse his direction and get back to the Altoona station."

"The lay of the land says any attack will come from the inside. What's the cover?"

"There's a narrow band of woods between the track and the reservoir in spots. Other than that, it's open ground."

The group spent the next hour speculating over how an attack might unfold and what the response would be. In the end, it was obvious that much would be improvised. Finally, one of the Pinkerton men stood up.

"And likely all of this is for naught. I say the danger of attack is overstated. But our men will be ready none the less." With that, the meeting ended. On his way out, Joe stopped Charlie. "See if you can find mention of this Bako guy."

Joe was soon on his way back to Lawrenceville. The cab dropped him off at Miss Hall's home just after six.

Joe stood for a moment, surveying the three-story, red brick house, complete with dormers and a wide front porch. While not a mansion, it was the biggest house on the street. Joe noticed many windows of stained glass and the fancy Victorian trim. *No, not quite a mansion, but a fine place. Just fancy enough.* He climbed the stairs and gave the doorbell knob a twist. The door was answered by an old woman in a black dress and white apron. She gave Joe the once over and fixed him with a stare. "Yes? May I help you?"

Joe doffed his cap. "Evening Ma'am. Name is Joe Zajac. Is this the Hall residence?"

Before she could respond Grace came out of the parlor. "Joe, right on time. Give Anke your things and join me."

Joe handed Anke his coat and hat but held on to his briefcase. He took it with him into the parlor, where Grace was already sitting in a chair by the fireplace. Joe sat in another. A small round table was between them. Anke returned with two glasses and a bottle, and sat them there.

"Nothing strong tonight Joe. Just a little aperitif. It's a dry sherry." She filled the glasses half-way. "To your studies Joe. May the seeds of wisdom sprout in thy fertile ground." They clinked glasses and took small sips.

"And to the university, and the learned instructors who plant those seeds."

They took another sip, then sat back in the chairs, both staring at the fire. Finally, Grace broke the silence.

"This is my favorite spot in the house, especially on a cold day. I usually prepare my lecture notes here."

Joe looked around, the parlor also a library, with bookcases built on two walls. Both were jammed to overflowing. "You've quite the collection of books."

"And this is just the overflow. I have a small office in the back and it's filled too."

"Lived here long?"

"Almost five years. Bought the place after my mother died."

"I've been living in a two-room joint for longer than that. It's time for me to spread out some."

"How was your weekend? Anything exciting happen? Are you hot on the trail of Mr. Straub?"

Joe laughed. "That trail got too hot." Joe offered an abbreviated version of his weekend adventure and today's meeting with the Carnegie Steel men. Grace listened in silence, a serious look on her face.

Joe was wrapping it up. "So come Friday we'll know one way or another. I wish I had a better idea of how it might all play out but we'll be ready as we can. One thing I do know is I've had good luck guessing what Straub is up to and somehow stopping him."

Grace sat her drink down. "That is a fascinating story Joe, yet told calmly. And now you're going to go shoot it out on Horseshoe Curve, a band of mountain men at your side. Are you brave or foolhardy?"

"I'm working hard at avoiding foolishness this go-round. In fact, I'm a bit fearful to be honest. That should help keep me on my toes. And it's time

Straub is stopped once and for all. There's blood on his hands that needs to be accounted for."

Anke appeared at the parlor entrance. "Dinner is ready Miss Hall."

"Right on time. Joe, this way." She gestured across the entry hall. Joe followed Anke into a formal dining room, a china cabinet built into one end. More elaborate woodwork decorated the room, broad crown molding and intricately carved panels. Two places were set across from each other in the middle of the table. Joe held Grace's chair then took his seat.

For the next hour, Joe and Grace enjoyed a fine meal and friendly conversation. *Haven't know her long but she's not too hard to figure out. What's the word she used? Had to look it up. Unpretentious. Suits her too.* They were back in the parlor, finishing with coffee and little cookies. Anke stopped by to clear the plates. "If that's all for the evening Miss Hall, I'll be going to my rooms."

"Yes Anke, and thank you." Anke turned away and climbed the steps. "She has the apartment on the third floor. We keep each other company in this big house."

Joe yawned and stretched. *Another long day. I'm beat.* He stood to leave. "I'd say that's all for me too Grace. I've a full day tomorrow. Don't want to miss my train."

Grace stood too, her face close to his. "I have a guest room here. Spend the night. We'll get you to the station early tomorrow."

Spend the night! Joe's mind was racing. "Thanks, but I better get back to town. I've some loose ends to tie up."

"Would your friend Peggy be one of those loose ends?"

Joe smiled. "Yes, one I intend to tie up one way or the other very soon."

Grace reached out, holding Joe's hands. "You are an honorable fellow then. I thought you'd be nothing less." She leaned forward and gave him a quick kiss. "See you on Thursday."

Chapter 58

*　　　*　　　*

A bead of sweat stood out on Joe's lip. He'd just signed several papers and would momentarily be the owner of 1 North Third Street, New Haven, Pennsylvania. He pulled an envelope from his jacket pocket and passed it to Mr. Morton.

"Here you are. Payment in full."

Morton opened the envelope, examined the check and nodded. "Indeed it is, Mr. Zajac. Best of luck with your ventures." They stood and shook on the deal, then Norton departed.

"Hooray!" Joe turned to Tony, cheering at his side. The two remained, along with Porter Newmyer, in his meeting room.

"Now we can get started." Joe passed Tony the building keys. "But first we've got more papers to sign."

Newmyer pulled another file from his briefcase. "This first one is a partnership agreement between you and Joe as owners of your restaurant. You are named as the restaurant manager and draw a salary. Joe is the business manager. He funds the capital requirements and keeps the books. You split the profits equally."

"Joey, you sure we want this? I thought a handshake is all we need."

"This protects us both Tony, in case something happens to either of us."

"Like you get blown up."

Joe smiled. "I'll try not to." Tony signed and passed it to Joe, who also signed and returned it to Newmyer. He pulled a second paper from the file. "This is a lease agreement between you two as partners in the restaurant and Joe individually as the building owner. If defines a variable rent for the first year based on gross sales, with the option to set a fixed rate then for the remainder of the term."

"Joey, how you rent something from yourself?"

"It's legal magic Tony, and why the world needs good lawyers like Mr. Newmyer."

Tony and Joe signed again and the paperwork was complete. "The restaurant account has $2,500 in it. Get receipts for what you buy. I've a new ledger book at home to keep track."

"You got it, boss. I get Franco started this afternoon."

They left Newmyer's offices, Tony back to work and Joe to The Star. Once there, Joe quickly got on the office telephone with Sheriff Miller.

"Yes, I sent my deputy poking around Dawson and environs. Other than that mine explosion on Saturday, wasn't much in the news. He did find one item of note. Four fellows were staying at a Dickerson Run boarding house, checked out Sunday morning and left on a northbound train."

Could be anywhere by now. "Much obliged sheriff. You still have Gus in custody?"

"Yes, and will for quite some time. His trial is set for early March."

Might want to talk to him again. "Put me on his visitors list at the jail."

Joe hung up and pulled out his notes. The sheet was headed "Friday Plan." Item one was "where to sit."

Need to spread out. What Henry said. Hide in plain sight. Put Franco at one end, Buck at the other. The boys can sit together. I'll already be in the baggage car. He wrote the next item: "weapons."

"Hello Joe. What brings you by?" It was Peggy, at the office door.

"Mostly just to use the telephone."

Peggy came in and sat at the desk across from Joe. "I was pleased to see you at our meeting last night."

"You had a big crowd. Even Aunt Margaret came to town."

Peggy smiled. "Yes, and she also noted your attendance. I told her what you said."

"And what did she say to that?"

"Something about 'your studies haven't proven to be a total waste then,' or words to that effect."

"I'll take that as a compliment. We still on for tonight?"

"Yes Joe."

"I've more errands to run. As Lloyd likes to say, 'I'm busy as a one-armed paperhanger.'" Joe gathered up his papers and left Peggy to her business. *One way or another we'll resolve our troubles tonight.* His next stop was Tony's. *See if Franco is there.* Which he was, mopping the floor as Joe entered.

"Franco, park the mop and have a seat."

"Glad to boss." They took a table in the corner. "What can Franco do for you."

"The plan for Wednesday—I've been considering our weaponry. The Harkins men will all have pistols on them. A half-dozen rifles and ammunition will be loaded in the baggage car."

"I'll have two pistols. And this." He pulled a sap from the waistband of his trousers. "This make a big man take a nap presto."

Joe smiled. "I've one like it I'll bring. My concern is that our attackers will have explosives. Their intent will be to get close enough to the railroad car to destroy both it and its occupants."

"I was thinking too boss. I go down to Pittsburgh yesterday. I come back with some special surprise for them. Come back to the kitchen." Joe followed him back, where Tony was busy washing pots. "No mind us cousin."

Next to the back door sat a small wooden crate. Franco lifted the lid to show six round metal balls stored inside. He took one out and handed it to Joe.

What the hell? It's got a long fuse. It's an explosive. Joe held it appraisingly. *Heavy but a big guy could toss it a ways.* Joe looked at Franco, who was smiling and nodding.

"We got our own little surprise. I use these a couple of times in New York. They pack a big punch for a little bomb. The casing, she turns into shrapnel."

Joe handed the bomb back to Franco. "It's up to you to see they get used to their best effect. We'll load them into the baggage car too. Meet me at the Dinner Bell tomorrow night at seven. I'll introduce you to the Harkins men. Plan on being on the first train out of here to Altoona on Friday morning."

Chapter 59

*　　　*　　　*

Joe arrived at the Patterson's family home just before 6:00. Peggy answered the bell, a full apron on. "Good evening Joe. Join father in the parlor. Dinner will be a few minutes."

Joe hung his coat and hat on the hall tree and went to the parlor. Andy was sitting in a red plush chair, feet up on a matching ottoman. A warmth spread from the gas fireplace. Joe sat on the sofa across from it.

"How do Andy. Thanks for having me to supper."

"You're always welcome here my boy, you know that. In fact, I've not seen enough of you lately. It's more than two weeks since you were here for Sunday dinner."

"It's been a busy two weeks for me, between school work and the case I've taken on for Carnegie Steel."

"Listen Joe, when you've done that, don't ever feel you need to take on more of it to make a buck. I've got a plan, could use some help on."

"What's that?"

"You likely don't realize, but I own all of the lots running east of here, up Patterson Avenue to Isabella Road. The south side is having a real estate boom. Won't be long until all these streets are built up. I'm going to start putting up houses on my lots and selling them off."

Other business interests. Old Andy is no slouch. "That's an offer I'd seriously consider."

"And what the hell's with you and Peggy? She's been in a mood of late."

"I'm here to resolve that."

"Dinner is served." Peggy stood in the doorway, removing her apron. The three made their way to the dining room, where the table was loaded with a fried chicken dinner. "Joe, say Grace please."

"Lord bless this meal and all at the table. Amen."

The three had a pleasant conversation during the meal, Andy continuing his story of the south side real estate boom. "Who you think owns the lots on Newmyer Avenue? Porter is who. He's already built on a half dozen."

The meal ended with a chocolate pudding, after which Andy quickly excused himself. "I'm going up. I've a new book just started." He left the two clearing the table and soon, the dishes done, Joe and Peggy were back in the parlor, sitting at either end of the sofa.

"I remember the first time you fed me dinner. Was that fried chicken too?"

"No, a pot roast as I recall."

"And after, here in the parlor."

"Joe, why'd you want to see me tonight? Not to talk of old times."

"No, not exactly. But it does no harm to recall. I'm here to learn where we stand, as a couple. Two weeks is long enough. You need to decide. If we go on only as friends, so be it. I'd prefer we let the past sit, see if we can move on together."

"Oh Joe. I am sorry. And there is no harm in the recollection of that night. In fact, the memory is cherished. But if we move forward, it is as equals, deserving of the same treatment. I'm past the point where I'd pledge my obedience to any man."

"And I'm past where I'd be asking for it." Joe moved toward the middle of the sofa. Peggy did the same and they held hands. "You said I never even asked, so I'm asking now. Peggy, will you marry me?"

Her eyes moistened as she nodded. "Yes Joe, I will." They joined in an embrace, sweet kisses sealing the deal.

Chapter 60

*　　*　　*

"It's been just two weeks since I first imposed on your good nature." Grace paused to take a spoonful of French onion soup.

"And an educational two weeks at that." Joe had already finished his bowl. "The French soup the least of the them."

"And you are a fast learner."

Joe paused for a moment to compose his thoughts. "I expected Peggy and I to call it quits last night, instead I'm engaged to be married. I hope you don't feel I've led you on."

Grace smiled and shook her head. "Not at all Joe. You're an honest man, your conduct proper in my book. Best of luck to you and Peggy."

*　　*　　*

By midafternoon, Joe was again with Charlie Kilpatrick at Carnegie Steel.

"I can confirm Zajac. The meeting here is scheduled to start at 4:00pm tomorrow. The train pulling Morgan's car will depart Altoona just after noon. It's #73, destination Chicago."

"We'll get into Altoona before ten."

Charlie pushed a paper across to him. "This letter is signed by Alexander Cassatt, President of the Pennsylvania line, telling all employees to render you any and all assistance." He pushed a second paper across. "And this one is signed by J.P. Morgan and H.C. Frick identifying you and your men as temporary Pinkerton agents for that day. Should keep you out of trouble with any local authorities that might get involved."

"Much obliged Charlie. You have any luck with that name I gave you?"

"Bako, Barko, Bucco, there's a dozen more like it. Could be one of a hundred or more hunkies worked for Carnegie over the years."

"How about mill deaths? Limit your search to that."

"I'll see what I can do. Don't think we keep a master list of those."

"Might be of some help somewhere down the line."

* * *

By 7:00, Joe was back in Connellsville and at a big table with the Harkins men and Franco. Introductions had just been made. The table was loaded with platters and bowls of food.

"Serving family style tonight. We're in for some fine eating."

Buck was already shoveling a load of mashed potatoes onto his plate. "I have to admit, the larder starts getting bare this time of year. This is a feast."

Franco piled slices of roast beef onto his. "I love the meat. Pass the gravy."

For the next half hour, the six men ate and traded stories, Buck for the most part telling tales of his younger days and the Civil War.

"I tell you I saw things I wish I could forget. Gettysburg was a hell hole."

The waitress finished clearing the table. Joe pulled out a piece of paper on which he'd drawn a rough map of the Horseshoe Curve. He'd added the train as boxes in a line, each labelled in its turn: engine, tender, two passenger cars, baggage car and, finally, Morgan's private rail car. On another sheet of paper, he'd drawn a bigger box of a passenger car, showing the rows of seats.

"We need to spread out some. I'll go directly to the baggage car. Franco, you sit as far from that end as possible. Buck, you find a spot at the other end closest to me. Hawk, Sky, John, just scatter around in the middle. Be on high alert as soon as we leave the station. First sign of trouble, move to the baggage car."

Franco leaned in, examining the map and car layout. "What kind of sign you thinking of boss?"

"An explosion would be the most clear. Or if the train stops for any reason."

Buck pointed to the reservoir. "That's surely frozen over, be an easy way to advance. What's your plan once we're in the baggage car?"

"I'll go out the back door with Franco, to observe. You be ready to open the windows and lay down fire."

"That's it? Don't sound like much of a plan to me. I'd say take the two boys with you. Work your way down behind the private car, here." He pointed to a spot near the end of the train. "Then be ready to attack at the first sign of the enemy. We'll open up from the baggage car and have them in a cross fire."

Joe considered it. *Makes better sense.* "We'll do just that then. You all think on it tonight. We depart from the Pennsylvania station tomorrow at seven. See you then."

*   *   *

In Homestead, eight men crowded together in the kitchen of Istvan Bako. He was pointing to a similar drawing laying on his table. "If the events unfold as planned the train will stop here. We'll be waiting in a grove here. The Morgan car should be nearly adjacent. There is 20 feet of open space between."

Kurt Straub spoke up. "And the big bomb. It's already in Altoona?"

"Yes, and loaded on a sled and ready to travel. Let us prepare to depart. We take the night train."

Chapter 61

The sun was still not quite up when the six men reconvened the next day at the Connellsville Pennsylvania Railroad station. All were silent as they watched the train pull in. Franco supervised the loading of their two crates, then joined the others, their seats in the front end of the passenger-baggage car combination. There were no other occupants in the compartment. With only two other passenger cars ahead, the train departed for Greensburg just after seven. They would change trains there, onto an express to Altoona.

Joe watched the sunrise, a brightening behind a gray sky. *I'm guessing we've some snow on the way.* Franco had been talking since they left town, telling the Harkins men of his bombs, and the last time he'd used them.

"So these fellas, they holed up in a garage, behind a big plank door. Me and my cousin, we sneak up and light two next to it. Then we run. Next thing you know 'kabloom!' like the Fourth of July. These fellas, they come running out, hands up. The door, she's gone."

Buck leaned back, hand to his chin. "Never been to New York, don't reckon I'll make it there. Hell, I thought the mountains were rough."

"New York, she can be a tough town. But I had a rough job. And so many people. We cousins live in two rooms. Eight of us. I think I like the small town life better."

By 8:00, they'd arrived at Greensburg, soon making the connection to Altoona. The men had scattered themselves about the compartment, Joe sat alone, his mind uneasy. *Don't want any harm to come to these good men due to my judgement.* His thoughts cleared as a whistle blew. They were descending toward Altoona, the Horseshoe Curve visible in the distance. Off to his right lay the reservoir. And, as described, patches of woods were interspersed with open ground along it. To his left was a rock wall, the rail line close to it. *Just like I pictured it.* From his seat in the middle car, Joe craned his neck as they turned the curve, able at one point to see the engine and the last car at the same time. *That's some tight turn.* Ten minutes later they arrived at the Altoona station.

Franco was at the baggage car seeing to the crates. *He's a valuable man to have along.* The Harkins men had moved into the terminal building. Joe decided to take a little walk. *Stretch the legs a bit.* He found a lunch counter and stopped in for a coffee. It was 10:30 when Franco came in.

"I figure I find you eating somewhere."

Joe wiped his fingers. "Just a bite. The doughnuts are fresh."

"I have the crates waiting to be loaded. You got the conductor's name for our train?"

"I do. A Mr. Casper Taylor. The train arrives at 11:40, has a 15-minute layover, then we're off. I'll speak with him and see the crates are loaded."

They returned to the waiting room, where the Harkins men were sitting in a row. Each had a box lunch. Franco and Joe sat across from them. "Good idea to have a bite. Might be awhile until lunch. I'd split up after in case someone is watching out." Joe moved to a bench near the platform door. Time passed slowly until finally he heard the whistle of an approaching train. The station clock said 11:35. A few minutes later the train pulled in with a screech and a hiss. Joe watched as the passengers unloaded. He made for the door and down the platform toward the engine. Then he walked toward the back. *Laid out just like they said.* He ran into the conductor just before the baggage car. Pulling out his letter from the railroad president, he approached.

"How do. You be Mr. Taylor?"

"I am sir."

Joe handed him the letter. "Those are my two crates there. I'll see to the loading."

Taylor handed him back the letter. "I've been worrying on this since we left Philadelphia. I'm the one responsible for the train and its passengers. I pray your concerns are excessive."

"As do I. If anything unexpected happens, get all of the passengers down on the floor, under the window line."

The color drained from Taylor's face. "I'll be ready. The baggage car is all yours. I've told the man to sit up front."

Joe nodded and went to help with the crates. Behind the baggage car was the Morgan private car. A Pinkerton guard stood at each end. Joe gave the baggage man a quarter, who then closed the center doors and left. Joe went to the end and stepped up between the cars. He could see his men already onboard.

"All aboard. All aboard." The conductor was one car up, waving a lantern up and down. With more hissing and chugging the train departed Altoona station.

Chapter 62

The train moved forward with a chorus of clunks, as the slack between the cars was pulled out. Then, more smoothly, it gained speed. Joe sat alone in the baggage car, at a small table used by the luggage man. Both windows were already open a crack. The town passed by until they left it behind, then Joe could see across the reservoir to the other side. The train continued to gain speed as it climbed the grade. Joe stood, feet braced wide, as they rounded the horseshoe. From his vantage point he could see through the doors at the end and into the passenger car. He could barely make out Franco sitting at the far end.

They'd rounded the curve and, still climbing, traversed the long straight-away, Altoona still visible across the valley. Then Joe heard a muffled boom. The train shook and, almost at once, the engineer hit the brakes. The train screeched to a sudden halt, Joe thrown to the floor. He picked himself up at once and could see the other passengers doing the same. He hurried to open their crates.

Meanwhile, in the adjacent car, the Harkins men were up and moving toward the baggage car. Two men jumped up, pistols drawn, just in front of Franco.

"You men. Stop or we shoot."

The Harkins men stopped and turned. The two advanced toward them. Franco pulled his sap and fell behind. Then, without warning, he cracked the man on the right across the side of the head. He crumpled forward and as his partner turned he was met with a blow across the cheek. Now both lie in a heap in the aisle.

"Go on. I clean up here." Franco collected their guns as the conductor entered from behind.

"Everybody to the floor." Franco handed him the weapons. "Keep down and shoot them if they wake up. But I think they sleep good." He crouched low and moved to the baggage car, where the Harkins were already pulling their rifles out. Franco grabbed three of the bombs and put them in a sack over his shoulder. "Franco is ready." Shots rang out as the four left Buck and John. Once out and behind the car, Joe surveyed the scene. Up ahead he could see the engine, half buried in an avalanche. *There will be no reversing.* To the rear stood the Morgan car. More shots rang out. Joe moved toward the space between the baggage car and it. "Buck, Sky, set up here. Don't shoot until you can see them." The sky had darkened and a snow squall had blown in. A near blizzard, visibility was limited. "Come on Franco."

The two moved to the end of the Morgan car. He could not see inside as steel sheets had been placed over the windows. *With gun slits in the middle. I guess Morgan is prepared.* Once at the end, Joe surveyed the other side. *Woods in front. That's where the gunfire's coming from.* He could see rifle barrels pointing out of the gun slits on this side. More gunfire and Joe could see something being pushed from the woods. *Looks like a little sled.* Two men crouched behind it, pushing. Another stood and tossed a bomb toward the car. *Just like Franco's.* It rolled near but not under, and went off with a roar. The gun barrels retreated.

At that moment, gunfire erupted from the baggage car. The two men abandoned the sled and fell back to the woods. Ten yards back, Straub and Bako huddled with them.

"The men inside, something's happened. They should be attacking by now. Forget about the bomb and attack the baggage car. Their fire has us pinned down"

They all crept through the woods until next to the car. Under the cover of his mates, the bomber ran out, bomb lit in hand. Hawk jumped from between the cars and shot. The bomber fell back, bomb in hand. Seconds later, he disappeared in a cloud of snow. The baggage car rocked back, its door blown open. Sky joined him and they filled the woods with gunfire.

From the rear of the Morgan car, a man emerged. Joe recognized him from the meeting at Carnegie. He held up a finger, then, using sign language, pointed to himself and Franco, then to the woods. The man nodded and returned inside. Franco and Joe crossed the open space quickly and moved toward the front of the train. Straub and his men were pinned down. *Old Buck had it right. We have them in a crossfire.* Joe had his pistol drawn. Franco had one bomb in hand, a lighter at the ready.

From the woods two men made another run at the sled. More shots and one went down holding his leg. The other retreated. The scene quieted, then Joe could hear the sounds of sticks breaking. *They've broken off the attack, making their escape.* Joe and Franco ran straight toward the bank of the reservoir. Up the bank 20 yards, a sleigh and several horses stood. Three men emerged from the woods there. Two boarded the sled. *That one fellow, he's wearing an eye patch.* The other jumped on a horse. *And there's Straub.* Joe fired in their direction, his shots wide. Straub looked his way, recognition causing him to frown, and pulled his pistol. Franco charged forward as Straub fired in Joe's direction. He dove for cover onto the frozen pond, then rose and advanced.

By now the sleigh was well across the reservoir. The snow squall had passed and a strong sun was out. Straub had the horse underway but it struggled for footing on the snowy ice. Franco was closing the distance, now almost to him. He stopped, dug out his lighter and lit the fuse. Then, like a little bowling ball, he rolled it across the ice in Straub's direction. He pulled his pistol and fired a shot in the air. The horse bucked, tossing Straub off, then it ran off following the sleigh. Straub righted himself just as the bomb exploded. It was far enough away that it did not blow him up, but the explosion cracked the ice. The cracks ran off in all directions. Soon a hole opened and the surface started tilting. Joe ran toward Straub as he slowly slid toward the water. His pistol was long gone. A surprised look crossed his face.

"Franco, go get a rope. I want this man to stand trial for the harm he's done." Franco ran back toward the train. Joe, gun still in hand, watched from the bank.

"Looks like the end of the line for you Straub. Just calm down and we'll get you off of there."

Straub laughed. "As you say, the end of the line. But I'll not be going to jail." He leaned back, accelerating his slide. With a plop he entered the water. Almost at once he began to shiver. He held onto the edge of the ice.

"You crazy man. Hold on."

"No thank you."

Joe realized it was too late. *He's going to kill himself!* "Tell me then. Your hatred of Frick. Is he your father as you claim?"

"That, yes. And he killed my mother."

"What? How?"

"Killed my mother. Johnstown." With that Straub let go of the ice and exhaled. Slowly his head sunk beneath the surface. One final burp of bubbles hit the surface.

Crazy bastard. He's sure enough gone for good this time. Franco showed up with the rope. "Too late. He's gone under."

Chapter 63

*　　　*　　　*

J oe and Franco returned to the train. No one was seriously injured there. The fellow by the bomb sled turned out to be Charlie Krouse. Joe walked over to him as the conductor administered first aid.

"Hello Charlie."

He looked up. "You!"

"Yes. And here you are, all shot up again. I wager you'll do more than 60 days this time. Attempted murder might get you a life sentence."

He hung his head. "Straub."

"Gone, for good this time. But it might be spring before he pops back up."

Joe left him and found the Harkins men. Franco was telling them about the end. "And I blow him up, just like a bowling pin. Hahaha."

He's a rough fellow. Glad he's on my side. "Any injuries?"

Buck rubbed his shoulder. "Got struck with a piece of the door when it blowed. It's just a bruise."

"We'll get it checked in town."

The conductor, finished with Charlie, joined them. Charlie was led past and loaded into the baggage car. Another of the attackers was there, captured as he fled down the tracks. "The railroad has help on the way. We've got a yard engine coming to pull us back to town. Then they can get the track cleared. It's mostly snow."

Joe left them and walked to the end car. The Pinkerton man was on the platform. Beside him stood two men, one of which Joe knew to be H.C. Frick. He stepped down from the platform and approached.

"Mr. Zajac. We meet again. And once again I'm in your debt." The other man joined them.

"John Morgan here. That's a hanging good job you've done there Sir. Add me to the debtors role."

They both shook Joe's hand. "I just managed to be in the right place again. I think we've seen the end of our troubles from that fellow."

Across the lake Istvan Bako pulled the sleigh into an old barn. He untethered the horse and saddled him up. Leaving his accomplice behind, Bako rode off toward Altoona. *This fellow Zajac. Somehow he spoils the good plan. Bah! Straub was an idiot. But Mr. Zajac, we will meet again.*

Chapter 64

✳   ✳   ✳

After a quiet weekend spent with Peggy, Monday found Joe back at Frick headquarters in Scottdale. Once again, he was sitting at Tom Lynch's desk. Joe had just finished telling him about the action at the Horseshoe Curve.

"The two that got away, any sign of them?"

"The authorities followed the sled tracks and found it. A fellow there was arrested."

"Wearing an eye patch?"

"No, nor was he carrying any identification." Lynch opened his desk drawer, pulled out an envelope and handed it to Joe. "This is for you."

Joe took the envelope and opened it. Inside were two checks and a note. Joe pulled out the note, written on the personal stationery of H.C. Frick.

"Dear Mr. Zajac, Mr. Morgan and I would like to thank you once again for your efforts on our behalf. Please accept the enclosed as a token of that appreciation. If ever I can be of service, please let Tom know. Regards, H.C. Frick."

Joe examined the checks, one each from Morgan and Frick. *Five thousand each!* He looked up to see Lynch smiling at him.

"You've made a loyal friend there, Joe. Henry is a good fellow despite his reputation."

Joe shrugged, returning the checks and note to the envelope. "May he see the error in his ways. I've come to see his labor methods as unjust." He put the envelope in his brief case. "I've a question for you then."

"What's that?"

"Straub told me twice that Frick was his father, first on the Leisenring bridge and again before he went under on Friday. Any truth to that?"

Lynch shook his head. "Not that I have any knowledge of. I will say that 'Clay' as H.C. was known in his younger years, was considered a good prospect, thanks to his grandfather's position. And he was never shy with the ladies."

"I paid him no mind the first time, considered it the ravings of a madman. But it might go a ways to explaining his hatred of Frick. He said something else just before he sunk. 'He killed my mother. Johnstown.' I know of the flood, but how's that Frick's fault?"

"He was on the board of the South Fork Fishing and Hunting Club. They owned the dam that broke and the reservoir behind it. Some say they failed to keep it in good repair."

"And thousands died."

"That's right Joe, over 2,200. And I do know this. There were several from West Overton died there, including some young women who worked at the club."

Joe nodded and rose. "It's of no further interest to me then. I'll not speak of it again."

Lynch rose, the two shook hands. "Good luck Joe. Come by any time."

Joe left the office and was soon on the streetcar back to Connellsville. *Might just as well go right to the bank. I think I'll ask Andy how much he wants for the lot at the top of the hill.*

Chapter 65

*   *   *

It was Saturday, March 2, 1901. It had been a busy month for Joe. He'd stuck with the school work, his relationship with Peggy was back on track and he'd supervised the buildout of "Joey Z's." Tonight was the grand opening party.

Tony was hurrying about the room, straightening tables and such, his nervous energy making it hard to sit. Franco was behind the bar, stocking a cooler with bottles of beer. A wine rack surrounded the mirror behind the bar. The bar top was Carrara marble, white with gray veins. Joe sat at the end, his feet resting on a brass rail. *And no spittoons. No chewing.* Joe was keyed up, but also at peace. *Cost way more than I planned, but it's a first class joint. Such is life.*

Slowly, people started arriving, all of the friends Joe had made since coming to town. Tony's family and Franco. Even Mr. Morton and Porter Newmyer showed up. Henry arrived and came over.

"Best of luck Joe. And I think you can consider the spiking case closed. Once we figured out all of us having troubles were being approached to be bought out, we put two and two together. We all three went over and called out Mr. Prinkey the elder. He claimed no knowledge, but agreed to check into it. Came to see us yesterday, apologized. Said it was the fool idea of some distant relation. He also offered restitution." He reached into his pocket and pulled out a knife. "And look what we found up at the mill site."

Joe took the knife and examined it. *Nice little folding knife.* The wooden handle had a silver metal back. Joe opened the blade. *What's this?* The blade was engraved, "DB '88." He closed the blade and handed it back. "I guess that's what Delbert was looking for."

"I'd wondered what caused him to return."

Joe stood as the restaurant door opened. "All's well that ends well I'd say. And here's my girl." Peggy joined them at the bar. "Now we can start the party." He moved to the front of the room, a glass of wine in his hand.

"Ladies and gentlemen. Welcome to Joey Z's. Now, I wanted to call it Tony's Place but there you go. The managing partner has the last word." The crowd laughed. "So here's to Tony and Joey Z's." He lifted his glass. Tony stood next to him.

"And to my friend Joe. He make my dream come true."

The crowd replied. "To Tony and Joe."

Joe returned to the bar and Peggy. He pulled a small box from his jacket pocket.

"I went shopping today. That extra reward money from Carnegie and Frick was burning a hole in my pocket."

"Ten thousand, and you more than earned it. Did you see the Courier? The Carnegie transaction was announced. Morgan made the deal, worth hundreds of millions to Carnegie, Frick and the rest of the shareholders."

"You don't say? I've got friends in high places."

"Don't let it go to your head."

Joe opened the box and pulled out a diamond ring. "I thought we could make it official tonight, if you're willing."

She held out her hand. "Yes Joe, I'm willing."

He slid the ring on and held her hand. "May our years together be many and happy."

Very-Vera:
Cookbook
AMAZON

Made in the USA
Middletown, DE
16 January 2019